THE NARROW PATH

This Large Print Book carries the
Seal of Approval of N.A.V.H.

THE NARROW PATH

GAIL SATTLER

THORNDIKE PRESS

A part of Gale, Cengage Learning

GALE
CENGAGE Learning™

Detroit • New York • San Francisco • New Haven, Conn • Waterville, Maine • London

GALE
CENGAGE Learning

LIBRARY OF CONGRESS CATALOGING-IN-PUBLICATION DATA

Sattler, Gail.
  The narrow path / by Gail Sattler.
    p. cm. — (Thorndike Press large print Christian romance)
  ISBN-13: 978-1-4104-2988-9
  ISBN-10: 1-4104-2988-1
  1. Mennonites—Fiction. 2. Large type books. I. Title.
PR9199.4.S3575N37 2010b
813'.6—dc22   2010019422

Published in 2010 by arrangement with Abingdon Press.

Printed in the United States of America
1 2 3 4 5 6 7 14 13 12 11 10

Dedicated to Joy Maher: I couldn't have done this without you, my friend. Everything is in God's timing and in God's hands, including those West Coast blueberries.

Special thanks to Christa Henning and Michael Aulisio. You two really do make a cute Mennonite couple. Also special thanks to Mary Stehman and Martha Thiessen for your vast experience and willingness to share. Honorable mention to my pastor, Harry Loewen, who may or may not be related to Pastor Jake Loewen in this book.

1

But small is the gate and narrow the road
that leads to life, and only a few find it.
— Matthew 7:14

As passengers began to exit the security area, Ted Wiebe raised his sign showing the name MIRANDA KLASSEN written in bold, black ink.

A group of chattering women rushed by, their coats billowing open to display skintight T-shirts, which left their midriffs exposed above jeans that were far too tight.

Ted lowered his head so the brim of his hat shielded his eyes. None of these would be Miss Klassen. Being a modest Mennonite woman, Miss Klassen would not dress in the ways of the women from the cities. Pastor Jake had researched her background before examining her portfolio. Miss Klassen came from a highly regarded Mennonite church with a large membership in Seattle.

Miss Klassen would be wearing a sensible ankle-length skirt or dress with heavy black leather boots. In the photo she had sent, her hair was dark brown and combed back. Here, in public, her head would be respectfully covered, probably using a casual veil instead of a prayer covering.

However, the only woman Ted saw wearing a head covering was Sarah's *grootmutta,* who had gone to visit Sarah's cousins in Pennsylvania and was now going to visit more relatives in Minneapolis before returning home. He nodded and smiled graciously to acknowledge the older woman as she walked past him, then returned his attention to the dwindling crowd.

Nearly everyone had already disembarked, yet he still didn't see Miss Klassen. If she had missed her connection, then he would have to wait for two hours until the next flight, which he didn't want to do. Despite often being required to travel for business meetings, he always hated the congestion of large, crowded airports, including the busy Minneapolis airport, even though it was the closest one to home, and therefore the most familiar.

He continued to hold the sign until the last straggler passed through the security walkway. This woman wore jeans, but they weren't as tight, so he continued to watch her while hoping Miss Klassen would soon appear.

This young lady definitely wasn't dressed for Minnesota winters. Her open, waist-length jacket showed a thin, non-padded lining, and she wore only a bright red T-shirt under her lightweight jacket. As she crossed into the exit area, she tottered on insanely high shoes — open-toed high heels. Not boots. When snow lay a foot thick on the ground outside.

A jingling electronic tone sounded. Entranced, Ted watched as the woman slowed her steps while she fumbled with a paperback book, tucked an umbrella under her arm, pulled out her earbuds, and still managed to balance a satchel strap on her shoulder. She nestled her purse under her chin as she patted all her pockets, then reached into the back pocket of her jeans and pulled out a ringing cell phone. As she answered it, she hung her purse strap on her pinky finger, flipped her hair away from her cheek, and stuffed an iPod into her jacket pocket.

Ted started to lower his sign and was about to leave when the woman laughed, capturing his attention. Instead of turning away he stood transfixed, with the sign at half-mast, staring while she talked into an intensely red cell phone, an exact match to her fire-hydrant-red lipstick. Her hair bounced as she nodded, causing her huge, dangling earrings, also shocking red, to swing.

With another laugh, she snapped her phone shut and tucked it into her red purse, which was so small he didn't know how her phone fit into it, even if all she carried was her wallet. The woman shuffled to the side of the walkway and scanned the now nearly empty area.

Ted's breath caught as her eyes locked on his sign, then his face. Her movements froze. For a second, her eyes flitted to his hat, then she blinked and looked him straight in the eyes. At the searing contact, Ted's stomach dropped to the bottom of his boots.

Like a scene from a childhood nightmare, she began to approach him.

"Ted Wiebe?" she asked.

Ted's heart pounded so hard he could feel it beneath his heavy coat. This was wrong. This could not be the woman he had been sent to fetch back to their church. He had come for a quiet, gentle woman of the same traditional Mennonite heritage as his own — a woman who had been blessed with a special gift and lived to serve others. Even though it was unusual for a Mennonite woman to be a musician and composer, her references stated that her love for God shone through in everything she did, especially the songs she wrote for God's glory. Even though she came from a big city, she had been born and raised in a Mennonite home and community. Her father was a pastor. Surely this could not be her.

Ted stared at the woman before him, dressed not much differently than the group who had just passed him, one of whom had made an immodest display of her belly button ring. Even though this woman's midriff was covered, she came equipped with all the latest city trends — a nonfunctional purse, a brightly colored cell phone, a collection of electronic gadgets, plus a laptop computer slung over her shoulder, and showgirl shoes.

She extended one hand. "Thank you for picking me up."

His mind went blank as he slowly accepted her handshake. He'd never shaken hands with a woman before.

Ted cleared his throat and tried not to stammer. "Miranda Klassen?"

"That's me." She grinned from ear to ear and gestured down the walkway. "It's snowing out there!"

"Do not worry," he said, as he tried to focus all his attention on her face, not her snug clothing and plethora of accessories. "It is windy enough that the highways are still clear. The forecast said it would not become heavy until midnight."

Yet, even though the roads would be clear, the blowing snow would drift and accumulate against the houses and existing piles of snow at the sides of the driveways and sidewalks. By the time he got home, he had a feeling he would welcome the exertion of shoveling his driveway before he could park his car in the garage.

"Is there lots of snow in Piney Meadows?"

"*Ja.* It is February, after all."

She blinked at his confirmation, as if this was a strange concept. "Oh." She released his hand and then jerked her head to the sign directing travelers to the baggage claim area. "Before I pick up my luggage, I need coffee. Do you have a Starbucks here?"

Starbucks. Not just ordinary coffee. She wanted the expensive, specialty kind. "I am not sure. I do not drink coffee."

"If I don't get some decent coffee soon, I think I'll die. Oops, but first, can you hold this for a minute?" She slipped the satchel off her shoulder and thrust it, the book, and the umbrella at him so fast he feared he might drop them. Things were not quite secure in his arms before she turned and dashed toward the ladies' restroom, her heels clicking as she sprinted off. Unable to take his eyes off her until she disappeared through the doorway, Ted's cheeks burned red. While he stood cradling her belongings, people shuffled past him.

He turned slightly so he wasn't staring at the entrance to the ladies' room, then shook his head so he could think.

How could he bring this woman back to his people? Of everyone in his church, he had the most experience with people from the cities, but she would be a shock to everyone else. More importantly, she couldn't possibly understand or relate to the project in their church. His people had chosen to remain distant from the ways of the world to maintain their Old Order tradition. Some modern conveniences had crept in, but out of necessity. He was one of only a few people who owned a car, and many depended on him because of it. But wherever they could, they protected themselves from the contamination of the world around them.

Miranda Klassen appeared to be entrenched in her city ways and actually enjoyed them. Starbucks!

He didn't know what to do. His inclination was to take her to the ticket counter instead of the baggage claim area and put her on the next plane back to where she came from. But he had been sent by his church, his people, and his pastor. Even though no one had experienced her yet, it wasn't his place to judge her.

Ted had promised to drop her off at the home of Leonard and Lois Toews, who had graciously invited Miss Klassen to live with them for the next year, and he always kept his word.

But first, he would take her to the one person who could make the decision to send her back to Seattle — Pastor Jake.

For the first time in his life, Ted wished he owned a cell phone.

Hoping to find a pay phone and make the call before she reappeared, he looked around for a map of the terminal. Before he could find one, Miss Klassen emerged from the entrance to the ladies' room. As she walked she draped her jacket over one arm while she rummaged through her miniscule purse. With the movement, the shoulder of her red T-shirt drooped, exposing a black bra strap.

He turned his head. The heat in his face

meant his cheeks were probably as red as her lipstick, which she must have retouched because it was even brighter than when she had walked off the plane.

"I'm so sorry," she muttered. "This is going all wrong. Can we start over? I'm Miranda Klassen, but my friends call me Randi. Thank you for driving all this way to pick me up."

Ted's mind went blank as he turned back to her, keeping his eyes fixed on her face until she adjusted her clothing. "Randy? But that is a man's name."

Miss Klassen shook her head as she tugged her T-shirt back into its proper place. "No, when I write it, that's Randi, with an 'i.'"

"I have never heard of that."

She shrugged her shoulders. "It's just the short form of Miranda."

He had never known anyone by that name either, but at least it was clearly feminine. As to Randy, or Randi, he didn't care how she spelled her name, it would always be a man's name to him. He couldn't do it.

Not that he would have to. By this time tomorrow, after meeting with Pastor Jake and possibly the board of deacons, *Miss Randi with an "i"* would be on her way back to Seattle.

She looked down at the sign still in his

hands. "The sign was a good idea. I had no idea who would be picking me up, and I wasn't sure you would have recognized me by the picture I sent."

He studied her face. She was right; he hadn't recognized her. He still wasn't sure this was the same woman as in the photograph.

"No, I did not," Ted replied.

She ran her fingers through her hair. "I just got my hair streaked a couple of days ago. Usually it's darker but this time she used a lighter shade, and I think she put a bit too much red in it. I hope it's okay."

Chemically dyed hair. He bit his tongue so he wouldn't ask if she had any tattoos.

If only he could save himself the gas and the wear on his nerves and send her back right now. But he couldn't. Only Pastor Jake could make that decision. "The luggage carousels are that way." Since his hands were still full, he jerked his head toward the right.

She reached toward him. "I'll take those now."

Her bright red nails caught the glare of the overhead lighting as he returned the umbrella and the book.

Because it was the heaviest of the three items, he retained the satchel containing her laptop computer. "I will carry this for you."

"Oh." She nibbled on her bottom lip. "Of course."

She reached up to flip a strand of bicolored hair out of her eyes, showing another flash of red — this time a narrow, single strand of red ribbon tied in her hair. The same red as her painted fingernails. And her phone. And her purse. And her earrings. And her T-shirt. He would never be able to look at anything red the same way again.

When her hands dropped to her sides, a glitter at her throat sparkled — a dainty gold cross that hung on a chain around her neck. Finally, an outward sign. But it didn't make up for the rest of her appearance. Nor did it change his mind.

He couldn't believe this Miranda Klassen was the person who had composed and directed the moving songs of faith and worship that had impressed the pastor and everyone on the church board so much that they had brought in a stranger to oversee the biggest event in their church's history. Especially without meeting her in person. Everything had been done over the phone, which was a mistake they would never repeat.

He crumpled the sign and tossed it in the

17

nearby waste container. "Let us go retrieve your suitcase. The sooner we do this, the sooner we can go."

"Don't forget my coffee. I see a sign." She pointed down the length of the terminal. "That way. Starbucks. I need a venti mocha really bad."

2

They were well clear of Minneapolis by the time Miranda's teeth stopped chattering. The hot coffee had helped warm her fingers, and finally she had some feeling back in her toes, but the only things that would truly take away the chill that had seeped into her bones would be either the quilt off her bed or a roaring fire.

Beside her, Ted had unfastened all the buttons of his coat. "Are you warm enough? I am finding it becoming hot. I would like to turn the heat down."

She didn't want to lie, but neither did she want her host to feel uncomfortable. "Go ahead," she said, trying to sound cheerful. "I'm feeling much better."

A silence hung between them, made worse because Ted didn't have a CD player or even a radio in his car. The silence was really . . . silent . . . except for the hum of the tires on the highway and the regular

19

double thumps when they crossed the expansion seams between the sections of cement.

"You are feeling better, but you did not say that you are warm." He looked down at her feet, which made her automatically wiggle her toes. "Can you feel your toes yet?"

At his words, she stopped moving them, even though they were now thankfully covered. "Yes. Thank you. That was a good idea."

By the time they had walked through the parking lot and arrived at his car, she could no longer feel her feet. Ted had graciously suggested that she open her suitcase and change into what he called "more adequate footwear." It had been rather embarrassing, but worth the sacrifice of her pride. She had never had such a hard time pulling on socks or stuffing her feet into tennis shoes. Everything below her ankles was numb, and her hands shook so hard she could barely tie the laces.

"It made no sense that you should be so cold. I did not mind waiting."

"I've got to be honest with you. I really had no idea it would be like this. I checked the weather channel before I left and saw that it might snow, but it's different at home. On the West Coast it usually only hovers around freezing when it's snowing. Even when it's cold enough for the snow to stick, it's never windy." Just thinking about it made a cold shudder run down her back. For the first time, she understood what people meant by the phrase "wind chill."

"I've never experienced such a cold wind in my life."

"I do not understand why you chose to change into your tennis shoes instead of your boots. I would have waited for you to repack your suitcase."

"I didn't bring boots. I don't own a pair. Do you know where I can buy some?"

"You do not own boots?" He turned and stared at her as if she were some poor homeless waif, underfed and underdressed.

She glanced down at his feet, protected by large, plain black boots, no doubt cushioned with thick wool socks.

Not only did she need to buy boots, she would also need to buy a new jacket. Today she had learned the hard way that the coat she'd bought in Seattle was woefully inadequate if this was a sample of normal Minnesota winter weather. Unlike her coat, Ted's heavy, padded wool coat was so long it hung below his knees. The fabric wouldn't be the least bit rainproof, which was probably why she had never seen anything like it in Seattle. A dull monotone shade of dark gray, it was plain and functional — made for warmth, not for looks.

Miranda raised her hand to the window and wiped away the fog. The snow was coming down heavier now than it had been when they first drove out of the airport. She'd never seen anything like it, and just looking at it made her even colder.

As Ted drove, he lifted one hand from the steering wheel and grasped the top of the collar of his coat. He fanned it a few times and blew out his breath.

"I am stopping the car," he said as he checked the rearview mirror.

Miranda opened her mouth to ask him why, but he braked so hard she lurched against the seatbelt and lost her breath. The center lane where most traffic drove was clear, but the falling snow was beginning to accumulate on the outside lane, and the shoulder was covered. Instead of pulling over onto the shoulder, Ted aimed the car so only one tire went into the snow; half of the car blocked the lane — a danger if anyone were to come up behind them. The second the car stopped, he clicked off his seatbelt with one hand, pushed the door open with the other, and bolted out.

"What's wrong? Should I —" Before she could finish her sentence, he'd shucked off his coat, thrown it in the back seat, and was again in the driver's seat, fastening his seatbelt.

In two seconds, the car had resumed motion. He eased it into the center of the driving lane and quickly picked up speed. As soon as they were back at the posted speed limit, he shifted into fifth gear and reached over to turn the heat on full blast.

"I needed to do that quickly before someone came up behind us. Now you will be able to get fully warm."

She stared at Ted, barely able to believe what he'd just done. She would never have pulled that maneuver on the I-5 at home, but then, this highway only had two lanes in each direction, not five, and nowhere near the same volume of traffic. Also, it was getting dark, and they were the only car on that stretch of road, at least for a couple of minutes. He'd removed his coat so efficiently that she suspected this wasn't the first time.

Automatically, she raised her hands to the vent, now blasting out hot air instead of merely blowing warm.

"Thank you. I think . . ." her voice trailed off as he turned to look at her, probably gauging her reaction.

"*Ja?* What is it?" he muttered as he straightened his hat, then returned his attention to the road in front of him.

Her thoughts froze as numb as her toes. She stared at his profile, taking in the whole picture of him, now that he'd removed his bulky coat.

The hat was the reason he had been the first person she had looked at in the crowd when she got off the plane. She'd never seen one like it, at least not in person. Made of solid black felt, completely unadorned, with a wide unrolled brim, it looked like hats she'd seen in some of the books at her church — the books about Mennonite history that her father had given her to read to learn about her heritage.

And the accent. *Ja.* Not *yes,* or *yeah.* Not only did he speak with a bit of an inflection to his words, he enunciated every word clearly. The more he spoke, the more prominent his accent. From the first moment she had heard him speak, she'd been intrigued and charmed by it.

Without his coat, he looked like he'd been pulled right off the pages of the book that was now packed in the bottom of a box in her closet. Like his coat, the rest of his clothes were just as basic. He wore a plain cotton button-down blue shirt, and his pants were loose and made for comfort to the point that he used suspenders to hold them up. Plain suspenders. No lettering proclaiming his favorite rock band. No Harley Davidson or other motorcycle logo. Just plain black suspenders.

"I'll be fine now." Miranda turned her head as if she were watching the passing scenery.

Before she boarded the plane, she'd had a long talk with her father. They had both had a gut feeling that aside from being a small town, Piney Meadows would be a place quite different from what they were used to in Seattle. During the interview process, Pastor Jake had overemphasized traditional values and strong family ethics. Since their own church felt strongly about those same things, neither Miranda nor her father understood why Pastor Jake had been so emphatic about it. They'd simply agreed, yet they both felt something neither of them could define. If Ted was a typical member of the church . . .

Miranda cleared her throat. "Well," she said, trying to keep her voice from shaking. "Tell me all about your town and Piney Meadows Full Gospel Mennonite Church."

For the first time since she'd met him, Ted smiled.

Her breath caught. The smile changed him. His eyes sparkled, and he was downright handsome in a country boy sort of way. Pastor Jake hadn't told her how old Ted was, but she guessed him to be a year or two older than herself, which put him at about twenty-six.

"I have lived here all my life, as did my parents before me. It is a small community, made of both townspeople and those who live on the nearby farms."

Miranda was content to listen to Ted recap some of the history of the town as they drove, including a few amusing stories of some of the residents and descriptions of the countryside that, unlike Seattle, experienced four distinct seasons.

When they passed the town's welcome sign, Miranda couldn't help but compare it to something she would see on television as a caricature of a hick town. There was probably a main street, but she couldn't see even a hint of a tall building and she had a feeling the reason wasn't just because it was so dark. In contrast to her neighborhood in Seattle, houses here were large and spaced well apart on large lots. Most had detached garages, something she never saw in Seattle, and rarely saw in the suburbs, except in the older neighborhoods. The town was small enough that not only did the population number show on the sign, it looked like it had recently been changed.

This was a town that wasn't likely to have a Walmart. Ever.

"Where are we going?" Miranda asked, wondering what time everyone went to bed in a town like this.

Ted checked his watch. "We are going to the church. I would like you to meet Pastor Jake."

Miranda looked around the neighborhood as they turned off the main road. The covering of snow gave everything such a pure and pristine feel. Yet, in addition to the quaintness, she had the impression that in the summertime, some of these yards would hold a goat or a chicken or two.

As they drove past the darkened houses, not one of them showed the glow of a television through the window. "Are you sure it's not too late? Everyone seems to be settled in for the night."

"No. He will be there. Pastor Jake is always at the church late on Thursday evenings. I am sure that he is anxious to meet you."

Just as Ted had promised, the church was

well lit when he stopped the car on the street. "Are you sure he's here? I don't see a car."

"The lights are on. He is here. As I do, Pastor Jake has a car, but he walks to church. He only will drive the car when someone needs a ride."

When Ted opened his door, an icy blast of wind pierced the haven of his small car. He visibly shivered and quickly reached into the backseat for his coat. He moved so fast he was almost a blur as he hopped outside, slipped his arms into the sleeves, and wrapped the coat around himself without fastening the buttons. "*Kom.* Come. Let us go inside."

Ted guided her up the stairs without speaking. Slogging through the ankle-deep snow, she was even more grateful that he'd given her the chance to change from her best dress shoes to her tennis shoes. Even though snow spilled over the sides and stuck to her socks, it was better than freezing her exposed toes.

At the door, he sidestepped ahead of her to open it, bowing his head slightly as she walked past him. Once inside, Miranda compared Ted's church to what she'd read about. It was just like the history books. Beside the doors were two sides of a community coatrack — one side for women and the other side for men, complete with pegs for the men's hats. Out of the corner of her eye, she saw Ted remove his hat and hang it on one of the pegs, but he didn't remove his coat.

Taking one step further, she looked up. The foyer's ceiling, made from old wood, had been stained deep and rich. Pillars of the same wood stood proudly throughout the large space. The room was elegant and beautiful, but at the same time warm and comfortable. Stepping closer to one of the pillars, she saw words carved into it, as well as an intricate carving of a shepherd and a few sheep.

"The Lord is my shepherd," she read, running her hands over the words as she spoke them. "This is magnificent. Where did your church get this?"

"One of our founding fathers carved all the pillars to be ready for the original construction."

"Wow," she murmured as she again tilted her head to study the ceiling more carefully.

With the foyer displaying such craftsmanship, Miranda's heart quickened at the thought of what artistry proclaiming the glory of God would be in the center of His house. "I can hardly wait to see your sanctuary."

"But —"

Ted raised one finger in the air, but Miranda didn't wait for him. She continued forward and pulled open a set of closed double doors. Sighing, he followed her into the looming blackness, and she heard the sweep of his hand against the wall. A click sounded, and one light came on at the front.

Just as she had imagined, wooden pews lined the slightly triangular room, layered in levels as the entire floor sloped toward the front where a small, bare stage held a wooden podium. Behind it, high on the wall, hung a large cross made of the same wood. The plainness of the room focused all attention on the cross, making a vivid statement. Even though the building had to be more than seventy-five years old, considering the shape of the room and the choice of materials for the wall covering, she suspected the acoustics were excellent.

"This is outstanding. Majestic, yet simple."

"It meets our needs. Let me introduce you to Pastor Jake." He stepped back, allowing her to exit the room before he flipped off the light switch and pulled the door shut behind him.

She hadn't taken more than a couple of steps when a middle-aged man wearing a suit about ten years out of date stepped out of one of the rooms leading into the foyer. Beneath the suit jacket, he wore suspenders too.

"Miranda Klassen, please meet Pastor Jake Loewen."

Miranda approached him. "Pastor," she said, and extended one hand.

Pastor Jake's face froze with an expression similar to that of Ted when he had first seen her at the airport. He blinked a few times, and his eyes met hers. Slowly, he smiled, but it didn't reach his eyes. Gradually, he extended his hand and wrapped his fingers around hers. "I am pleased to meet you, Miss Klassen."

"Please, call me Randi."

"With an 'i,' " Ted piped up beside her.

Pastor Jake's grip tightened.

Out of the corner of her eye, a movement caught her attention. A woman walked out of the pastor's office. It didn't surprise Miranda that this woman was dressed the same as the elderly lady on the plane, the one who wore a prayer *kapp.* It made Miranda wonder if that lady was a member of this church and community; perhaps she should have spoken to her.

31

Pastor Jake released her hand and smiled. "Miranda Klassen, this is my wife, Kathleen Loewen."

Miranda forced herself to breathe normally as she took in everything she'd seen in the last few hours. Nothing had been like she thought it would be. Her head spun as she combined images from her history book with what surrounded her now. The quaint neighborhood. The old building. The clothes. Like *Little House on the Prairie* — with cars.

Miranda smiled graciously. "I'm pleased to meet you, Mrs. Loewen."

Mrs. Loewen smiled and nodded briefly. "And I am very pleased to meet you. Did you have a nice flight?"

Miranda nodded. She'd had a nice flight. But suddenly she was unsure of the landing.

"You are looking tired."

Not as much tired as overwhelmed. She'd been so excited at the thought of putting together a project like they'd discussed over the phone while not under her father's wing. Not that she wanted credit or glory, but even Jesus felt the sting of not being taken seriously in His own hometown. Here, she had thought she could spread her wings and fly like an eagle. Instead, she felt like a colorful parrot among sparrows — a parrot that had just had its wings clipped. But God loved each and every sparrow, exactly the same as parrots. She sucked in a deep breath.

"Yes, I am a little tired, and — I have to admit this isn't exactly what I'd expected."

Ted's eyebrows arched, and he crossed his arms over his chest. "Really?" The deep tone of his voice bordered on sarcasm. ❧

The pastor narrowed his eyes and glared at Ted for a moment before he turned back to her and scanned her from head to toe.

Miranda tried not to cringe at the inspection. She had worn her best jeans and her favorite T-shirt for the flight, but she had a feeling that her choice hadn't been the right one for this mission. And it was a mission.

She had come to help this church with their Christmas program because they lacked the resources and had sought experienced help. She had composed and directed three musical Christmas dramas for her father's church, and every one of them had met with tremendous response, both from established members and newcomers.

That was why she was here. Even though she didn't have much in common with this lifestyle, she and these people did share one thing — the thing that counted the most.

She was a Mennonite too.

Pastor Jake cleared his throat. "Are you having second thoughts?"

Ted stepped closer. "I will not go to work tomorrow and take you back to the airport."

Miranda stood tall, making eye contact first with Ted, then with Pastor Jake. Suppressing a shiver from the cold of the melting snow that soaked her socks, she tucked her purse under her arm, reached up, untied the ribbon in her hair, and stuffed it in her pocket.

"No, I'm not having second thoughts. I just need to buy a new jacket and a good pair of boots, and I'm ready."

3

Ted hoisted Miranda's heavy suitcase out of the trunk and set it on the ground behind him.

He couldn't believe she was staying, with Pastor Jake's blessing. Although he knew Pastor Jake and his wife would be long in prayer about it, probably at this very moment.

For tonight, anyway, she was here. Tomorrow, she was required to attend a church board meeting, so that would probably change her mind, as well as the pastor's.

"Since the sidewalk is not shoveled, I will carry this for you; it is not possible to pull it through the snow."

"Thank you. I know it's pretty heavy. I had to take out one of my books at the check-in counter so I didn't have to pay extra."

He handed her the backpack that had been her second piece of checked luggage and waited while she tucked her umbrella and book in the outside pockets.

She slipped on the straps, then slung the laptop satchel over one shoulder, and picked up her purse. "I'm ready."

Ted nodded as he lifted the heavy suitcase and began walking the length of the sidewalk. "When Sarah's grootmutta flies, she always packs too much as well."

His bad mood lightened slightly, thinking of Gretta's homemade *wassermelone pokel* that she'd tried to take on her last trip. He couldn't believe she had taken a glass jar containing liquid into the security line. Before the TSA threw it out, he'd recovered it, planning to take it home. But it had been a long day, and he was hungry. Using a plastic fork from the airport's food court, he had nibbled the watermelon pickles in the car on the way home. After eating the whole jar like a heathen he suffered from a stomachache, but every bite had been worth it.

Ted set the suitcase beside the front door and pushed his fist into the muscle he'd overworked. A shadow came over Miranda's face as she watched him.

"I'm so sorry. It's heavy because I had to bring some work with me. I'm on a tight deadline at the office."

"You have a job? I thought you were the worship leader at your church."

"Yes, I am. I'm also the church treasurer. But I also have a day job. I think any of the other accountants could have done these reconciliations, but the client wanted me or they threatened to leave. So I ended up agreeing to work part-time and do everything remotely until my return."

Ted clenched his teeth. His friend, William, was the accountant for his *onkel's* company. It was more than a mere job. Being an accountant was a career, one he doubted Miranda would quit when the day came for her to be married. The church board didn't know she was chasing a career instead of preparing herself for a family of her own. They only knew she was a pastor's daughter, who happened to be a talented musician and composer.

He looked at her again — frazzled, chemically treated hair, bright red lipstick, city-woman jeans, insane shoes. The more he discovered about her, the worse it became. She was not a match for his people, or their congregation.

He had no doubt that the rest of the church board would feel the same way as he did. They would have her back on the plane before she had finished unpacking.

Just as he raised his finger to push the doorbell, barking echoed from inside. "Leonard and Lois are anxious to meet you, as is their dog."

"I hope they didn't go to a lot of trouble."

He paused, his finger poised in midair. Of course they had. Leonard and Lois Toews had been the first ones to raise their hands at the committee meeting when they discussed where Miranda would live for the year she stayed with their congregation.

"Leonard and Lois truly have the gift of hospitality. They also have an empty room since their daughter got married, and a piano."

Ted pushed the button. The door opened before the ring finished playing. Leonard stood in the doorway, Lois slightly behind him, both smiling brightly.

It was too bad that when the shock hit them, they were going to be so disappointed, especially Lois. Lois anticipated their visitor would want to do many of the things she had done with her daughter. However, instead of joining the ladies' sewing groups, Miranda would spend most of her time working on the computer she had brought with her.

If she stayed. Which she wasn't.

Ted guided Miranda inside. Once she

crossed the threshold, he hauled her suitcase in, closed the door behind him, removed his hat, and reached to the side to hang it on the rack. By the time he turned around, Lois and Miranda were already hugging each other, not waiting for him to introduce them properly.

Leonard reached forward to shake his hand. "How was the highway?"

"Starting to drift and getting packed in places. More snow is coming."

Miranda stepped back from Lois. "Another snowstorm? Oh, no!"

Ted turned toward her. "Snowstorm?"

Miranda extended one arm to the door. "Look at how much there is! You say there's more on the way?"

Leonard frowned and peeked through the blinds. "Did I miss something? No, it is not snowing hard."

Miranda also stepped forward and peeked outside. "I see at least three inches on the driveway."

Ted cleared his throat, causing everyone to look at him, then jerked his thumb over his shoulder in the direction of the door. "In Seattle, this is considered a lot of snow."

Without commenting, Leonard and Lois looked down at Miranda's tennis shoes. Her red tennis shoes.

"*Ach,* your feet. They must be cold," Lois said as she rubbed her hands together. "*Kom.* Let me show you to your room and get you settled. You have had a decent supper, have you not? I know they do not feed you on the plane anymore, either, and what they call food at the airport!" She shook her head and mumbled a word Ted didn't quite hear. "Horrible. I have some *Alles Tzsamma* that will only take a few minutes to heat up."

Miranda pressed one palm over her stomach as it grumbled. "That would be great, thank you. I haven't eaten since lunch. I wasn't hungry at the airport, but I'm sure hungry now." She glanced at Ted, then back to Lois. "As long as it isn't any trouble."

Lois waved one hand in the air. "*Verdault nicht.* For sure not. Take off your shoes and come inside. Len, take her things to her room, and I will warm up some *Alles Tzsamma.* Ted, would you like to stay?"

"No, *danke shoen.* I must be on my way." Ted placed his hat back on his head. "I will see you again tomorrow evening at the church for the introductory session." Where the church board, the deacons, and committee leaders will all meet *Miss Randi with an "i."*

Just as he started to turn toward the door,

40

Miranda looked at him with eyes wide, like a puppy dog with a thorn in its paw.

For a moment, his heart softened. Even though she didn't belong here, he didn't wish to see her hurt. However, less damage would be done the sooner she returned to her city life. As well, the sooner she went back, the less damage would be done to his people.

He was only doing the right thing. When he got home, he would pray for the meeting and for wisdom for all, including Miranda. And for her to have a safe trip home.

He took one last look at her and walked out the door.

Miranda stood in the bedroom doorway while Len lifted her suitcase onto the bed.

He turned around, winced slightly, then smiled when they made eye contact. "Lois says there are plenty of hangers in the closet, but if you run out, please ask. We have more." He smiled again, nodded slightly, and left the room.

Miranda immediately sat on the bed and pulled off her wet socks. While she dug through her suitcase for a fresh pair and her slippers, she glanced over her shoulder at the room that would be hers for the upcoming year.

41

It was small, but furnished in a classic, homey style. Everything was simple and comfortable — a quiet, private place to work, or the perfect spot to wind down after the day was done. The only flaw was that the room was crowded. The furniture had been squeezed tight in order to add the desk.

As soon as her feet were covered, she walked across the room and slowly ran her fingers along the smooth edge of the dresser. Like all the furniture in the room, it was plain in design, hewn in dark wood, and styled in clean and distinct lines that were pure country classical. The simple craftsmanship displayed little ornamentation; yet instead of looking bare, everything had a warm and cozy ambiance. Lovely inlays accented the curves of the more ornate pieces, giving them a subtle beauty and emphasizing the workmanship. The accompanying chest of drawers was a perfect match, along with a headboard and footboard on the bed. A colorful quilt, which Miranda knew from the unique design had to be handmade, covered the bed.

Although the desk wasn't from the same matched set, it had a distinct appeal as well. The simpler design made Miranda wonder if it was an antique, even though it didn't

42

have a roll-down cover. Everything was a perfect blend of simplicity, practicality, and comfort.

When her electric piano arrived, however, she would have a difficult time finding a place for it because it would destroy the atmosphere of the room.

Lois appeared in the doorway. "Your supper will be a few minutes longer. Would you like to see more of the house until it is ready?"

Miranda nodded. "Yes, I'd like that. Your home is charming."

Lois's cheeks darkened, and she smiled nervously. "Before I show you the living room, I know where you will be spending most of your time."

Lois led her into a small family room, but instead of a television and video game center being the main attraction, it was a piano: a square, brown rosewood grand piano. If Miranda remembered correctly, square pianos dated back prior to 1880. She was almost afraid to touch it. It was probably worth more than her car.

"This is incredible," Miranda said as she approached the piano. Her hand shook as she lightly played a B7 chord, resolving it into E. The rich, harp-like sound resounded all the way to her soul.

"It was Lois's grootmutta's piano, and her grootmutta's before her. It has been in the family for many generations."

Miranda did the mental math. For this to be Lois's grandmother's grandmother's piano meant the beautiful instrument could well date back to 1880.

"I've seen pictures, but I've never touched one of these before," Miranda murmured. She ran through a few basic chord progressions, without sitting down on the hand-embroidered seat cushion, clearly as antique as the piano. As the notes soared, she imagined a lady from Lois's family playing this antique piano — dressed the same as Lois was now, in a long, dull-colored, loose-fitted, ankle-length dress. In her own home, Lois didn't wear a prayer covering, but like the pastor's wife, she probably did when she went out.

"My electric piano will never sound like this." Or feel like it, either. Playing her electric piano would never be the same, regardless of its weighted keys or how she set the sound. The keys on this piano were slightly yellowed, meaning they were real ivory, something else she had never touched.

Lois stepped beside her. "It will be a joy to hear you play. I miss the sound of music in the house."

Len slipped one arm around his wife's waist. "Kathleen said she would give you lessons. One day, you could make music just like your mama used to."

"Kathleen has no time for such things. She already does so much."

Miranda stepped back from the piano, her mind reeling from the thought of being able to play on such a fine instrument every day. "I teach piano lessons to a few members of my congregation. I'd love to give you lessons as a small way to thank you for opening your home to me."

Lois raised one hand to her throat. "Do you mean you have given up your students to come here? That must have been so difficult. And such a sacrifice."

Miranda shook her head. The wonders of technology allowed her to keep her treasured students, still do her job, and keep in touch with her friends. "It was no sacrifice. I'm going to continue their lessons on schedule over the Internet."

Len frowned. "I am sorry, but we do not have a computer."

Somehow, she knew he would say that. "That's okay. I'll just set up a remote connection and use my laptop. Would you mind if I arranged for an Internet hookup? I don't know what's available to this area, or the best price — dialup, cable modem, or DSL."

Both Len and Lois looked at her as if she had spoken in a foreign language. To them, she probably had. But saying it made her suspect that their phone was still on the old hardwired system. Being so, she wasn't going to run wires through their house.

"Don't worry. I can probably do it from the church. I've exchanged email with Pastor Jake, so I know he has a computer and an Internet connection. I'll ask him what kind of setup he's got when I see him tomorrow."

Lois raised one hand toward the door. "*Ja.* That is tomorrow. For now, the *Alles Tzsamma* should be ready."

In reply, Miranda's stomach grumbled. She didn't know whose face turned redder, hers or Lois's. "That would be wonderful. I don't remember the last time I've had *Alles Tzsamma.*"

Not many people in her church still made the traditional Mennonite dishes on a regular basis. They usually required too much preparation time, and everyone had a job. After fighting the Seattle rush-hour traffic, the last thing on anyone's mind, including hers, was spending hours in the kitchen preparing a meal. Once a year the church's social committee held a traditional potluck dinner, and Miranda always brought the same thing — farmer sausage bought from the deli on her way home.

As they approached the kitchen, a timer dinged — the bell of an oven timer. Not the electronic tone of a microwave.

The kitchen table was set for one, with a beautiful china plate and a knife and fork that matched. Miranda sat down in the chair.

Lois transferred the food from a metal tray to the plate, set it before Miranda, then politely stood back to allow her to give thanks in private.

Miranda's prayers were heartfelt, but quick. She openly savored every bite. "This is delicious. Thank you so much. I have a feeling that I'm going to gain weight while I'm here, and it will be worth it."

Lois smiled. "It is not healthy to be so skinny as the girls in the magazines. For those girls to do that to themselves, this is wrong."

Miranda noticed that while Lois wasn't anywhere near skinny, for a woman old enough to be Miranda's mother, she wasn't chunky, either. She smiled at Lois.

"Fortunately, I have a good metabolism. I don't have to starve myself to keep my weight down." Her father told her that her mother used to be the same way. "I just don't want you to go to a lot of trouble for me. Please cook exactly the same things as if I wasn't here, and I insist that you let me help, including doing the dishes." Unfortunately, that meant doing them by hand because Miranda didn't see a dishwasher anywhere. "Housework too. I don't want to be a burden. I want to do my share."

Although now that it had been said, Miranda hoped her share of vacuuming the carpets meant exactly that — vacuuming — not hauling rugs outside and beating them by hand.

"*Ach,* but not. You have so much work to do for our church. But if you insist, then I think the dishes will be a good thing for you to do."

"Great." Finished eating, Miranda stood, automatically turning toward the cupboard beside the sink, where the dishwasher should have been and wasn't. "Then I'm going to start by washing my plate."

Lois removed it from her hand. "Do not be wasting water for one plate. This will be fine to sit in the sink until morning. Now go finish unpacking your suitcase, and then we can talk for a while before bed. It is getting late. You must be tired."

Although the time change traveling eastward had been in her favor, she was tired. However, the reason was probably more stress-related than time-related. "Yes, it's been a long day. Thanks."

Before Miranda continued putting her things away, she pulled out her cell phone and sent her father a text message to ask him to start recording *CSI* every week, because along with no microwave or dishwasher, the Toews didn't own a television either.

She flipped off the phone and then back on again to send another text message to remind her father to buy a big pile of blank DVDs or a new external hard drive to store a year's worth until she could watch them all — in order.

As she turned the phone off again, Miranda stood in one spot, staring at the now-black touchscreen. When she got on the plane this morning, she thought she was stepping into a dream — a dream that was part of God's ministry. She had never looked forward to anything so much in her life, including her university graduation.

The decision to move to a small town, even for a short year, had been difficult because she loved the busy city life. She worked in a high-rise office tower in downtown Seattle that looked over Puget Sound and the Pacific Ocean. In Piney Meadows, the tallest building she'd seen stood three stories. It probably didn't even have enough elevation to look out over the nearest farm.

Miranda squeezed shut her eyes. She was here, and she intended to honor her promise — one she had made to the pastor, the church board, and most importantly, to God — that she would put together everything they needed to celebrate Christmas and their seventy-fifth anniversary. This church wanted to reach out in ministry to everyone within driving distance, which was why they had brought her here.

At least this wasn't a commune with horses and buggies. Unless the horses had all frozen to death, forcing residents to buy cars. She shuddered at the thought.

She looked into the open closet, which now contained about half of the clothes she had brought, then stared blankly into her half-empty suitcase. She had packed only her favorite items and a few basic staples. Nothing resembled anything close to what she knew the ladies here wore every day. She owned a few skirts, but all were fitted and none hung lower than her knees. She had brought only one with her.

While she was here she wanted to fit in, but in doing so, she didn't want to lose herself. She hated neutral colors. She hated boring monotones even worse. Everything she owned was bright, cheery, and colorful. Her favorite color was red. Except for her tennis shoes, every pair of shoes she had brought had at least three-inch heels.

Miranda covered her face with her hands and peeked out between her fingers. It wasn't *all* bad. She had been picked up in a car, and she'd been hired over the Internet.

The Toews owned a dog, but from what she had seen, she wouldn't be surprised if some of the people nearby might have a pet goat. That wasn't bad, either. She had always loved to play with the goats at the petting zoo when she was a child.

The men's clothing was as boring as the women's, but she had to admit Ted sure looked good in that hat.

Miranda sucked in a deep breath, hung up the rest of her clothes, and piled her paperwork on the desk.

She could do this. She *would* do this.

Miranda set the suitcase and empty backpack in the back of the closet and closed the door. At the same time as she let go of the door handle, a kettle whistled from down the hall. Tea was on the way. She forced herself to feel some enthusiasm. She had a feeling it was going to be a long time before her next visit to Starbucks.

Lois had filled the teapot with water and dipped a teabag in as Miranda arrived in the kitchen.

Miranda lowered herself into the chair and wrapped her hands around an empty mug. "Your little dog is so cute. I've always wanted a dog, but Daddy and I have a lot of people visiting, so we can't take the chance that someone will be allergic."

Lois nodded. "*Ja,* Fidette is a good little dog, but sometimes she is too friendly. We do not encourage it, no, but often she sneaks onto the bed at night, so I am glad you like dogs." Slowly, Lois poured the tea, looking down as she spoke. "Tomorrow will be your first time to meet our church board."

Miranda swallowed hard. She hoped she could meet their expectations. Since this was not what she had expected, it could be reasonably assumed that she was not what they expected, either. "Yes. Now that I'm here, I'm not sure I'm ready."

She vowed that just as soon as she retired to her bedroom, she would first thank God for a safe and uneventful flight, and then she would pray for wisdom not to put her foot in her mouth until she learned more about these people. She also would pray about being a better listener than speaker, a trait that had never been her greatest strength.

"Still, the person you will be spending the most time with will be Ted, since he is our worship leader. He is a hard worker. He will help you very much."

"I know he plays guitar. He told me on the way here from the airport."

Lois chuckled softly. "Poor Ted. He does not like going to the airport. Pastor Jake said he would be the best one to pick you up because he visits the cities so often."

"Yes, he did seem to know his way around the airport."

"Having you here is such an answer to prayer," Lois said. "Ted had already started working on this program, but he is so busy, and he became frustrated looking for the right music. When your portfolio arrived, after seeing the photos of what you have done and listening to the tapes you had sent, we knew that this surely was God's timing. When you replied so quickly, we knew this was surely His will."

Miranda nearly choked on her tea. "Ted had already started? I didn't know that."

"*Ja*. But the project is too much for him. When we voted to bring you here, he graciously stepped down."

The delicious supper she'd eaten suddenly sat like a cardboard lump in the pit of her stomach. The same thing had happened to her once before, and it was an experience she would never forget. She had been chosen to compose the background music for a university function. A week later, after she'd had it half completed, they told her that they had reconsidered and given the honor to the professor's niece. It still stung, even after so much time had passed. Only now, years later, could she think of Sally without hating her — at least most of the time.

Now she was doing the same thing to someone else.

"I was thinking that he doesn't seem to like me very much. Now I know why."

Lois waved one hand in the air. "That is not so. Ted is a good man; you must get to know him."

Miranda stared into the bottom of her empty cup. She had a feeling that was a task easier said than done. •

4

Ted sat stiffly in his chair at the boardroom table, trying to appear relaxed even though his mind whirled faster than *Tante* Odelle's spinning wheel. He'd participated in the initial planning meeting for the church's combined Christmas and anniversary celebration, but under different circumstances from today.

In the three years he'd served as worship leader, he had proven himself in his abilities and strengths. Without fail, he had successfully put together all the music for every worship event, whether Sunday services or larger celebrations. But for this one, because of some initial difficulties, the deacons and church board declared Miranda Klassen an answer to prayer. He'd prayed about it, too, but *Miss Randi with an "i"* was not the answer he'd received.

As they waited for the last board member to arrive, he couldn't help but be aware of every move Miranda made since she sat across the table from him. Every time he turned her way, she was already looking at him, and as soon as he looked back, she glanced away. When she wasn't looking at him, he tried not to stare at her fire-engine-red lipstick, her worldly clothing, or her uncovered, unbound hair.

He gritted his teeth. She was the only woman in the room not wearing a prayer *kapp*. Even though they sat in the meeting room, it was still God's house, and they would still have a short prayer. As a woman, she should be wearing a head covering.

Last night he'd gone home in a state of shock, which had only begun to wear off. He had tried to remain a gentleman, yet his mind had been mostly numb about this woman.

Now his thoughts were clearer. Everything about her had been the exact opposite of what he had expected. He could not in good conscience give this city woman full blessing and a free rein on the most important event in his church's history. Even though she called herself a Mennonite, she knew nothing of his people or their culture. Although it was true that he had never executed a project of this magnitude before, he did know his church and his people.

As the general manager for Onkel Bart's furniture factory, the largest employer in town, managing was his job. He made decisions on purchases for all supplies and materials and approved or amended all design changes. He also did all the hiring, and occasionally he needed to fire someone, which was never pleasant, but he did what had to be done. He ran the company proficiently, with a profit, even when economic times were difficult. The current fiscal year end was approaching, and it held good promise of being their best year since Onkel Bart had retired and given Ted full control of his corporation.

Certainly he could run a church musical as efficiently as he ran a company. Only the church board didn't think so.

On purpose, Ted dropped his pencil on the floor, then bent to pick it up. With his face below the table, he closed his eyes and quoted to himself a verse from Psalms he'd memorized to help him deal with the stabbing feeling of betrayal: A man's wisdom gives him patience; it is to his glory to overlook an offense.

He had prayed about this, but he needed to pray some more. He still felt angry about being pushed aside, and his anger had begun to leak out in inappropriate ways. At work, where he'd always been considered fair and reasonable, he'd been irritable almost to the point of being short-tempered, which wasn't like him at all. Or at least, he thought it wasn't — something else he needed to pray about. He certainly had not been in his glory lately, nor had he used much patience. He was convinced that he had been a poor leader and a worse example. Perhaps now, here at church, in front of his elders, his pastor, and his Lord, he needed to repent and overlook the offense of being thrown in the recycle bin like a bent nail.

Ted righted himself in the chair and laid the pencil alongside his notepad.

Pastor Jake addressed everyone seated around the large wooden table — the table Ted had made for the church with his own hands, sparing nothing for the Lord's work.

"We are all here now. Are we ready to start?" Pastor asked.

Everyone, including Miranda, nodded, so Pastor Jake opened the meeting with a prayer.

After everyone's "amen," Pastor folded his hands on top of the notepad in front of him. "I know all of you have met Miss Klassen, but I would like to make our introductions formal for the sake of the minutes."

Miranda held up an odd-shaped pen. "I know the minutes of the meeting are being written down, but does anyone mind if I also record the meeting?"

Kathleen smiled. "Of course not. I can also let you read the minutes of our past meetings if you want to see what ideas we had before we decided to bring you here."

Miranda's eyes widened. "Really? That would be great. Thank you."

Pastor Jake nodded his agreement, then opened the meeting by introducing everyone on the church board — Leonard and Lois Toews, who were the head deacon couple; Elsie Neufeld as the Ladies Ministry Coordinator; William Janzen as the treasurer; Kathleen Loewen as the church secretary, and Ryan Schofield as the youth leader, who would organize the younger people to build all the sets and maintain the stage.

Pastor Jake turned toward Ted. "You have already met Ted Wiebe. Ted is our worship leader."

Ted felt the heat of everyone's eyes on him. He cleared his throat. "Welcome," he said.

A silence hung in the air, but he didn't know what else to say, or even if it was wise to say anything. He'd seen the shock in everyone's eyes as they came into the room, wondering why this city woman was at their meeting. When Pastor Jake introduced her, he'd thought Elsie might faint. For now, everyone needed time to think and evaluate.

Miranda blinked a few times, then stared directly into his eyes. "Thank you for picking me up at the airport yesterday."

Not a single head turned away. Everyone's concentration remained fixed on him. "It was not a problem," he muttered. Manners dictated that he say, "It was a pleasure," but it wasn't.

The room remained silent until Pastor cleared his throat, thankfully drawing everyone's attention to where it belonged, away from him and to Pastor.

As the meeting continued, everyone discussed ideas Ted had already heard before, some of them his own, while he listened. At the last meeting, he'd taken meticulous notes, scrawling out ideas and schematics. Now he sat with crossed arms.

When everyone finished speaking, Miranda picked up her pen, clicked it, then set it down in front of her. Her notepad remained completely blank. Either she had a photographic memory, which he doubted, or she wasn't really interested in anything they'd discussed.

Pastor Jake also put down his pen, but at least he'd been writing with it. "Does anyone have any questions or comments?"

Ted could see it in everyone's eyes. In addition to the expected questions about the presentation, the most important considerations were those closer to everyone's hearts and homes — how would Miranda Klassen fit in here, and how would she affect everyone, especially their young people, many of whom already struggled with the limitations of their protected community versus the freedom, dangers, and vulnerabilities of life in the cities.

No one said anything; no one asked any questions. But Ted could understand this. It had taken him an entire day to collect his thoughts. He could only think that others would need time as well. But time was something they didn't have. They only had the length of the meeting, and they were already running late.

Ted turned to Miranda. "I am sure this will be very different than what you have done before."

"Yes, but the message behind Christmas is universal. After I get to know more people, I don't think I'll have any problems. At home, I consider everyone who wants to be involved before I put anything together.

Here, I will do the same thing. It will work. But first I need to study the area, including all the demographics."

Ted blinked. Demographics? "This is not a political rally. It is a celebration for our church."

"Exactly. I need to know who I'm trying to reach."

He narrowed his eyes. "Which we made clear in our proposal to you." He lowered his voice. "Nothing has changed."

One of the ladies made a quiet gasp.

"But in order for this to work, we have to reach everyone we can. We want to pack this place, which seats four hundred people, with more than friends and relatives for five performances. We're going to reach souls as far as we can go. We need to do what it takes to get people excited and to come from miles around. That means advertising in all the local papers and doing promos. I need to check into the cost of a few radio ad spots during rush-hour traffic. We can do a movie trailer and put it on YouTube and anywhere else we can online. We'll set up a website for the church and run it there too. I'll start a blog and gather a chain of Internet influencers."

Words he'd heard in Sunday school all his life and had taught himself in Bible study meetings roared through his head: *Be ye in the world but not of the world.*

"Not over the Internet," Ted blurted out. He stood slowly, leaning forward over the table, glaring at her, deliberately towering over her. He was the only one besides the pastor who had significant dealings over the Internet. While there was much good, the evils far outweighed the godly content on the wide-open computer networks. With the Internet came temptation of a magnitude no one here had ever experienced. He could not expose his people to that. *"Niemols,"* he snapped. Never.

Beneath the table, clothing rustled and boots scraped on the tile floor.

Ted gritted his teeth. Of course they wanted to reach the unsaved. But they weren't going to risk their families or compromise the traditional lifestyle they'd worked so hard to guard. Like everyone here, he wanted to bring new people into God's kingdom, but he wanted those who came to their church to be family people of good morals. If she sent open invitations over the Internet, all the unsavory characters of the area would come and poison their innocent members. He knew how ugly it was out there. Every time he had to travel, it took him days to wind down after being thrust among the evils of the modern world.

Pastor cleared his throat. "Uh . . . well . . ." he stammered, "we do want this to be an outreach."

Miranda sat tall in her chair, turning as she spoke, making brief but definite eye contact with every person around the table. "Then we have to do more than just put a note in the church bulletin. We have to speak to people the way they're used to listening, and that means using the modern media to our full advantage." Her voice lowered, both in volume and in pitch. "Or I can pack up my things and go back to Seattle."

Ted held his breath. It had finally been said. But somehow it didn't have the same effect coming from Miranda as it would have from one of the church board members, the pastor, or himself.

No one said a word. No one suggested that they take this to a vote to see if it would work.

He sank back down in his chair. Their church had worked hard over the years to maintain a close bond of tradition and spirituality, keeping their members pure by minimizing temptation.

Miranda was now saying they could use her city ways, everything they'd wanted to keep out, to bring people in. It was like offering another apple from the Garden of Eden.

Pastor Jake tapped his pen on the table. "I have thought about this, and Miss Klassen speaks the truth. We agreed that we want to reach as many people as possible. Miss Klassen thinks we should do more than what we have done before, and we will be able to reach even more souls. This is what God wants us to do."

Ted's stomach tightened. Of course God wanted all His children to show His love and reach out in fellowship. But that didn't mean putting their families and their children at risk. Successful outreach happened when you got to know people and then invited them into the fold — not when you opened the doors to the evils and poisons you had worked so hard to avoid. Most of the people in their church had no idea what life was like outside of the safe boundaries of their burg and surrounding farms.

He did. He'd been exposed to all sorts of distractions and temptations when he traveled. He did his best to keep himself pure, and sometimes he failed. But by God's grace, he could keep himself as unscathed as possible.

If this was what his church decided they

wanted, there was only one thing Ted could do.

He turned to Miranda and hooked his thumbs in his suspenders. "Then I will help you do this. I will do everything I can to assist you." *And Lord, protect us.*

"*Ach,* you should not be here in my kitchen getting your own tea. You are a guest." Susan extended one arm in the direction of the doorway. "You should be showing your pictures and good ideas to the men. I will bring you more tea when it is ready. Go into the living room."

"Thanks," Miranda said. Nervously, she ran her hand down her slim skirt. She didn't know why she had brought it, but now she praised God for His divine intervention. It wasn't exactly suitable for church, but it had saved her from being the only woman in the entire Sunday morning service wearing slacks. With the hemline just above her knees, it was the shortest skirt in the congregation, but at least it was a skirt. Still, she wondered if she had made the wrong choice and should have worn dress slacks this morning. At church, most of the men had averted their eyes, as if seeing her legs was too shocking.

Now, here, at Susan and John Friesen's

home, she felt as exposed as if she were at the beach wearing a bathing suit two sizes too small. In the smaller crowd, in a private home, she could tell when one of the men stared at her legs, then turned his head when she caught him looking.

At church it had been worse, even though she sat on the women's side with Lois. There, where the men could no longer be disturbed by her legs, the women had stared at her shoes. She'd heard a few "tsks," but no one had made any specific comments. After the service Lois ignored the obvious disdain and introduced her around to the ladies, and Ted had introduced her to a few of the men.

Lois entered the kitchen just as Susan began to shoo her out. She rested her hand on Miranda's arm. "You do not need to be so nervous. Your ideas, they are good."

"I know," she mumbled, running her hand once more down her skirt, smoothing out yet another imaginary wrinkle. "But I'm worried that I didn't make a very good first impression this morning. I had the feeling Ted usually stays longer after the service, but he seemed to be rushing me out the door." Ted, more than any of the other men, made a point of keeping his eyes glued to her face and not her legs.

Lois's eyes followed her hand. "Ah, you are feeling strange about your skirt. *Ja,* it is very different from the rest, but it is not something that cannot be fixed. I love to sew. Let me work with you, and we will have a lovely new dress for you by next Sunday."

Miranda glanced down at Lois's dress, then back up to the woman's face. All morning, even though she knew it would be that way, she had been stunned by the mass uniformity. All the men, including Ted, had worn plain dark suits, blending together in a sea of sameness. The women's side had shown slightly more color, but the effect was no different. She couldn't remember anything specific or eye-catching about a single thing anyone had worn, male or female.

She swallowed hard. "Thank you, Lois, I would really appreciate that. No one has ever made anything for me before. I'm honored."

Lois waved one hand in the air. "*Doats jau neuscht.* It is nothing. I used to sew dresses for my daughter. It was something we both loved to do. Now I get to do it again. It is something I enjoy."

"Thank you. I'd love your help. I only own one long skirt, and it's quite different from what I'd wear here." It was a satiny formal gown she had worn only once at a college party. Even though it hung to her ankles, the right side had a slit that went up to her thigh. She bit her bottom lip thinking of the reaction that would get from the men here. Especially Ted. So far nothing she had said or done had met with his approval.

"But I feel I should be in the kitchen with the rest of the women." As at church, the separation of men and women continued here at John and Susan's home. After the meal the men had naturally moved into the living room to share ideas while the women had silently cleared the table and retreated into the kitchen. A few minutes had passed before Miranda realized she was the only woman in the living room with the men — the only one wearing the shortest skirt these men had seen in years, maybe even in their lives. She had nearly run for the kitchen.

"At home I take the leftover food and put it in the fridge, then go back and join my guests. My father and I do the dishes together after everyone leaves."

Lois gasped. "Your father is the pastor, is he not?" She pressed one hand to her mouth, as if the thought of the pastor doing his own dishes was too horrible for words.

"Yes. It's just him and me. My mother passed away a long time ago. It seems that lately the only time we get to talk is when we do dishes. So in a way, sometimes we look forward to doing them." Although at home the process wouldn't take as long, because unlike anyone in Piney Meadows, they had a dishwasher.

"Let us not talk of dishes. You go. There is Ted, waiting for you."

Inwardly, Miranda cringed. She didn't want to talk to Ted.

Today he blended in like everyone else, but yesterday, after presenting her thoughts, she had felt like an invading rival in a *Star Trek* movie. Ted had risen from the quiet void of nothingness, emerging like a Klingon Bird of Prey decloaking with battle stations engaged, while all around him men cowered, knowing death was near. But instead of speaking Klingon, he'd said something in Low German.

She would have understood Klingon better. But the message was clear. Ted disagreed with pretty much everything she'd presented. And Klingons showed no mercy to their enemies.

She couldn't remember if Klingons wore suspenders. The thought made her want to giggle. She would google that to find out — if she could ever obtain Internet access.

Miranda blinked and focused on Ted,

standing quietly beside the couch, patiently waiting for her with all the other men in Susan's living room.

Lois nudged her from behind. "Go. Show everyone what you showed me last night. It is good."

Slowly, Miranda made her way into the living room, needing that cup of tea more than ever. She sat on the couch, positioning herself behind her laptop, and flipped open the cover. The couch moved as Ted settled into the space beside her.

He turned and gave her a half-smile. "Your church must be very much different from ours."

Miranda quickly turned so she didn't have to look at him. Her skirt had crept up slightly as she sat, and here she couldn't hide herself under the table. "Yes," she said softly as she hit the power button. Unless it was communion Sunday, like many in the congregation, suitable clothing was her best jeans and her most comfortable shoes. She'd never felt so out of place in her life as she had during the service.

In the gap waiting for the operating system to boot up, Miranda tugged at her skirt, for all the good it did.

"Don't worry about me embarrassing you like this again. Lois offered to sew me a few

71

new skirts. I didn't want her to go to all that trouble, but she insisted."

"*Ja,* Lois likes to sew. She used to sew with her daughter."

"Where is her daughter now? I wasn't introduced to her this morning."

"Deborah had gone to one of the Christian universities to become a teacher. She used to come home most weekends, but she met a man and they got married. They are both living on campus, and they will both graduate in September. They do not know where they will live, but everyone doubts that it will be here."

"Is Lois okay with that?"

"She misses Deborah, but she is waiting for grandchildren. Lois dislikes travel, but she will do it to see babies."

"I can imagine her on the plane; she's so warm and friendly. Everyone near her would do anything to help her relax. In exchange, Lois would probably mail them cookies."

"*Ach,* no. She would mail them *pasching puffa.*" Ted closed his eyes and sighed, making Miranda imagine how good Lois's peach fritters must be.

Even though she had only been in their home a couple of days, she'd never experienced such an example of old-fashioned domestic bliss. Lois truly enjoyed keeping the house clean and performing all the domestic duties the hard way and accepted that as her contribution.

Being the pastor's daughter, Miranda had developed a sense for people. Usually she could tell when someone was acting happy on the outside, but inside they were miserable. Lois wasn't miserable. She seemed genuinely happy, inside and out.

The graphics program finally finished loading, so Miranda set the photos to slideshow mode, then sat back to allow the men room to watch.

"For the last cantata, we had two soloists, and the choir behind them."

Ted pointed to one of the costumes in the photo. "I see that someone in your church also has a talent for sewing."

"Actually, people were responsible for their own costumes. Most of them were bought at shops."

The next photo was of the band. From behind her, she heard a few sharp intakes of breath, making her wonder what the men found more shocking — that the drummer was a woman, or that the woman drumming wore pants. Or that she was using a computer to show photos.

"I brought a DVD of the concert." As the words came out of her mouth, she wished she could take them back. There would be no electronics in John and Susan's home. Not even a television.

"There is a DVD player at the church," Ted said. "We will have to plan for a meeting to listen to it. But some of your songs from this were on what you mailed, were they not?"

"Yes. Here are a few more pictures from last Christmas. The tickets went so fast we had to put on an extra performance. Which is what I hope will happen here."

"Tickets? We are not going to charge for tickets. This is to be by open invitation."

"The tickets will be free. They're just to reserve seats — so we know how many people will be there each night, and we won't have more people come than we have seats and need to turn people away." *Although from the looks of things so far, I doubt that will happen.* But she could dream. And pray.

Almost like a domestic parade, all the ladies appeared from the kitchen. Lois set a cup of tea beside her laptop, and Susan carried a plastic container filled with a variety of leftovers, which she placed near the edge of the coffee table. "For you, Ted."

He smiled graciously at her. "*Danke shoen,* Susan. I am always grateful for your left-

74

overs, and one day when I am fat, I will know who has done this to me."

Miranda smiled. This one thing was the way it was at home. Many of the older married ladies gave handouts to the single men. Ted, being the only single man in attendance, probably would receive enough food for a few days, and be happy for it.

She turned to ask if anyone in the congregation ran a print shop and was stopped by the sight of John grinning and patting his rounded stomach. "Ah, Ted, my friend, this truly is what will happen to you when you get married. This is also why I am going to get only one sandwich for lunch all week long."

Beside him, Len laughed. "You are doing fine until your wife starts packing a salad for your lunch."

The men's smiles dropped, as if Len had proposed a fate worse than death. Behind them, most of the women giggled.

For the first time that day, Miranda felt herself relax. This was a similarity that her church shared with this one — in Mennonite circles, one did not entertain without mass quantities of food.

Maybe the culture shock wasn't going to be so bad, once she got a new wardrobe. She had already texted her father to stop the shipment of all but one box of her clothes, and her piano. If she wanted to look at the bright side, this was a good reason to go shopping. Yet, no matter what she wore, she still feared that she would never truly fit in with the women here. She was university-educated and fully immersed in the business protocols of the modern world, as were many other women in her church, certainly all of her friends. Here, the lines were distinct. The men were the providers and head of the house. The women took care of hearth and home. Yet no one seemed unhappy. In fact, Miranda suspected the divorce rate here was almost nil. In some ways, she almost envied them, while at the same time she knew that she could not be happy here on a long-term basis.

For one short year, she could do it, and probably enjoy it. It could be like a working vacation. Except she wasn't exactly on vacation, she was doing two jobs — first writing and directing the church's Christmas drama, plus the job she couldn't leave behind in Seattle. The key would be settling into a routine.

Tomorrow, when all was calm and everyone went back into their weekday activities, Lois would allow Miranda the privacy she needed, which she would use to full advantage. She wouldn't have an Internet connection, so she planned to walk to the church and visit Kathleen, who could discreetly answer many of her questions.

Once more, she studied the group, while they were all busy studying the display on her laptop.

Even though Ted obviously shopped at the same store as all the other men and his trusty hat hung at the rack near the door with all the rest, he seemed to have a different way of thinking than everyone else. Something about him wasn't quite the same, but she didn't know what.

When the last picture finished and the screen went to black, Miranda began the process of shutting down the computer. As she closed the laptop, Ted sat forward, capturing her attention. "In the meeting, you had talked of demographics. I will help you familiarize yourself with Piney Meadows. I have taken tomorrow off work to show you around."

Miranda's throat tightened. "Tomorrow? You took the day off work?"

"*Ja*. All arrangements have been made for someone else to look after my duties, so I have booked a vacation day. I will pick you up at ten."

rage. She would have an impulse control, so she planned to wait to the
porch and confront Miranda, who could the
clearly observe many of her emotions.

Once more, she studied the group; noth-
they were anxiously manning the display on
her laptop.

Even though Ted obviously shopped at the
same store as all the other men and had

5

"What I wouldn't give right now for a Starbucks," Miranda sighed from the chair.

Ted turned his head to stare at the growing pile of boxes on the floor beside her.
"Would that help you decide? You have tried
on every pair of boots in the store. Soon we
will be asked to leave."

Whenever Ted bought boots or shoes, he
picked the ones he liked best from the shelf,
tried them on, and if they fit, he bought
them. Within five minutes his transaction
was done, and he was on to his next task.

Instead of again taking off the current
boot, she slipped the matching one onto her
other foot. One eye narrowed as she con-
templated both booted feet side by side,
then she tapped the heels together.

"I'll take these." She turned to look up at
the poor clerk, who sagged visibly with
relief. "Can you put my tennis shoes in the
bag, and I'll just wear these out? I'll put

that on my credit card."

When her transaction was complete, Ted stowed her package in the trunk of his car. He checked to make sure the lock was engaged, then turned to see Miranda digging for something in her new purse, which was serviceable, large, and a good neutral color.

"Will Lois need her coat back today? I need to know, in order to plan what time we need to return."

She shook her head without looking up. "No, she said she has no plans for herself, or her coat. But I need a trip to Walmart as soon as possible to get my own."

While she continued to dig, a gust of wind whipped up her hair. Ted pressed his hat down to his head until the gust stilled.

Even with Lois's coat, he knew Miranda would still be cold because she wasn't used to Minnesota winters. He was cold. Her jeans would keep her legs warm, which, even though he hated to admit it, was a wise choice. Some of the young ladies the same age as Miranda wore pants in casual situations away from church, although none of the ladies over the age of forty ever did. While he valued tradition to the core of his soul, he often thought those ladies would be very, very cold with the winter wind blowing, and had concluded that was why all ladies' winter activities were held indoors.

Miranda pulled something out of her purse, stuffed it in her jacket pocket, and raised her head to look at him. "Are you going to start my tour, now that I have my boots? Before I freeze to death?"

He cleared his throat. "As you can tell, this is the main street in town."

She pulled the smallest camera he'd ever seen out of her pocket, aimed it at the street sign, pressed the button, and turned to smile at him. "Ya think? After all, the sign says we're on Main Street. Before I forget, on our way home, can we drive in the same way as we came from the airport? I'd like to take a picture of the welcome sign with the population count for the opening page of my album."

"You take pictures of signs?"

"Of course. They're like a road map, directing me through my photo albums."

He'd already seen too much of her camera. Everywhere she went, she took photos, often when she thought no one was watching. She had taken a few at the church on Sunday, plus Len and Lois caught her taking photos of their antique piano. As if she wouldn't see it enough in the coming year.

He looked at the camera again. At least it

wasn't red, but it was pink. "My friend Brian also has a digital camera, although it is larger." It was also black and looked like a camera. "Whenever he shows me his photos, we have to turn on his computer, just like you and your laptop. I like to hold photographs in my hand when I look at them."

"Tsk. And you call yourself a Mennonite."

Ted reached up to straighten his hat. He had always been proud of his heritage. Above all, he was never ashamed. He didn't stop wearing his hat when he was in the city on business, even though people often stared at him, and sometimes they whispered and pointed. But God was gracious. When he was away on a business trip, the way he carried himself and his refusal to dress like the city people identified him with Onkel Bart's furniture business, which their purchasers liked. His success at marketing told him God had blessed their business.

She smiled a little too sweetly. "I am being a good steward with my digital camera because it doesn't take film, and it uses a rechargeable battery."

"Taking many pictures does not make you a good Mennonite."

"Still, they help me remember where I've been."

Ted had been many places in North America, and even though he didn't own a camera, he remembered them just fine.

She snapped more pictures. "This area is so quaint. I like it."

"This is the older area of our downtown. We do not have a mall here. We chose to keep the atmosphere friendly with the traditional shopping area."

He wondered if she had visited the Mall of America.

She lifted her camera and snapped more pictures. "I've seen pictures like this in books. All these stores look so old."

"That is because they *are* old."

Ted started walking at a reasonable speed, but Miranda slowed her pace to take more pictures as she continued on. He slowed so she could catch up, but the more he slowed, the more she did, until she was at a dead stop in front of Bess's store. "Can we go in here?"

"It depends. Do you want to take pictures or buy something?"

She smiled as if he'd made a joke. "Buy something. I need to buy some yarn to knit myself a scarf."

He lowered his head. "This I must see," he grumbled to himself as he pulled the door open and waited for her to enter. He

82

couldn't imagine her knitting, but if she truly did, maybe there was some hope for her after all. Maybe.

He stood, waiting less than patiently, while she introduced herself to Bess, then bought all the yarn Bess said she would need for a hat and scarf. It shouldn't have surprised him that it was red.

Once again, they returned to his car that was parked on the street. Not that he'd needed to drive the short distance. In fact, it had probably taken longer to warm the car up than it would have taken to walk. But he was glad he had brought it, because she had bought so many things they had to keep returning to the car to stow them. The trunk was almost full, and they hadn't yet been inside every store. Almost every store, but not all. However, he had to admit he was getting an education. Until today, he had never been inside a fabric store. He hadn't known there were so many components involved in the construction of a dress.

For the fourth time, he rearranged the contents of the trunk so he could close it without squashing anything. "This shopping trip has taken longer than I had planned. I would like to stop for lunch."

She looked up one side of the street, then the other. "I don't see any burger joints. I guess this means we're eating healthy."

"*Ja.* A good meal should be wholesome and not rushed."

Miranda's mouth opened as if she was going to ask a question, but instead she shook her head and turned in the direction of the only few stores they hadn't visited, which was also where Elena and Mary's restaurant was. "That sounds great. I'm starving."

As they walked, Miranda continued to compare the main downtown area of Piney Meadows to the Pike Place Market in Seattle. There, the theme was variety in crafts, unique items, and collectables, as well as the markets for fresh fruit, vegetables, and delicious snacks. Here the theme was much the same, but it was Mennonite through and through. For the Mennonite people who lived here, these were their normal places of business. Therefore, the prices were modest.

But good prices or not, after buying so much fabric, she didn't dare go inside any more stores. She had overspent her budget by about double, and needed to wait for her next paycheck before buying anything else, down to a pack of gum.

On her next shopping trip, she wanted to spend more time, and money, at the craft store. That's where she'd seen most of the materials used in many of the handcrafted items she wanted to take home, and she knew that it was probably the ladies in the sewing group she planned to join who made these things. She would ask them to teach her how to make these things herself.

That was a group she needed to join — the sewing group. It was the best setting to meet the ladies, learn to fit in, and make friends. Fortunately, no one had called her an "Englisher" as the Amish did with outsiders. Her last name assured them that she was one of them, and yet she had to earn the right to be welcome in any of their inner circles.

"If one day you would like to get your hair cut and you do not want Lois to do it, here is where you can go."

Miranda slowed to take a picture, again from the outside as they passed, since Ted had started to refuse to walk inside any more of the shops. "Are you sure? This looks kind of like a barbershop, but different."

Ted nodded, slowing only slightly while she caught up. "*Ja*. It is more than a barbershop. Dave Reimer cuts the men's hair on the right of the shop, and his wife Gerta cuts the ladies' hair on the left."

Even the hair salon was divided down the

middle. She didn't dare ask if Gerta could touch up her roots. The next time she got her hair streaked, it would be back at Roxi's at home. Next January.

"Here we are. You will enjoy this. Elena Rempel and her *sesta* Mary Dueck do all the cooking. You have met William Janzen, their *brooda*. He is the church treasurer. He works for Onkel Bart and me for four days a week, and for one day he takes care of the restaurant."

From the second the door opened, wholesome cooking smells tantalized her — onions, sizzling meats, the unmistakable aroma of roasting chicken, and something sweet that meant dessert. "Mmm!" Miranda closed her eyes and inhaled deeply. "This smells just like my church's last potluck supper, only better."

While Ted held the door open, Miranda stepped inside, then moved to let him pass.

"I see a good table that is empty," he said as he stepped onto a burlap mat and stomped the snow off his boots. "We will go there."

The door had barely closed behind them when one of the sisters called out from behind the counter. "Ted! *Na woa laet et?*"

"It is looking good," he said, then smiled to return her greeting. "As usual, it is a

86

pleasure to see you."

The woman didn't approach them but continued to speak loudly across the room. "I see you have brought our guest, Miss Klassen. Sit down. I will be there very soon."

Ted removed his hat, then carried it with him, leading Miranda to a table beside the window. Instead of sitting, he pulled out one of the chairs and waited behind it.

Miranda had almost aimed herself to go around the table to the other side before she realized what he was doing. "Thank you," she mumbled as she moved toward him, then lowered herself into the chair as he pushed it in for her to position herself comfortably.

She draped Lois' coat on the back of her chair while Ted walked casually around the table, as if this was normal for him. She couldn't remember the last time a man had seated her at a table. Bradley had never done that when he'd taken her on a date.

Ted deposited his coat and hat on the seat of the extra chair, then sat opposite her. "All this shopping has made me hungry," he said, as he rested one hand on his stomach.

"What shopping? All you bought was a tin of shoe polish."

"I needed nothing else." ✻

A lady with "Elena" on her name tag appeared with two menus in hand. "Enjoy! Of course we will give Miss Klassen's meal the same discount as we give you. I must run. The pies are coming out of the oven. I will be back."

Miranda opened the menu, but leaned forward toward Ted. "Discount?" Ted opened the menu, skimmed it quickly, then closed it and laid it on the table. "I come here often."

Between the leftovers she knew people gave him and his spending so much time at the restaurant that they gave him a standing discount, she wondered if he even cooked. "I almost was going to tease you about not cooking, but I can't really. I don't cook much either. My father does most of the cooking at home."

"Your papa? I know life is different in the cities, but your mama does not cook?"

"My mother died when I was a little girl. It's just me and my father."

"*Ach,* I am sorry. Both my mama and papa have also gone to glory, so my heart is with you."

A wave of guilt rushed through her. On Sunday, she had wondered why she hadn't been introduced to Ted's parents. She'd simply assumed they hadn't gone to church that day, even though in this community that would be rare. Now she knew why as a single young adult, Ted lived alone.

"I'm so sorry. If there's anything I can do for you, please ask."

"Do not worry. My house is often messy, but Tante Odelle helps me."

Miranda blinked. "Not housework — I meant if you needed help with something I'm good at. Like if you need some advice with your income tax return, because you probably have a lot of things that could be written off as business expenses that you don't know about. Or if you need your spark plugs gapped or changed, I'm not too bad under the hood of a car, unless it involves lifting the engine."

"Oh." He paused and looked at her arms, then back up to her face. "I thought —"

Miranda held up one palm toward him and sighed. "Please, don't say it. I know that's not typical girl stuff around here. It's going to be a huge adjustment for me, but I'm going to do my best to fit in. You can't begin to guess at how much I'm out of my league here."

His frown tightened. "I think I can."

Miranda thumped her elbows on the table and buried her face in her hands. "I'm sorry. You do know how much I don't fit in here. I want to do whatever it takes to make this work, but I don't really know what to do. Dad and I aren't exactly a typical family unit. Without my mom, and because Dad was so busy as a pastor, I've had to learn to do a lot of nontypical things for the two of us to survive. You know, instead of shopping today, I should have been at the library, learning the history of your town and community."

"After we eat, I can take you to our museum, if that is what you desire."

She spread her fingers and peeked between them. "You have a museum?"

"*Ja.* It is at the end of our downtown area. A few more blocks."

She lowered her hands to grasp the edge of the table, and leaned toward him. "That would be great!"

Elena returned to take their orders. She looked at Miranda first, her pencil poised above her notepad.

Miranda stared at the menu. It wasn't in English. If she sounded some of the entrées out carefully, many of the dishes were familiar to her. But many were not. "There are so many choices, I can't decide. Ted, what are you having?"

He left his menu on the table. "Today I will have *Graesht Mehl Grumbara Supp.*"

Miranda slapped the menu closed. "I

90

think I'll have the same."

Ted smiled as Elena returned to the kitchen. "As you can guess, Elena and Mary have a different menu for the tourists."

"Yes, that's a terrific idea. These tourists are just non-Mennonite people who live in the area, right?"

"*Ja.* Right."

Miranda nodded. Then those were the people his church wanted to attract on Sundays and spread their ministry to. "Elena and Mary are definitely doing something right. All the shopkeepers here are doing great at attracting the tourists. I can see why they keep coming, and I've got some great pictures. Do you want to see what I've taken so far?"

He shrugged his shoulders. "I hope I am not in any of them."

"No, you're not." But the fact that he mentioned it set her mind racing. She hadn't yet had the chance to e-mail home, and she hadn't told her friends or Bradley what she had walked into. A photo of Ted in his hat and frumpy coat standing against any of the old storefronts, the sidewalks piled high with snow, would say more than a thousand words.

She hadn't finished showing him all her pictures before Elena returned with two bowls of steamy, fragrant soup.

Since no one brought soup to the pot-lucks, she had no idea what was in it. As a classic Old Mennonite dish, she doubted it would contain green peppers, which was the only food she truly hated.

Ted bowed his head to lead a beautiful and heartfelt prayer, thanking God for the time they would spend together at the museum and asking a blessing on the food they were about to share.

"Amen," she said quietly.

Ted blew gently onto the soup as he stirred it a few times, then began to eat.

He closed his eyes and sighed. "Mary makes the best *Graesht Mehl Grumbara Supp* I have ever tasted. It is even better than my mama's."

Cautiously, Miranda took her first taste. It was some kind of potato soup full of tender vegetables, but it wasn't the same color as she'd had before. Still, she liked it. "Yes, this is delicious. Was your mother a good cook?"

He smiled, and his eyes glazed over. "*Ja.* This was why my papa said he married her."

Even though the ability to cook meant more to the Mennonites in Ted's world than it did to Mennonites in suburban Seattle, it was still important for hospitality and showing love for others. Even though it wasn't the same, some of the best times she had with her father were when it was just the two of them in the kitchen sharing a meal, even if it was the special from the local Chinese takeout.

She watched Ted, who still seemed lost in thought over the relationship between his parents.

Being initially attracted to a woman because of her cooking and family skills was better than some of the things she had heard in some of her clients' workplaces. One of the men proudly proclaimed to everyone in the office that he'd married his wife for various parts of her anatomy.

"I'm afraid I don't remember any of my mother's cooking. The only thing I really remember is making chocolate chip cookies, but I don't remember eating them. So either they weren't very good, or once we finished mixing them, I was no longer interested. Did you ever make cookies with your mother?"

"No." His face closed up, reminding her that in his world, a boy spending time in the kitchen was a fate worse than death.

Miranda sighed and continued to stir her soup. "When I get married I dream about making cookies with my kids. But I know realistically that I'm not going to do a lot of cooking, so I'm going to have to marry a man who knows his way around a kitchen or we'll all starve to death." *Either that, or they will all learn to love Chinese takeout real fast.*

"The woman I marry will be a good cook, like her mother, so there will always be plenty of food on the table."

Since the soup was now cooled to a more comfortable temperature, they ate in silence until the last drops were gone from both bowls.

"Come. We can go to the museum now. They will put this on my account. Elena and Mary make my lunch every day, and I stop here on my way to work to pick it up. It is easier to pay once a week."

That shouldn't have surprised her. As he stood to slip on his coat, and probably because they'd just been talking about him not cooking, Miranda noticed that while he wasn't carrying too much extra around his middle, he wasn't exactly starving. She suspected he received many invitations to supper from mothers of the single ladies.

The soup had warmed her from the inside out, but by the time they reached the end of the block, Miranda felt as if she had made a trip through a deep freeze. Back when she'd had a part-time job at the local supermarket, even the freezer hadn't been this cold.

The museum, small and smelling of old books and newspapers, had a plaque near the door proclaiming that the building used to be a school. One corner of what appeared to be the main room was dedicated to the history of the area and the early colony days, before the community had allegedly modernized and settled on the outskirts of this town, which had now joined theirs in its population growth. Faded black and white photos displayed a blacksmith, a gristmill, and many old sod houses that she had never realized were built so low in the ground.

She pressed her finger to the glass in front of a picture of an old windmill. "Is this still intact?"

"*Ja.* If you want, I will take you there. But it is only open to people in the summer. Would you like to go into the other room now? This room is all pictures, everything else is over there."

She could have spent the rest of the day looking at the old photos. One day she would return by herself. But since Ted wasn't as interested in the pictures as she was, she followed him to the other, smaller room.

"Wow. Look at this stuff . . ." The expected farm and kitchen implements were displayed, as well as clothing and a prayer *kapp,* which wasn't much different from what the ladies wore now. The precision in the crafted items caused her to stop. "I've never seen a quilt like this in my life."

A glass case in the center of the room displayed what looked like children's arts and crafts. Each item had been dated back to different stages of the school's growth, up to the time when one-room schoolhouses were discontinued and this school was closed.

She studied the dates. "Everything here was made by people who actually lived in the area, right?" She had never met anyone who had gone to a one-room schoolhouse. A million questions about what it must have been like bounced through her head. But she doubted there was anyone left who had lived through that kind of history.

"*Ja.* That picture over there was made by Gretta, who is Sarah's grootmutta. We should be going. They are going to close soon. And it is almost dark out."

Miranda checked her watch. Sure enough, it was nearly five-fifteen. She turned to smile at him. "I doubt you're thinking the same thing as I am about the dark. For me, I worry that the nutcases come out worse at night, and it's dangerous when you can't see them coming."

"When I go to the cities, I am cautious about unsavory characters too. Here, I say this about the dark because I know how cold you are feeling, and it is colder after dark."

"I don't want to think about that." She immediately started fastening Lois's coat, which was so large it hung on her like a sack. At least it was a warm sack. "I guess I'm as ready as I'll ever be."

"I do not know if I told you. We have been invited to Pastor's home for supper tonight. He said to be there at five-thirty."

Miranda looked down at her jeans and grimaced. "Great."

6

Ted swung the car door open, holding it from being blown shut, until Miranda got all the way in. While he waited, watching her struggle to gather up the length of Lois's coat so it wouldn't get caught in the car door, her desperate words about trying to fit in came back to him.

He believed that she would try. But the fact that she openly admitted she didn't fit in proved the truth of her statement. Some things, no matter how hard one tried, were not attainable by any means except through the grace of God, and this was truly one of those times. At the same time, the Bible also warned about not putting God to the test.

As Miranda finally pulled the coat hem into the car, he closed the door, jogged around to the driver's side, and got in. Miranda was pulling down the sun visor.

"You do not have to worry," he said as he started the engine. "The sun is almost set.

98

We will not be driving into the glare. Pastor's house is to the north from here."

She quickly clicked on her seatbelt, then began digging through her purse frantically. "I hope you drive slowly."

"The roads are clear. There is no danger. You have already learned that I do not speed. I have never had a ticket. I . . ." His words trailed off as she pulled a small, square plastic container out of her purse.

She flicked it open and fumbled for a miniature brush with a solid foam end instead of bristles, and brushed it through a cake of brown powder. "Please drive real slow. This won't take me long, but I know his house can't possibly be far from anywhere in this town." She closed one eye, stretched her neck to look at her face closely in the visor mirror, and began to apply the powder to her eyelid. After a few seconds, she looked at herself, blinked three times, then applied more powder to the brush and began the same process with the other eye.

"What are you doing?"

"I'm putting my makeup on. I can't go out like this."

"Like what?"

She sighed loudly and snapped the container closed. She then pulled out a thin pencil and pulled the cap off, although why a pencil would need a cap, he didn't know. Then she moved the pencil up to her eye.

He didn't know what she was about to do, but he didn't want her to poke her eye out. "Wait!"

"Just don't move the car until I'm finished with the liner. Then we can go. I don't want to make us late." She drew a line under each eye, then smudged the lines with her finger. "Okay. We can go. I'll do the rest while we're moving."

"But —"

She waved one hand in the air quickly, then continued to dig in her purse. "Don't worry. I do this all the time in a moving car on the way to work. Just tell me if you're going to hit any potholes."

He considered the engine to be sufficiently warm, so he started moving, but it was difficult to keep his attention on the road. Even though he knew women in the cities looked very different from everyone he knew at home, he'd never witnessed the process of making the change.

Next she pulled out a cylindrical container, which unscrewed in the center. When she pulled at each end, a black brush with a strange curly shape came out. Again, she held it up toward one eye.

Ted gritted his teeth, slowed his speed,

and drove slower than he usually did, keeping a close watch for potholes, yet at the same time glancing to the side to see what she was doing. She brushed a dark substance to her eyelashes, taking more care at the sides of her eyes than the middle, then screwed the pieces back together and returned them to her purse.

The next procedure involved a short tube-shaped container, which pulled apart into two pieces, but this time there was no applicator. He feared it was broken until she started to turn one of the halves, and a red extrusion appeared. She pressed this gently to her lips, which transferred the red color.

He thought she was done, but next she pulled out another square plastic container, larger than the first one. This contained a skin-colored powder, and this brush was larger and actually had bristles. She swiped the brush into the powder, and this time brushed the powder onto her cheeks.

She snapped it shut and dropped it into her purse. "There. It's not perfect, but it's done. Do I look okay?"

He stopped the car in front of Pastor's house and turned to her.

"*Ja.* You look . . . uh . . ." At her request, he studied her face. He didn't know why, but even though she looked exactly the same as she had before they got in the car, something was different about her. Prettier. Somehow more interesting to look at. Although it didn't make sense because he'd seen exactly what she had done. The entire process had only taken seven minutes. The small bit of powders and applied colorings enhanced the flecks of green in her eyes, and the darker color of her lips drew his attention. Looking at her face, he could feel a difference in himself. Then her lips quivered, and she licked her top lip. Something fluttered in his stomach.

Ted looked away.

If he could feel this way while looking at their exasperating visitor, then he could understand that this was exactly why young unmarried people required a chaperone.

He turned off the engine and pulled out the keys. "You look fine. Let us go in."

The second the door opened, Ted could tell Kathleen had been working hard all day. Unless he was mistaken, he could smell *brotevascht mit eppel,* which meant that Kathleen would probably have *schnitz* pie for dessert.

"*Kom ein!* Welcome!" Pastor greeted them and waved them inside, to the living room.

Miranda tugged off her boots, wiggled her toes, then sighed. "It's so cold out there. Is it like this every winter?"

Pastor nodded. "*Ja.* But we have not yet had the coldest part of the winter. That will be in a couple of weeks, in the middle of February."

She mumbled something about a mistake, but Ted couldn't quite hear. Before he had a chance to ask her to repeat herself, she started walking toward the kitchen. "I think I'll see if Kathleen needs me."

As she disappeared into the kitchen doorway, he couldn't help but wonder if she would be more of a hindrance than a help. He didn't understand how any Mennonite woman could know so little about cooking. Life was different in the cities, but he had no idea that it would be that different in the church as well.

Pastor motioned him to sit on the couch. "How was your day with Miss Klassen?"

"Uh . . ." Ted tried to think of something encouraging. "Uh . . . she is very friendly."

Pastor waited. "And?"

And she didn't poke her eye out in the moving car.

Miranda appeared from the kitchen. "Kathleen says supper is ready."

Pastor looked at him, but Ted deliberately looked away. Once in the kitchen, he seated Miranda, then took his place at the table.

After bowing their heads for the blessing, everyone completed the prayer with an "amen."

Miranda closed her eyes and inhaled deeply above the fragrant main dish.

"Mm . . . sausages and apples. Mindy at my church makes this. It's one of my favorites, and yours smells even better."

Ted grinned. A quick glance at the counter proved he was also right about what Kathleen had prepared for dessert.

Miranda's grin widened. "I see you also made apple pie. I'm so awful with pies. My crust is always too thick and never tender."

Pastor smiled. "I am sure your talents are in other places."

Ted could only hope so.

Not only did Miranda help herself to a portion of *brotevascht mit eppel* suitable for a man, she also piled a large amount of buttered green beans onto her plate.

She smiled as she chewed. "This is so good. Thank you."

Kathleen watched, then smiled back. "It does my heart good to see a young woman eat like this. From what I have seen, women from the cities are always on a diet."

Miranda shook her head. "Not me. I've got a very high metabolism, thanks to my mother. It drives my friends crazy."

Pastor Jake cleared his throat. "Speaking of the cities and the difference to our little town, how did you enjoy our shopping area? Ted told me he was going to take you there today."

"It was great. I got some fabulous pictures, and the first thing I'm going to do when I get back to Len and Lois's home is to start knitting myself a nice warm scarf, and hopefully a hat. You've got a wonderful market area. I can see that it's very popular, both with your residents and with people from farther away."

"*Ja*. Opening the market area has been very good for us. We are no longer a farm community. Our young people are leaving the farms as machinery can do more and they are doing other things. Some have opened shops and are running businesses, and many of our people work in town instead of on the farms as they did a few generations ago. Others of our young people have gone to the cities to get an education. Some return, but many do not come back because we do not have jobs for them. Ted, he returned to us, and has doubled the size of the furniture factory."

Her eyes widened, she stopped chewing, and stared at him. "Really?"

Ted did not have fond memories of college. "Many of our people do not come back, but I did not enjoy my time in the cities. There are many evil things there. Alcohol. Illegal drugs. Most people are always in a hurry. Even at the dormitory, where students were supposed to trust each other, there were thieves and people often did not treat each other well."

"You took a business course, then?"

"*Ja.* I took extra classes so I could graduate with all I needed in two years." Which was why he stayed at the dormitory. He wanted his time in the city to be as short as possible. He hated crowds, and the college was always crowded. Starting early and finishing late every day, he got enough extra credits so he could graduate in two years instead of three. Besides that, Onkel Bart needed him back as soon as possible.

Miranda's eyes narrowed. "You didn't go to a Christian college, did you? I know they would probably be brutal to you."

"The Christian college was too far away. I made some friends where I went, but we were not together all the time. On campus there was much disrespect."

"Didn't you go to church on Sundays? Surely there were enough Christians on campus."

"The service was multi-denominational,

including non-Christian faiths. I was not comfortable there. I tried to come home once a month to be with my own people."

She reached toward him and wrapped her fingers around his hand. "That's too bad, but you did it, and you can be proud of yourself for your accomplishments. I did all my courses for my BA in accounting at an excellent Christian university in Seattle. I was there for four years, and it was a wonderful experience."

He looked down at her hand, then pulled his out from under hers. "I was not at college to have a wonderful experience. I was there to study and prepare myself to return to take over Onkel Bart's company."

Kathleen smiled, but yet her smile was sad. "We have found that those who go to Christian universities are the ones who seldom come back. This means we are seeing more and more of our people leave us and not return."

Miranda nodded. "That's happening all over the country in all small towns. It's expansion and progress. A small town can only support a certain population, and then the town either grows, or people leave so they can find jobs. There's probably only enough work for one or two doctors here. You've only got a small community hospital that would barely be called a clinic in Seattle. I would think there's also only enough work here for one lawyer, and he or she probably wouldn't do many interesting cases. It would be the same for all professionals. There's a limited marketplace in a small town."

Pastor glanced at his wife, then looked back toward Miranda. "I am not saying it is bad for our people to leave. In these times, often there is no choice. For them, we do our best to make them ready to spread God's word wherever they go. But just as we want to spread God's word into the cities, we wish to do the same here. Our town has many people who are not of our faith, or any faith. We wish to reach these people, and the people in all the towns around who are close enough to join us in worship every Sunday. We do not want to lose our heritage, but at the same time we want to welcome strangers to join our family. To show them God is good. As you learn about our town, and our area, this is what our church wishes for you to think about. How can we bring these people in, but not lose or compromise our heritage? This is why we want to bring many people to celebrate our church's anniversary at the same time as we celebrate Christmas."

"My Mennonite church in Seattle is very different from yours. I won't say our heritage is lost, but we have made some big adjustments over the years to meld ourselves with life in the fast-paced, big city."

Ted looked at her. His opinion hadn't changed since he first saw her at the airport. To call the difference "adjustments" was an understatement of monstrous proportions.

"As long as you are right with God in how you conduct your worship, this is what is important. Just as we are also sure that we are right with God in the way we live and conduct ourselves here." Pastor leaned back in his chair, a position he usually took when he was comfortable and knew his point had been taken and accepted.

Ted leaned forward. "There is more to living your faith than how you conduct yourself during the Sunday worship service. And what is right for one group of people will not be right for another. We are not willing to compromise ourselves."

Miranda cleared her throat and set her fork down beside her empty plate. "I know that."

He waited for her to put her thoughts together and say something. Visiting the museum was a start, but it wasn't much of a local history lesson. She knew nothing of their way of life. They probably hadn't shared a common ancestry for at least three generations.

Kathleen rose from the table. "*Ach,* it is time for pie. I hope everyone will have a large piece."

Miranda smiled graciously. "Yes, I would love a piece of pie. Just not too large. I think, despite my claims, that I ate too much of your good supper."

Ted did not smile. Today had been a day not just for Miranda to learn more about them. It had also been a day for him to learn about her. What he had learned did not fill him with confidence.

The church board had withdrawn from him the task of putting together their celebration event because of his inexperience with such a large-scale production. But he at least knew his people, and he knew their boundaries.

Miranda had the experience, but he didn't know what her boundaries were. Or even if she had any.

And there was only one way to find out.

7

"I'm not doing very well," Miranda muttered around the finger in her mouth. The bitter taste of blood made her wince. She pulled her finger out and pressed the injured spot with another finger.

Betty waved one hand in the air. "*Ach,* you have never done this before, so you are doing very well. Show everyone your square."

Miranda had never been afraid to try new things, but here in Betty's living room, among this group of the quietest and most humble women she'd ever met, she felt totally incompetent.

As she looked around the room, everyone looked back at her. When they saw her obvious hesitation, they all smiled warmly. Even though she participated in many of the ladies' functions at her own church, she'd never experienced anything like this.

The room was small, at least compared to the homes of her friends, and even her own, in Seattle. It wasn't furnished for *feng shui,* but rather for function. Every inch of wall space had something pressed against it, mostly for seating, because Betty's home was the meeting place for the weekly quilting circle. It should have been too small for fifteen, and now, including herself, sixteen ladies. Yet these women didn't mind squeezing six of them onto what was supposed to be a couch for four; in fact, they were quite happy. Perhaps because they were so close, it made a closer group for conversation.

Across the room from her, four more ladies squeezed onto a worn loveseat. As Miranda was a newcomer, they had insisted that she sit in the armchair, and two ladies sat back to back on the ottoman in front of her. Betty had dragged three chairs from the kitchen, and squeezed them into the living room, supposedly with enough elbow room to do their quilting.

Moving around was another matter. Every woman had brought her own sewing basket stuffed with fabric scraps and different colors of thread, all with an extra hoop. All the bags were on the floor near their owner's feet. Betty had dragged the coffee table into the center of the room for tea, coffee, and mountains of delectable cookies, buns, cakes, and muffins brought by all the ladies in attendance.

Miranda should have been embarrassed by the fact that she'd eaten the most while everyone else just nibbled, but between the alluring scent of Lois's fresh-baked cinnamon buns, the close-your-eyes rich smell of Betty's chocolate cake, and Helen's fragrant melt-in-your-mouth chocolate chip cookies, she had a hard time concentrating on sewing. Not that it was a valid excuse.

Slowly, Miranda held up a square of her alleged quilt. Everyone else had done at least three. She wasn't even halfway through one. Everyone nodded and clucked their approval, even though Miranda had no illusions about the quality of the workmanship, or lack thereof.

"At home, I made a baby quilt for a friend once," she said as she lowered it into her lap. "I bought a piece of fabric with a picture already on it, put some padding under it, added a back piece, and then I stitched on the lines. It looked really nice." The instructions had been really simple, and it had only taken a few hours. Not a few months. Or a few years, the way she was going with this one.

The entire room fell silent.

Miranda lowered her head and did another stitch. A little blood wouldn't matter.

This was cotton and washable. *By machine, I hope.*

Sarah, who appeared to be the same age as Miranda, was one of the two sitting on the ottoman. She looked up at her and smiled. "I am so glad you came today. I think you are learning very fast, since you say you have never sewed by hand before. Your quilt will be very beautiful when you are done. What kind of sewing machine do you have at home? My mama uses our sewing machine so much that mama and I went into the city with Ted and we bought a new one for me. Now we can both sew at the same time." Sarah lowered her voice so no one heard her except Miranda. "It is very modern."

She suspected that the modern abilities of Sarah's sewing machine were much different from what she and her friends had at home. "I don't do a lot of sewing, so I don't have a fancy machine, either. Lately all I've used it for is sewing on buttons."

The room fell silent again.

Sarah's grandmother, who was seated across the room, gasped. "You sew on buttons with your *sewing machine?*"

Miranda lowered her square to the table. "Yes. It's got a special foot for that. I love it, but I do go through a lot of needles." With it, her buttons were always sewn on tightly; they never came off.

Sarah's eyes widened. "I was so excited when I saw that this sewing machine made buttonholes. I made sure to buy that machine quickly."

"That's a wonderful feature." Miranda didn't say anything about the computerized sewing machine that her friend owned. It embroidered pre-programmed pictures and even threaded itself.

"I have decided to get a job with my sewing machine."

Miranda nearly stabbed herself with the needle again. "A job?" She glanced around at the circle of women, all in various stages of making their quilts. Every stitch by hand. No change from the way it had been done since the 1800s, except they were using commercially produced fabric and thread. "What kind of job?"

"I will hem pants and skirts, and make the city people's clothes fit them better. It is called alterations. Ted said that since I live near the same street as the shopping area, if I put a sign in front of my house, people will come. Not many at first, but they will."

"Ted said that?" She nearly choked at the thought of Ted encouraging one of these women to get a job, even if it was in her home. Even more surprising, she couldn't imagine him encouraging a local lady to be in contact with people from the city. •

Sarah nodded. "*Ja*. Those who come here know that our people are very careful with our work, and they will trust us. He even told me how much money people in the city charge for doing this. He told me to charge a little less, and people will be very happy to come here. Then they can shop while they wait. If it is a small job."

"Very astute. There's marketing for both the individual and the community." Now that she knew Ted had a business degree, she could appreciate where his ideas were coming from.

Elsie, whom she'd met initially at the church board meeting, nodded her head enthusiastically. "*Ja*, our Ted. He also has given jobs to Sarah's brooda and sesta. David and Anna, they work at the factory."

"That's really nice. Does Anna sew cushions for the chairs?"

"*Ach*, no. She talks to people on the phone when they wish to buy furniture, and she puts all the orders into the computer."

"Really?" Miranda tried to picture a woman dressed like Sarah, in a long dress and the most boring shoes in the world, typing eighteen thousand keystrokes per hour on a computer. She couldn't. She tipped her head at the thought. Sarah and the younger women here were not wearing prayer *kapps,* even though every woman over the age of forty was. There truly was a move toward modernization in the younger generation here, just as the pastor had said. It was just happening about thirty years behind the times.

Sarah sighed. "Yes. She sits at the desk next to William, Mary's brooda. I think one day they will get married. If only William would open his eyes."

When that happened, Miranda wondered which one of them would get home from work first to start making dinner.

While she didn't know exactly how big this community was yet, she guessed that perhaps up to a third of the church population could work for Ted. Ted was probably responsible for a large portion of the economy here, either as a direct employer, or by encouraging and offering good suggestions to people like Sarah. He'd known everyone they'd spoken to when he escorted her through their shopping district.

She had badly underestimated Ted, likely because of his uneven speech patterns. He was college-educated, skilled in marketing and administration, and now that she thought about it, he spoke two languages. She knew only one. In the back of her mind, she could hear the lilt of his charming accent.

She still wasn't sure how to feel about him. Everyone seemed to like him. She couldn't count the times since she had been here that different people had mentioned his name in conversation — always fondly. He was certainly pleasant to talk to, and she had seen hints of a quick wit, if only he would let himself relax.

Just as Miranda once again took her chances with another stitch in her quilt section, the other ladies began to gather their projects and pack up.

Lois paused to look up at her. "Our time for today is up. We all must now get home to cook supper."

Miranda tried to be discreet about checking her wristwatch. It was only two-thirty in the afternoon. Even on a day off, starting to make supper so early would have been the last thing on her mind. However, these ladies all would be cooking something from scratch, including two servings of nutritious vegetables, not merely throwing a pound of ground beef with some Hamburger Helper into the microwave and then adding a sliced raw carrot at the last minute.

They also had to walk to get where they were going. However, she had come to realize that in this climate, it likely would take longer to warm up a car and scrape windows than it would to walk the four or five blocks home.

Miranda hadn't been able to go shopping for a new coat yet, but Lois had managed to find an old one she hadn't given away, so for now, Miranda would make do. With the addition of a sweater she was as warm as toast, even though she was so padded she looked and felt like the Pillsbury Dough Girl.

As she slipped them on, she praised God for her new boots. A few ladies left together while she wrestled with her newly knitted scarf. Since she hadn't quite finished the hat yet, she wrapped the scarf over the top of her head and under her chin, then around her ears, fastening it in a knot at the back of her head.

Behind her, Sarah giggled, but Miranda didn't care what she looked like. At home, she would have. Here she would rather be alive and breathing than a dead but fashionable icicle when she got to her destination.

Over her shoulder, she slung a tote bag that Lois had loaned her, tugged on her gloves, and then rammed her hands into her pockets anyway, following Lois out the door as they made their way back home.

Her breath came out in a white cloud as she walked, something that didn't happen often at home. On cold days when she was a child, she and her friends had laughed and pretended to be smoking. But at these temperatures here in Minnesota, it wasn't funny.

"Lois, I want to help you with the cooking today." Besides feeling obligated to do something useful, standing near the stove would help her nose thaw.

"Do not be silly. I know you have much paperwork that you brought with you that you have not yet touched. Also the library phoned about the books you have asked them about."

Again, Miranda gave silent thanks for her new boots. It would take fifteen minutes of walking at a fast pace to get to the library. "That's great news. When will they be ready to pick up?"

"You do not have to do that. I know how you are not yet used to our cold weather. Ted will pick up the books for you."

She thought of all the times in the last week she had seen Ted — every day, in fact. Wherever she went, he was there, including the Wednesday evening Bible study. "He

120

doesn't have to do that."

Lois grinned. "*Ja.* He does. Or else I will not give him supper."

Miranda squeezed her eyes shut for a second, then forced herself to smile as she trudged forward. "You don't have to give him supper just for picking up a couple of books. I can really go myself." She probably wouldn't die of hypothermia.

"It is no trouble. Ted, he comes to our home for supper every Wednesday. Because we do not have a single daughter."

Miranda nearly lost her footing over a small snowdrift on the sidewalk. "What do you mean?"

"Poor Ted. He does like to eat, but he does not like to disappoint the mamas when he does not court their daughters."

"Is he not interested in finding a wife?"

Lois laughed. "*Ja.* But he says God will show him the woman who will be his wife, not the girl's mama."

"Then he's not seeing anyone? I don't want him ignoring his girlfriend because he feels it's his duty to help me while I'm here." She also didn't like the feeling of being a burden to him.

"No, he is not with anyone. Do you have a gentleman waiting for you at home?"

"Yes. His name is Bradley, and he really is

121

waiting. He asked me to think about marrying him when I got back."

This time Lois's pace slowed. "You do not sound excited. This should be a joyous thing."

Even though she had spent more time with Bradley than with her best friend, his proposal had been completely unexpected. They were so close they finished off each other's sentences, but her father had recently pointed out that Bradley only held her hand when the other single women at church were watching. In retrospect, her father was right.

"He's really special." Almost like the sister she never had. Not that he was gay or anything. It was just that when he embraced her, and even when he kissed her, she didn't feel the sparks and fireworks like in the romance novels.

"He asked me to marry him at the airport just before I had to go into the boarding area, so he kind of caught me off guard. It wasn't the most romantic proposal in the world." She shrugged her shoulders. "But that's just the way he is, and I gotta love him for it."

Lois nodded. *"Ekj seene,"* she mumbled. "I see." As they trudged up the steps, Lois inserted the key into the lock and they went inside where once again, it was warm.

Miranda stomped the snow off her boots, then pulled the scarf off her head. "Do you mind me asking what happened to Ted's parents?"

Lois's hand paused on the closet doorknob, and all the sparkle left her eyes. "*Daut trüarijch.* So sad. Their house caught on fire late one night, and they did not make it out. Ted was away with Pastor Jake at a conference and he was not there to help. So tragic, but they are with Jesus, and we celebrate their good life and loving hearts."

"Is he an only child? No brothers or sisters?"

"No, no brooda or sesta. No one knows why. David and Evelyn wanted a large family, but it was not God's will. When his parents went to glory, he was left alone except for his onkel and tante."

"Is that why he's running his uncle's business? Didn't his Uncle Bart have any children?"

"*Ja,* but Bartholomew and Elsa had three lovely daughters who did not want this. All three went to college, but instead they became nurses and a teacher. Donna and Anita have gone to the city; only Sandra has stayed."

She cringed, but she had to ask. She

didn't know Ted well, but she didn't like the feeling that he had been forced to take over the family business when it wasn't his dream.

"Is Ted happy with this?"

Lois's smile returned. "*Ach. Ja.* He works very hard, and he is a good manager. He is very happy, and all who work there are happy with him too. The business is growing, and he is very proud of it. His heart is good." She waved her hands at Miranda in a shooing motion. "Now you go. I will be fine in the kitchen. You have important things to do, like Ted."

Miranda smirked. "I feel like you're sending me into my room to do my homework."

"Then you go."

Being sent to her room was not a bad thing. The house was quiet and she didn't have the temptation of the Internet, so she got more work done in one afternoon than she'd ever done before. The only distraction was the increasing aroma of cooking food — onions melding with rich meat and later the sweetness of a chocolate cake in the oven. Also, Lois hummed when she cooked, a comforting, encouraging sound.

Miranda had nearly finished the first fiscal quarter's reconciliations for her most important client when the doorbell rang. She didn't want to be rude, so she hit save and made her way to the front door, arriving just as Ted set his boots on the rubber mat. His hat was already hanging on the rack.

"*Goondach,* Miss Randi-with-an-'i,' " he said, nodding his head once in greeting. He smiled as he unbuttoned his coat.

Miranda stopped suddenly, causing her socks to slip on the polished hardwood floor. She managed to regain her balance just before she almost fell, then looked up at Ted. The smile looked good on him, making her realize that he didn't smile often enough. It was nice to see the smile at the same time as he said her name.

She cleared her throat. She had no idea why he'd suddenly called her Randi, even if it was the long version with the explanation. He hadn't called her by her nickname once since she'd been here, and it had been over a week. "Hi back to you. But that's just Randi."

The smile dropped. She wanted to kick herself for correcting him.

"I am sorry. But I have never called a woman by a name I have used only for a man before. This will take me time to get used to."

"Don't worry. It's not important." She smiled at him, hoping he'd smile back, but he didn't. "Miranda, Randi, Miss Randi, it doesn't matter. Call me anything you want. Just don't call me late for dinner."

His brows knotted. She could almost see his mind churning as he remained silent.

"That's a joke. A play on words."

He thought about it for a few seconds, and his face relaxed. "Ah. I understand now."

She wondered if he'd told "knock-knock" jokes as a child, or if he ever wondered why the chicken crossed the road.

"I brought the books that were ready for you at the library."

She accepted them with appreciation, set them on a side table, and followed him into the living room. The front door opened behind them as Len arrived.

"I am sorry I am so late."

Miranda waited for him to say that he'd been stuck in traffic, and then she had to give her head a mental shake. There was no traffic here. Very few families even owned a car.

Lois appeared from the kitchen. "Was there something at the school you forgot?"

Len smiled. As the principal, he made it his duty to be the last person out of the building every day. "No, I had to talk to Mark's son. He is not doing his homework, and his grades are too low for a boy of his ability."

Even as an adult, the thought of facing the principal made Miranda cringe. In high school, she'd always done her homework and had been a straight-A student, up until her last year when she had let herself get distracted with the band and too much social life. That year, she had received too many such talks.

Len followed Lois into the kitchen, but Ted lingered.

"I hope you do not have somewhere to go after dinner. There is something we must discuss. And we must talk away from other people."

8

Miranda sat on the other end of the couch, her back as stiff as a two-by-four. Her hands were wrapped around her mug so tightly it was as if they had been treated with cured resin.

Len and Lois had gone into the kitchen to give them some privacy, but not too much.

Ted stared at her, no words coming. He had not shared much in the conversation during the meal because he was thinking of the right words for this moment. However, he still had no clearer idea now that she was waiting expectantly in front of him, and that was unusual. At work he never had difficulties saying what was needed.

Miranda cleared her throat. "I have said something really stupid and hurt someone's feelings, haven't I?"

"No. You have not." He forced himself to look directly into her eyes, as he did when he spoke to an employee. "But what you have done is to encourage the ladies to, uh . . ." he struggled for the right words. He wanted only to stop her, not to alienate her. ". . . change their style of dressing. You have worn your denim jeans everywhere except to the Sunday service and now the young ladies and even some of the mamas think this is a good idea. They say just to keep warmer outside. I have already had three requests to drive to the Mall of America in Minneapolis."

She blinked repeatedly, and her mouth dropped open.

He waited for her to say something, but she didn't.

"I would like you to encourage them to make another choice."

"You don't want them to wear pants outside, do you? Even when they could get frostbite? And hypothermia? And die? Would *you* go outside in this weather with bare legs?" She tipped her head to one side. "No, you probably don't even wear shorts in the summer, do you?"

At the airport where he usually waited to pick up guests, he'd seen a large advertisement poster displaying men with wet hair wearing very small shorts and no shirts, promoting some kind of beverage. His face burned at the thought of their near-nakedness.

"I didn't think so," Miranda mumbled.

"I did not mean it in that way. I certainly do not wish the ladies to be cold. Elsie told me you were at the ladies sewing circle today. Can you not sew them?"

"Jeans aren't something you can just sew. They're very complicated, and not every sewing machine can handle thick denim like that."

"Jeans are very expensive. These ladies do not have a lot of money. Pants that are not jeans would be best."

Miranda nibbled her bottom lip. "I never thought of that. Very few of them have jobs. For the ones who aren't married, the only money they get comes from their parents."

"As well, if they sewed pants that weren't jeans they would not be found wanting in cold weather. Times are changing. My mama stayed inside for most of the winter, but now the ladies do not stay home. It is not right that they should be cold." Not that he'd deliberately looked, but once when he saw Mary walking to the restaurant early in the morning, the wind had blown her skirt before he could turn his head. She had been wearing pants under her dress to keep warm. He suspected many of the women who had jobs in their community already wore pants and the men did not know about it.

"The cheapest places for jeans are always the factory outlets. We could go to one of those."

"But these factory outlet stores are only in the cities. It is a three-hour drive to Minneapolis."

"Let me guess. You don't want to be stuck in the car with four single women for so long."

His cheeks burned hotter. When he took a group of ladies in his car, it was usually very quiet. They would whisper between themselves and every once in a while he would catch the ladies looking at him, and then they would giggle. He never liked that. However, if he took Miranda in the car, anything they whispered would be repeated for all to hear, whether he wanted to know or not. And then Miranda would be taking pictures of everything of interest, as well as things not of interest. Including him. He had caught her sneaking pictures of him the day he took her to the museum. He didn't like his picture taken. Most of his people didn't.

"I was thinking that the price of gas has gone up again."

"Wait." Her eyes narrowed. "What bothers you the most isn't that they want to break tradition and wear pants, it's the expense? And you don't want to go so far, not because we'd drive you nuts, but because the price of gas went up? You're a . . . a . . . cheapskate."

"I am a careful steward."

"You're definitely a Mennonite."

Something in her tone told him it wasn't necessarily a compliment. He pressed on. "Can you not help these ladies sew their pants? I am sure you could convince them that homemade pants are better than purchased jeans."

"I could. We can buy what we need from Agnes's fabric store and make it a special sewing day because I don't want to intrude on our quilting days."

Ted crossed his arms over his chest. "You are making a quilt?"

"We'll just say I'm attempting it. By the way, my stuff should be here next week, including my electric piano."

"Why would you need your own piano? Len and Lois have an excellent piano."

"Because I'll need it at night."

"At night?"

"When I get an idea in the middle of the night, I get out of bed and work on it. I don't want to wake anyone up, so I'll work on my electric piano with headphones." She closed one eye and tapped her cheek with one finger. "But I don't know what I'm going to do. There's no room in the bedroom for it. I'd have to move the desk out, but that would be rude after they went through so much trouble to put it in the bedroom. I guess I could put it in the big room next to the real piano."

Ted didn't want to picture Miranda tiptoeing through Len and Lois's house in the middle of the night wearing her pajamas and carrying headphones. He really didn't. "I have a spare room at my house where I can store it."

"Really? That would be great. In the beginning I'll need the desk more, but when I get all the lyrics done and the play written, I'll need the piano more. Then I can ask to trade the desk for my piano in the bedroom."

"That sounds sensible. Until then I can keep your piano at my home."

"That's really great, thank you. But you don't have to just store it. Go ahead and set it up and feel free to use it if you want."

"I do not play piano. Only guitar."

She waved one hand in the air. "I've seen you play your guitar in church. You're a very talented musician. I bet you could pick up piano in no time flat. If you want, I could give you lessons. I have a number of students back at home, and some of them are adults."

"Your resumé said you were also a piano teacher." It was one of the major points that had given her credibility to do the tasks they needed her to do.

She stroked her bottom lip. "Which reminds me. I need to get an Internet connection somewhere near the piano. Len and Lois's house is all hardwired, I already checked. I don't want them drilling holes in their walls to string cable to rooms where there isn't a phone line. What about your house?"

"My house?"

"You run a business. You told me that you don't have a computer, but really, think about it. If you had a computer at your home, you could do e-mail and connect remotely with your office and work from home when you needed to. I don't know what I'd do if I couldn't work from home sometimes. If you had an Internet connection, I could do my piano lessons back home from your house." She rubbed her hands together with glee and smiled ear to ear. "What a great idea!"

"People have mentioned to me that I

should have a computer at home." He refused to work on Sundays, at home or the factory, but he did see the benefits of being able to catch up in the evenings or Saturday from home, where he could work in comfort without the expense of heating the entire office just for one person. "I have considered it, but I do not have time to go all the way to Minneapolis to buy a computer."

"You don't need to. I'll help you shop online, and they'll ship it to your home. Most of the time shipping is free when you buy more than a single component."

"What does me having a computer have to do with your piano lessons?"

"I could do all my lessons remotely, with a webcam."

He'd heard of webcams, none of it good. "How would you do that?"

"They don't have to see my face, just my hands, and hear me. They would also just aim the camera at the keyboard, so I could see their hands. It isn't ideal, but it's the only way to do it. It's the next best thing to being there."

"When would you need to do this?"

"I'd like to start the online lessons next week. Then I'll give you lessons in exchange for letting me use your house and your Internet connection."

He didn't know how to refuse, so he simply gave in. "That seems like a lot of work for you, when all I am contributing is a room that I seldom use."

"It's an exchange for the commitment of letting me use the room, and having access to your house. We should go to your house now so you can show me the room. I might need to buy a new webcam. I can just add it to the order for your computer, and I'll pay you back." She set her cup on the coffee table and smiled at him. "This is going to work really well. Remember, you'll need to rearrange your schedule to give yourself time to practice. You don't need to practice an hour a day until you get to a certain level, but I do insist that you practice every day."

Ted closed his eyes and pressed his thumbs into his temples. "I think I am getting a headache. Were we not talking about sewing with the ladies?"

"Oh. That." She waved one hand in the air. "I'll talk to a few of them tonight and organize something. Don't worry about it."

Just her saying so made him worry more, although for all her flighty ways, he could see that Miranda did follow through on her word. He would remember to thank God in his prayers that night. He would also pray about her guiding the ladies for a modest choice of new clothes.

Miranda stood. "You've got a key for the church, right? I'll go get my laptop, and we can do some online shopping."

Miranda pressed the new sticker into Ted's lesson book. "Great work! You're going through the lessons even faster than I thought you would."

"I do not need stickers of cartoon animals in my book," he grumbled. "I know I have achieved the level of proficiency to pass each song."

She stroked the newest sticker with her index finger. "Humor me. As a teacher, I miss not being able to put stickers in my students' books. CyberStars just aren't the same. You've got to make up for it every time someone else passes. I would hate to think of how I'd feel if you didn't pass any songs one week. No pressure, of course."

Ted's lips pressed together and his cheeks tightened, which meant he was grinding his teeth. Which meant that again, she had won.

"Seriously, you're progressing faster than any of the adults I've taught so far. You really should have started taking piano lessons sooner. Especially after the way you taught yourself to play guitar."

"I did not teach myself. I bought a book."

Miranda refused to argue with him. Even when she praised him, he contradicted her. When the day came that they actually disagreed on something worthwhile, she would have to call upon divine intervention.

Brian entered the room. "The bell on the oven has rung."

Miranda stood. "Then that concludes our lesson for the week. I'll call you when supper is ready."

Brian rubbed his hands together. "What is for supper today?"

"It's a surprise. Keep out of the kitchen. Both of you." As if either of them would ever go into the kitchen to help.

Sure enough, Ted followed Brian into the living room without so much as a backward glance.

Miranda hurried to the oven and slid in the tray of fries that were waiting, now defrosted, on the counter.

She hadn't done so much cooking in the past year as she had done in the past month. But she was learning a lot from Lois, who was an excellent teacher, and an even better cook. Then, once a week, she cooked supper for Ted and Brian after Ted's piano lesson.

From the living room, she heard the two men laugh. Miranda sighed as she started peeling the carrots.

Ted never laughed like that over anything she said. She was hard-pressed to get an occasional smile out of him. Although, with Brian always present when they had supper together, they always had an enjoyable time. Brian was a good buffer.

She sighed again.

Brian. Best friend, chaperone, mechanic, and owner of the only gas station in this section of the town. He also repaired farm machinery, which was the majority of his business. Every Thursday Brian closed his business early and taped a note to the door that he was at Ted's for supper if someone had an emergency. Of course, no one ever did. Even if an emergency happened, they would wait until suppertime was over before calling.

In Seattle, Brian never could have stayed in business. Either he would have failed for lack of customers or someone would have noticed the note and broken in and stolen everything of value, knowing exactly how long he would be gone.

Here, everyone understood. Brian was the official chaperone for Ted's Thursday evening piano lessons, which had become a popular topic of conversation. Every Friday morning, Pastor Jake would phone to ask how it went. But that was only the start of the cast-in-stone schedule she had somehow fallen into.

Monday — the day for her accounting work and online meeting with her office in Seattle.

Tuesday afternoon — sewing day, which rotated between various homes.

Wednesday — quilting at Betty's in the afternoon, Bible study meeting in the evening.

Thursday — remote piano lessons at Ted's house, Seattle being two hours behind Minnesota's time zone. After the lessons, she prepared supper. On Thursdays, Ted and Brian arrived together. Brian spent his time on Ted's computer while Ted had his piano lesson, then she finished the preparations, and they ate together.

Friday evening she now taught lessons to some of the children and a couple of the young ladies. Of course, Friday night Brian wasn't required to be the official chaperone. The mothers always stayed for the duration of the lesson, and the next student arrived before the prior lesson ended.

So on Friday night, date night, Miranda was teaching piano lessons. The highlight of her week. Not that she exactly had an exciting social life at home, but when the guys at the office found out after she got back, she wouldn't hear the end of this one for years.

"Supper's ready!" she called over her shoulder.

The men arrived just as she set the third plate on the table.

Brian inhaled deeply. "Ah. I smell chicken. Is it *Hingle* potpie today?"

Brian sat, but Ted remained standing as he pulled the chair out for her to be seated. "It does not look like it. It does not look like anything I have seen before."

"It's Shake 'N Bake chicken with crispy coated fries, carrot sticks, and dip."

Ted sat, but didn't fold his hands in preparation to pray. "*What* kind of chicken?"

"Shake 'N Bake. I have this all the time at home. I got Susan to order it at the store for me. Let's eat before it gets cold."

All three of them bowed their heads while Ted unenthusiastically gave thanks to God for the food and their time together.

Instead of eating them, Ted poked at his fries with his fork. "I buy French fries when I travel, but they do not look like this."

Miranda popped one into her mouth. "That's because these are oven-baked, not deep-fat fried. These are good for you. No trans fats. I bought this for you too." She pushed a bottle of ketchup toward him.

"I've never known anyone who didn't have ketchup in the fridge." Next, she pushed the bowl of vegetable dip toward the two men. "I made this at Lois's house and brought it here. You dip the carrots in it. Like this." She leaned forward and dipped her carrot in it, then took a purposely loud, crunchy bite. "Remember, no double dipping." She popped the rest of the carrot stick in her mouth and smiled.

Ted poked at his coated chicken as if testing it, but Brian cut a piece and ate it without hesitation. He chewed slowly, closing his eyes while he savored the spicy flavor, then swallowed. "*Zehr gut!* This is very good. Did Susan order this just for you, or did she put the rest of the case in the store? I would like to tell my mama about this."

"It's there for anyone to buy." Since word traveled fast here, she had no doubt that Susan would be ordering a second case from the wholesaler within days.

Finally, Ted must have worked up the courage, because he cut a piece of chicken and began to eat. At his first bite, one eyebrow arched. "*Ja, zehr gut.* I hope you are going to cook this again."

Brian smothered his fries with the ketchup and then shoveled so many into his mouth that he could only nod in agreement.

"I imagine you don't have this kind of food often. I thought I'd start cooking more of the things I make at home, for something different. What I really wanted was bok choy, but Susan couldn't order just a couple; she would have had to order a full box, and I couldn't use that much."

"What is bok choy?" Ted asked.

"It's a Chinese vegetable. It's stir fried with other vegetables, and then you add soy sauce and noodles."

"I think this chicken is very good. I have never eaten anything like this before."

With the Shake 'N Bake being such a hit, her mind raced at other things she could feed them. "I was thinking, have you ever tried any ethnic foods besides Mennonite? I'm pretty good at —"

The ringing phone cut off her words.

"Excuse me." Ted rose to answer the phone. He greeted the caller briefly, then turned back toward the table. "Brian, it is for you."

While Brian asked questions about what sounded like a blown wheel bearing, Miranda watched Ted eat. It was a good thing she had made extra because it looked like he was going to ask for seconds, maybe even thirds.

He put the last morsel of chicken in his mouth and was spearing a few fries when Miranda looked over her shoulder at Brian. He was listening and nodding, looking as if he wanted to get back to his supper but was unable to interrupt the caller.

Miranda folded her hands on the table and sat straight in her chair. "Before Brian comes back, I need to tell you something. I was talking to Pastor Jake today. I've been here just over a month and I'm getting to know everyone, so we both feel it's a good time for me to start working on the Christmas musical. He suggested that I collaborate with you on the general theme and presentation."

Ted stopped mid-chew, and he swallowed laboriously. "So early? It is only March."

"It's time to start a rough draft of the storyline. I'm not saying we should do auditions this soon, but I've been paying attention to people as they sing. I think I know who the best potentials are for the lead parts, and what their vocal range is. I can't leave this too long. I have to have the whole thing written, composed, and in progress by June. We'll have auditions in April, and by the middle of May the people who get the main parts will have to start working on them. Remember, it's going to take more work and more time because no one here has ever done anything like this before. So I have to start now because this only gives me three months to write it with these people in mind. It's not a lot of time, when you think about it. Everything is going to move pretty fast from here on."

Ted set his fork down. "I am not sure about having auditions, but you are right, of course. It is time to start."

Brian hung up the phone and returned to the table. He began gobbling his food so fast that Miranda worried he might choke.

"I am sorry; I must go. Frank and Myrtle are in Bemidji, and their car is making a loud sound. I think it is the wheel bearing, so it is not safe to drive. They are afraid to go to a mechanic they do not know, far away from home. They fear that they will be cheated, so I must help them. Forgive me for being rude, but I will not waste this good supper." He shoveled the last of his fries in his mouth, then stared at Ted's plate. "Are you not going to eat those, my friend?" He poised his fork above the last three fries that Ted hadn't eaten yet.

Ted looked down at his plate, set his fork down, and pulled his napkin from his lap. "No. I am no longer hungry."

Brian stabbed the fries and had them in

his mouth before Miranda could offer him more from the tray beside the oven. He hadn't finished chewing, and he was already standing. "I am so sorry," he mumbled between chews. "Would you like me to take you home now? I will be driving past Len's home on the way to the highway."

"I can't. Everything is such a mess."

Ted stood. "Do not worry. This is my house. I will clean up. Phone me when you get back to Leonard's house, and we will talk."

9

Pastor = divine intervention.

Or at least the pastor was as close to divine intervention as she was likely to get during her time on earth.

Miranda pushed the paper with her outline across the table toward Pastor Jake. "I say this is the only way we can reach the people in the community and surrounding area who aren't Mennonites."

Spreading his fingers — which emphasized the size of his hand, something Miranda had never noticed before, even during piano lessons — Ted planted his palm on top of the paper preventing the pastor from picking it up.

"I say this is wrong. This is not the way our people are. Presenting them like this would be a lie."

She tried to tug the paper out from beneath his hand but only succeeded in ripping the corner. "I thought the purpose of all this was to evangelize."

Pastor Jake turned to Ted. "She has a point."

Ted's eyes narrowed, and his voice lowered to a gravelly rumble. "Everyone will be so uncomfortable that they will not be able to evangelize."

Pastor Jake turned to Miranda. "He has a point."

Miranda jabbed at the paper between Ted's fingers. "Evangelizing is never easy. Even Billy Graham struggled in the beginning of his ministry. We all need to step out in faith."

Pastor Jake shrugged his shoulders and turned to Ted. "She has a point."

Ted pressed down on the paper, moving it toward himself. "We are not having one person at the front, preaching. Everyone will have scripted lines and song. If they are nervous and make a mistake, then everyone else will make mistakes and get lost. People who come will not listen. They will go home remembering the mistakes, not the message."

Pastor Jake sighed and turned to Miranda. "He has a point."

Miranda turned to Ted. "This is a church production, not Hollywood. Of course there will be mistakes. That's one more thing that will make the whole thing memorable. Mistakes aren't important, only the effort. God will still be glorified."

Pastor Jake ran his fingers through his hair and turned to Ted. "She has a point."

Ted picked up the paper and waved it in the air. "God is better glorified through truth, not pretending to be something one is not."

Pastor Jake pinched the bridge of his nose with his thumb and index finger, then turned to Miranda. "He has a point."

Miranda gritted her teeth and counted to five. She couldn't make it all the way to ten. "What do you think acting is? Do you know how many people were reached by *Touched by an Angel*? Do you think Valerie Bertinelli is a real angel?"

Ted quirked one eyebrow "Who?"

Pastor Jake lowered his forehead to the table. "Have you two agreed on *anything*?" he muttered into the wooden surface.

"Yes," Ted snapped.

"No," Miranda ground out between clenched teeth.

Ted turned to Miranda. "We agreed that Sarah Janzen should do the leading female role."

She turned back and glared at him. "And I said that's true, but she's too shy to pull it off. So we have to pick someone else."

Ted turned back to Pastor Jake, who had not raised his head from the tabletop. "No. Technically, we have not agreed on anything."

The silence hung in the air. Miranda could hear the old building creak, and it wasn't even windy.

Pastor Jake pushed himself upright, leaned back in his chair, and crossed his arms over his chest. "So this is the first thing you have agreed on, then."

She couldn't tell if he was making a joke or a sarcastic observation.

Pastor stood. "Tomorrow evening is the board meeting," he said, then left the room.

"I guess this means we have a deadline," she mumbled.

"That is something we can agree on. Len and Lois have invited me for supper. We will both work better with a full stomach."

"After much discussion, Ted and I have a proposal ready. We feel this will best meet our own needs, as well as fulfill our mission to reach out to the surrounding community. The important thing is that this isn't just for the choir and worship team. This is something that is going to involve every single person in the congregation, the young and, uh, the wise but young at heart. I printed a copy for everyone to read."

Ted smiled to himself as everyone else read the summary of the proposal. First, he'd noted Miranda's use of the word "our" in her introduction. That she now included herself as being a part of the church gave her a personal connection to everything that happened, good and bad. It made her more likely to want to make everything work because the benefit was not just for everyone else but herself as well.

He had also glanced around the group, especially at the "wise but young at heart" board members. Beneath the fire and bluster, she truly did have a kind heart.

Although she still possessed a rebel spirit, she now wore a long skirt to church like all the ladies. However, even though the dresses that she had sewn with Lois guiding her were moderately conservative, they were decorated with red over-stitching and large red buttons. Which, of course, matched her red earrings. Two weeks ago, realizing that winter was far from over, she went online to eBay, which she called her gateway to the outside world, and bought a pair of red boots, which she wore daily.

The shuffle of papers indicated everyone had finished reading. Now it was Ted's turn to speak.

He stood and nodded at Miranda.

"As you all know, we have had many changes in our church over the past few years. While we value our traditions, we also have realized that the world is changing, not all of it good." He paused to let his words to sink in, and waited for everyone to nod in agreement. "This also means that we are changing too. Three years ago we added the piano to our worship for our Sunday services, and a year ago we added my guitar. At Miranda's church, which is in Seattle, the worship at her church is done with a piano, two guitars, a bass guitar, and drums." This time he didn't pause as long, because not everyone, including himself, approved of setting up the worship team like a rock band. "The addition of instruments has been a good change for us because it adds beauty to our worship, and this pleases God." This time, everyone nodded. "We are going to make another change, this one for the sake of outreach. Because many of our guests will not know our traditions, and others who know some of them will not participate in them, many will feel unwelcome, regardless of our words of greeting. Most important, as Miranda has told me, they are very likely to leave. Even if they stay for our production, they will not come back."

All eyes focused on him. He knew that everyone here, with the exception of himself, Miranda, William, and Pastor Jake, had never known another way.

"On Sunday, the ushers will seat everyone as they enter the church. Married couples will sit together, and families will stay together — husband, wife, and children will all sit together."

Elsie pushed herself to her feet, something she had never done in all the time he had been on the church board. "It is one thing for a husband and wife to sit together in God's house, but what about all the others? Where will they sit?"

"Widows and widowers may still choose to sit on the right or left. We will reserve the back five rows for that purpose."

Elsie planted her hands on the table and leaned forward. "What about unmarried people who do not have family?"

Ted's insides churned. There were not many in their church who lived alone. In fact, besides those separated by death, he was the only one who was unmarried who lived in his own house. All his friends were living with their parents, where they would continue to live until they got married.

His mind raced. He couldn't see himself sitting with the widowers. All of them were more than double his age, and every conversation started with questions about why he was not yet married.

He turned and focused on Miranda. As soon as she felt his eyes on her, she turned all her attention on him, maintaining full eye contact as he spoke.

"It is my place to join Len and Lois." He could see when what he meant sank in, because her face paled. But he said it anyway. "And Miranda."

10

Ted had almost made it out of his office to check on a problem in the upholstery department when his phone rang.

Hopefully it was Karen, telling him that she had managed to find the correct upholstery material after all and that he wouldn't have to stop doing the quarterly budget projections and drive into Minneapolis to buy a replacement bolt of fabric.

But the number on the call display was an outside line — a number he didn't recognize. It had also come in on his direct line, not through the switchboard.

"Good morning, this is Ted Wiebe," he said, doing his best to take the frustration out of his voice.

"Ted? We have a problem."

"Miranda? Is that you?"

His mind raced. Their initial attempt to mix the men and ladies during the worship service had not gone well. After that, a few

155

of the board members had taken him aside to express their dissatisfaction at the proposal for the play. Then, some from the congregation complained that Miranda was causing unrest among the women, as well as with some of the young men. The only enthusiastic response he had received about Miranda was from Agnes's husband, Mark, about the sudden increase in business at the fabric store.

He checked the time. "Are you not supposed to be at Betty's house making your quilt?"

"That's not until after lunch. I'm calling from my cell phone. I'm in the parking lot. I need to talk to you."

Ted felt his chest tighten. That Miranda had walked all the way to the furniture factory told him something was very wrong.

"Why did you not come in? The door is always open."

"Because it's business hours. But I was hoping you could take an early lunch and we could go somewhere."

Once again, he checked the time, then walked to the window where he peeked through the blinds. Sure enough, Miranda stood in the parking lot, her red hat and scarf almost obscuring her face, her shoulders hunched against the cold, her cell phone pressed to her cheek. "I cannot take a lunch break today. If I do not find the fabric we had set aside for a special order, I will have to drive to Minneapolis to buy another bolt that is like it. Come inside, and we can talk in my office. It is warm." He smiled. "There is also coffee."

Her posture straightened at the word "coffee."

"You don't have to ask me twice." She flipped the phone shut and bolted toward the door. She was standing in the doorway of his office in less than a minute.

"I will show you to the cafeteria where you can pour your coffee. There are always a few people taking a break, I think you probably know at least some of them. I must ask you to wait for about ten minutes while I check for some fabric that has gone missing."

Miranda tugged off her gloves and stuffed them into her pockets, then nodded as she blew into her cupped hands. He helped her remove her coat, draped it over his own on the coat rack, then escorted her down the hall past Anna sitting at her desk, who watched every step they took.

As they neared the lunchroom, the fresh aroma of coffee soothed his nerves. Even if he didn't like to drink coffee, for some reason he always enjoyed the scent of it. Because it happened to be so close to the lunch break, Harold was the only person in the lunchroom, only because he had just made the fresh pot of coffee. If it had been a woman, Ted would have left Miranda here, but even though he trusted Harold, it was not right to leave her alone with a man she didn't know, despite this being a place of business.

"It now appears that you are going to receive an unofficial tour. Unless you wish to wait for me at my office." Miranda seemed to understand that it would be inappropriate for her to remain in the lunchroom. She wrapped her hands around the hot mug. "Am I allowed to take this with me?"

"If I said no, would you leave it behind?"

"Uh . . . no."

"That is what I thought. But I will say yes because as long as you are carrying the mug, you will not be taking pictures. Come this way."

The closer they got to the cutting area, the more the sharp tang of fresh-cut wood overpowered the coffee aroma, which next became overpowered by the oily smell of the industrial sewing machines in the upholstery section. Once past the assembly area, he found Karen madly searching through the racks that held the bolts of fabric.

"It must be in here somewhere," she muttered over her shoulder when she noticed Ted standing behind her. "I hope we did not use it for something else by mistake. I thought I had put it in a special place, but I cannot find it anywhere."

Ted glanced around the room. "Then why are you looking through the regular stock?"

"In case someone else picked it up and put it back."

Beside him, Miranda slurped her coffee, then began to giggle. "When I was in university, I had this one really awesome pair of earrings that I used to put inside my shoes."

Ted stared at Miranda. "You kept earrings in your shoes?"

She shrugged her shoulders. "Only one special pair. I didn't want my roommate borrowing them, so I had to hide them. Even if I forgot what I did with them, I would always find them when I put my shoes on. I couldn't go anywhere without my shoes, after all."

Karen froze, then rammed the bolt of fabric in her hand onto the nearest rack. "Wait . . . I think . . ." Before she finished her sentence, she ran off.

Ted stared until Karen disappeared around the corner. "I do not understand. What do shoes have to do with missing fabric?"

"Nothing that I know of."

"Did you have other clever hiding places for your special items?"

"I once hid a snake in the bathroom. That didn't turn out so good, though."

Ted didn't think he wanted to hear that story.

"There was also the time that I —"

Before she finished her sentence, Karen ran back into the room, with lengths of fabric folded over one arm.

Ted rested his fists on his hips. "Where did you find it?"

"In the thread cupboard. Because before I started to sew this project, I would first have to get the right color thread. So that is where I put it." She opened her arms to give Miranda a hug but noticed the cup of coffee in Miranda's hands and stepped back. "Thank you, Miranda. You helped me remember where I put it. Now if you will excuse me, I must get busy with this."

Ted ran his fingers through his hair. "*Ja. Danke shoen,* Miranda. You just saved me an unnecessary trip to Minneapolis."

"Uh . . . well . . ." she muttered.

Ted felt shivers up his spine. "I see. Maybe. Maybe not."

"This was very generous of Ted to give you his car, *ja?* I do not know of any time he has let someone drive his car."

"Yes, Ted is very generous." However, Miranda suspected it wasn't as much generosity as it was being able to avoid being trapped for hours with a carload of single women.

Miranda gripped the steering wheel tighter as she drove over another icy patch on the road. Ted had told her that it wasn't exactly dangerous, but she had to be cautious. He'd been right. Not only were there piles of frozen snow and ice, there were also unfilled potholes. The only reason she kept going versus turning around and going back was because he'd guaranteed her that once she got off the short country road that hadn't been plowed recently, she would have clear sailing the rest of the way.

Not that he'd used the words "clear sailing." He'd actually said "unhindered access." But she knew what he meant. However, she would definitely question him for his definition of "short." For her, short meant a few blocks. Out here in the country, she'd gone miles.

Not a yard too soon, she turned onto highway 371, heading south from Cass Lake, as her notes said. Ted had promised this road would be better, and it was, but not much. He'd also promised that the way wasn't that long, but now that she thought about it, on the day he'd picked her up from the airport, they'd been on the road for more than three hours. Which meant she would be spending at least two of those hours on highway 371. He'd promised that the highway would be significantly better at Brainerd. From there it was a shorter trip to St. Cloud, where she had the address of the nearest veterinary supplier.

However, since she had talked to Ted, she'd had a change of plans. Instead of just taking Sarah and Arlene along to St. Cloud for company, she now also had Theresa and Debra, and their destination was Minneapolis.

She spoke to Sarah, who was sitting beside her, although Miranda never moved her head, keeping all her concentration on the road. She'd never driven on such an uneven surface, one made even more scary because she was driving someone else's car. "Ted couldn't leave work, so he thought this was the best thing to do. Is this road always like this?"

"No. This is a very clear day. It is not going to have new snow. So this is very good for you."

"I've never driven on anything like this before. In Seattle when it snows, I stay home and the farthest I go is the corner grocery store. And then I walk."

All whispering from the backseat stopped. Theresa leaned forward, resting her hands on the seat between Miranda and Sarah. "You stay home all winter? What about Sunday services?"

"It's different on the West Coast. I didn't mean I stay home all winter. Only when it snows. Most winters we don't get any snow at all."

All four ladies gasped.

Debra raised her hands to her cheeks. "No snow in the winter? How can that be?"

"That's the way it is where I live. Mostly it rains. Sometimes for a week without stopping." In fact, she thought, as she hit another pothole that may have jarred one of her fillings loose, she couldn't believe she had left the nice safe rain for this.

"If there is no snow, then the grass is bare all winter? Is it green or brown?"

"It's green, but not bright green like in the summer."

"Then you never have to miss church in

the winter, *ja?*"

"That's right. But even if we do have snow on the weekend, I always go. I just walk." She held back from making any further comment. Most of the people here walked anyway, regardless of the weather. They probably thought it very strange to drive a three-block distance to church. But then, her best shoes weren't exactly made for walking.

"When it snows in Seattle, most people stay home, especially on the weekends. But Daddy still runs the service, even if there aren't many people there because it goes out on webcast."

"Webcast?"

Miranda forced herself not to groan. Apparently, Ted wasn't the only one who had a habit of echoing her when he didn't know what she was talking about.

"We broadcast our services over the Internet for people who are sick or who for any reason can't come. Anyone can watch, no matter where in the world they are, if they want to. You don't have to be a member to view our Sunday services."

Sarah turned sideways to face Miranda. "Does that mean we can watch too?"

"I suppose . . ." Miranda nibbled her bottom lip, hoping that none of these ladies ever found an Internet connection. The difference between her church and this one would seem like being transported to an alternate universe. At home, people stood during worship and many raised their hands. No one was shy about crying, or shouting out questions — her father even encouraged it.

Here, last week was the first time this church had husbands sitting with their wives. The tension was so thick even the young children were quiet. Order and structure ruled. These people worshiped quietly except for when they joined together to sing hymns. They always sang in perfect four-part harmony, and the first hymn was always done *a capella*. The rest were accompanied very subtly with a piano and Ted strumming gently on his guitar. Always hymns. Never contemporary choruses, not even choruses that were twenty years old.

At home, her church featured a full band for worship. Lately they had tried to incorporate one hymn in each service, accompanied by the driving beat of the bass guitar and drums.

Debra's voice drifted from the backseat. "Are we going to the veterinary wholesale supply first or the outlet clothing store?"

"First priority is the veterinary wholesale.

I didn't even know they made special diabetic dog food." What she did know was that she was very glad she wasn't going to be home when Len got there. When Lois opened the box that was supposed to contain Fidette's special dog food and found some of Len's tools, she had been one unhappy camper. Zebediah, who was the only veterinarian in town, ordered only two cases of the special food at a time, and the case Lois had opened was supposed to be that second case.

"Lois won't take the chance and let little Fidette eat ordinary dog food. Lois is so careful with her diet. Even if we don't get to buy any clothes, if all we get is the dog food, then we'll have done what we needed to do."

Theresa rested her hand on Miranda's shoulder. "Are you sure we are allowed to buy this special food? We are not a store."

Miranda glanced down at her purse, where her cell phone was neatly tucked inside the pocket. "Yes, I've already phoned, and they have a case waiting for us. I've also made a note of Zebediah's business registration number, so as far as the wholesaler is concerned, we're good."

Sarah shook her head and made a *tsking* sound. "I cannot understand how you write things down in your phone. Do you not have paper at your home?"

Miranda smiled. "I have paper. I can just never find a pen. Besides, when I make notes on paper, I lose them. I never lose my cell phone. So I keep all my important notes and stuff in my phone." Lately she hadn't used her cell phone much as an actual phone. But in order to keep track of what she was learning about the community around her, she had been using the note-maker, calendar, and word processor more than ever. Also, thanks to the wonder of automatic backups, one of the most important programs she had ever had in her life, which she thought she had lost, had been recovered and was now back on her cell phone.

"Will we get to the clothing store before they close?"

"Yes. But we can't take too long. I don't want to drive home on this road in the dark."

"When my mama was a girl, she said Grootmutta and Grootfoda would take all of them into the cities when they needed things they could not get at home. They would find another Mennonite family and stay with them and not have to travel in the dark or travel too much in one day. She said they would feed them and have them stay the night in their homes, and then they would be on their way the next day, when there was more time to go home in the sunshine."

"Really? I can't imagine staying with strangers."

Sarah smiled. "But Len and Lois were strangers to you when you first came to us. Now you are like their family. You have become family to all of us. I hope we will remain like family even after you return to your home in Seattle, where you do not have snow in the winter."

Miranda blinked to force the tears back. "Thanks for saying that. You're all very special to me. All of you feel like the sisters I never had."

Theresa rested her hand on Miranda's shoulder. "And sisters go shopping together, *ja?*"

Miranda smiled. *"Ja."*

Sarah, Theresa, Debra, and Arlene all laughed.

Debra giggled. "Your accent, it is very bad."

Miranda smiled, but only for a second. For the first time, these ladies were going shopping in the big city without their parents. Because of that, beneath their coats they were all dressed in their baggy pants with loose-fitting plain cotton blouses. Their purses were plain and functional, and none of them wore their prayer *kapps* today. They looked a little odd and definitely out of style, but nothing about them was particularly eye-catching, which was the way Miranda wanted it.

"Seriously, we have to talk. For the most part, you're going to blend into the crowd, but once you talk, everyone will know that you are Mennonites from the countryside. People might stare, and I want you to not pay attention to that."

They all nodded solemnly.

Once again, Miranda smiled. "Great. We're going to have a fun time shopping." She only hoped the fun they had outweighed the reaction they were going to get when they got home. "Since Ted doesn't have a CD player in here, how about if we make our own music? Who wants to sing 'How Great Thou Art'?"

11

Ted stiffened his back and stood tall. He crooked his elbow and waited. "It is time. Let us go in."

As soon as he felt Miranda's small hand on his arm, he began walking into the sanctuary. "This is not going well," he muttered as they stepped through the doorway.

"I don't know if I'd go that far," Miranda whispered as they walked. "But it's definitely interesting."

"Interesting?"

"Look at who is in here before us. Most of them are the couples who are the business owners who work together as partners. Zebediah and Rebecca Rempel. Frank and Susan Neufeld. Dave and Gerta Reimer. They are the ones who are bold enough to go to the front and sit together in church without being led in. I think it's great that they've come in so early. I know they're trying to make a statement to everyone else and be good examples."

"I think you are right." Ted also noticed that the older couples who maintained traditional lifestyles at home were still in the lobby area. They were in no rush to enter the sanctuary; they felt they were being forced to adhere to the new system. "But look in the back. There are still a few widows and widowers who are following our traditions. Since they have no one to sit with, they have also come early, to sit on the right, or the left."

"Everyone will get used to it. They'll have to. How do you feel about it?"

"I am not sure. While I think it is good for couples who pray together at home to sit together during worship time, it is also distracting."

Ted felt himself relax just a little as Miranda chose to sit on the right, the side that had up until two weeks ago been the men's side. She slid into the pew, and as he slid in beside her, she wiggled and shifted until her skirt was positioned properly. Then, just as she had done the previous week, instead of positioning herself with her ankles touching demurely, she crossed her legs and began to tap the toe of her boot against the frame of the rack containing the hymnals. Her red boot. That matched the large red buttons that decorated her dress in a long row extending from her neckline to her hem. That matched her red earrings. And her red cell phone that she had taken out of her red purse and had laid beside her.

He should have been praying to ready his heart to worship. Instead he stared at all the red.

"What are you doing?" he asked between his teeth. "If you are expecting a phone call, you should turn off your phone during the service."

"Shhh. It's time to pray." She patted his arm, then folded her hands in her lap and bowed her head.

All he could do was pray for patience as the church slowly began to fill up. When the time came, he left his seat and took his place at the podium.

"Welcome, everyone, on this glorious Lord's Day morning. Join with me in opening our hearts in praise and worship. Please turn to page 296 in your hymnals, and we will sing 'Standing By a Purpose True.' "

As the congregation sang the words to the chorus, "Dare to be a Daniel," Ted wondered if he'd chosen the right theme. He'd selected the hymns they would be singing today to encourage everyone to be faithful in following God's direction, and to have courage. Yet, in the historical reality, in staying close to God's ways, Daniel refused to make changes. Here, Ted truly did believe that the changes they were making were good and were God's will. However, not everyone did.

For the second hymn, he had chosen "Hark! 'Tis the Shepherd's Voice I Hear." He waited for the congregation to find the right page in the hymnals, nodded, and counted four beats to signal Lorraine on the piano, joined her with his guitar, then started the congregation singing. As he looked up between verses, as often happened, Miranda was the only one in the congregation with one hand raised. But this time, he saw something he hadn't seen before. While the congregation sang the words of the chorus, "Bring them in from the fields of sin," tears were streaming down Miranda's face.

He'd never seen anyone cry during worship before. Of course, until today, he'd only watched the men's side, since it wasn't proper for him to look at the women.

During the next repeat of the chorus, since he had it memorized, he was able to scan the congregation, including the women, since they were now mixed with the men.

Not one other person had tears, although Pastor Jake had his eyes squeezed tightly shut and his hands pressed to his chest.

When the hymn ended, Ted stared at the hymnal. Silence loomed in the sanctuary as he silently read the words, perhaps thinking about them for the first time. He'd sung this song countless times, all his life, from the time he was able to read, and never really thought about the words.

He cleared his throat. "We are going to do something we have never done before," he said, speaking loudly enough so everyone could hear him clearly, all the way to the widowers in the back who were hard of hearing. "I am going to read the last verse and chorus without singing. I would like everyone to read silently with me, and think of the meaning and how this will apply to you, in your own life."

Out in the desert hear their cry,
Out on the mountains wild and high;
Hark! 'tis the Master speaks to thee,
"Go find my sheep where'er they be."
Bring them in, bring them in,
Bring them in from the fields of sin:
Bring them in, bring them in,
Bring the wand'ring ones to Jesus.

At the close of the last word, the only sound in the sanctuary was Miranda sniffling.

"Let us now sing this hymn again. From our hearts."

At the close of the hymn, Miranda was still the only one whose face shone with tears, but he clearly saw a difference in many in the congregation. His heart beat strangely in his chest as he finished off the worship time with the other hymns he'd selected, feeling different than he'd ever felt before, including the first time he'd led worship. This time, he'd really read the words as he sang them.

He returned to the pew to sit beside Miranda as Pastor Jake directed the congregation to open their Bibles to the verses for his message. While everyone else was turning pages, Miranda picked up her cell phone and flipped it open.

He leaned toward her. "What are you doing?" he spat out between his teeth. He had just had one of the most insightful moments of his life, and Miranda was about to make a phone call.

"Shh," she whispered as she hit a few of the buttons on the screen. "You're disturbing people."

He leaned closer. "And you will not be?"

She turned to him. "Where is your Bible? Did you forget it at the front? Here, I'll share."

Instead of holding out her Bible, which he didn't see, she held out her open cell phone. Tiny lines of print spread across the miniature screen. "Wait, if we're both going to do this, I have to reset the font." She poked a couple of buttons, and the print became larger.

Ted opened his mouth, but his words froze in his throat. On the screen was Luke 4:14, as Pastor Jake had directed everyone to find. The words of Jesus were colored in red, just like in his Bible.

His real Bible.

"What . . . What is this?"

"Shh!" She smacked the side of his knee with the back of her hand. "Do I have to send you away with the children? Follow what Pastor is reading."

It wasn't King James, but it was easy enough to follow. When it would have come time to turn the page, she hit a button with her thumb that scrolled the text. He continued to read the words but couldn't concentrate properly on the full meaning when he was looking at the backlit screen of . . . Miranda's cell phone.

He was reading God's Word on a telephone.

He opened his mouth, but before he could speak, she smacked his knee again.

"Knock it off," she hissed. "Can't it wait?"

It could wait. In fact, he needed some time.

As Pastor Jake presented his sermon, every time the congregation needed to read part of a verse, Miranda's cell phone popped up between them. He kept telling himself that the technology wasn't important — it was still God's Word despite the electronic medium.

But it wasn't the same. It felt wrong.

A number of times she touched buttons on the screen, then tapped sermon notes into her phone, then turned it back to the verse, and continued to listen to Pastor Jake.

It was driving him crazy. *She* was driving him crazy.

When Pastor Jake ended his sermon with the closing prayer, Ted once again took his place at the front to lead everyone in the closing hymn, "I Will Sing of My Redeemer." When he returned to the pew beside Miranda, she was happily tucking her cell phone back into her purse while quietly singing both parts of the chorus, all mixed up.

She looked up as she snapped her purse closed. "There you are. Now what was it that was so important you couldn't wait?"

He pointed to her purse. "I cannot believe that you have God's Word displayed on your cell phone."

She smiled broadly. "Yeah. Isn't it great? It's got a concordance with it, and all the cross references, and I can add all the notes and highlights I want."

"But it is not right."

Her smile faded. "I have news for you. Because it's in this format, I take my Bible with me wherever I go. Sometimes I read my Bible when I'm stuck in rush hour traffic. I'll bet you can't say you've ever done that. No. Wait. You've never been stuck in traffic." She waved one hand in the air. "Why can't you ever be happy for me? I thought I lost everything when it crashed not long after I got here, but I finally figured out how to reload the archive files that were backed up on my laptop. I've recovered years of notes. How would you feel if you lost the Bible you'd been making notes in since you were a teenager, and then found it again after a couple of months?"

"Well, I would feel very good."

She hugged her purse to her stomach, stood straight, and raised her nose in the air. "That's right. I feel just like the woman who lost the silver coin, then found it. And now I'm going to celebrate." She spun around so fast her skirt twirled as if it were a windy day, and she stomped off to join a group of young ladies. Without turning to acknowledge him, she walked away with Sarah and her parents.

Len and Lois joined him just as Miranda disappeared through the main door.

Lois smiled up at him. "Will you and Miranda be joining us for lunch, or are you taking her to your Onkel Bart's?"

He should have been relieved that for the first time since she'd arrived, he wouldn't be responsible for her during a Sunday lunch. Instead, he felt as if he had been slapped. "Miranda is going to Peter and Susan's home. I am not going."

Lois's eyebrows raised. "Sarah is becoming good friends with her. But it is strange that you are not going with them. Would you like to come to our home for lunch?"

Ted stared at the door, watching people leave one by one.

"No. *Danke shoen.* I think I will just go home. I have some reading I need to do."

12

"Remind me to ask if you are available the next time I must negotiate a sales agreement contract," Ted grumbled beside her while they waited for Pastor Jake to return to his office.

Miranda tapped her fingers casually on the wooden desk while Pastor Jake attended to a paper jam in the photocopier. "What do you mean?"

"This is something Pastor Jake should have presented to the church board to approve. But he did not."

She smiled innocently at him. "What? I didn't say he couldn't run it past the board. All I did was ask if he trusted me."

"It was not what you said, it was how you said it."

Miranda fluttered her eyelashes and puckered her lips like a kewpie doll. "What? Don't *you* trust me?"

She could see him grinding his teeth,

180

something he used to do only occasionally, but now it seemed to be happening more often.

"I suspect that is one of those false questions where even though it appears that I have a choice, there is only one permissible answer I can give."

She bit her bottom lip until it began to sting. She didn't know how she answered with a straight face, but she did. "Trick question. It's called a trick question. Would I do that to you?"

One eye narrowed as he stared at her. "This appears to be another one, is it not?"

She stifled a giggle, which made him narrow both eyes. "Maybe."

He sighed, bowed his head, and applied two fingers to his eyebrows. "This is not the way of my people. We have never done anything like this before. Many will not want to participate."

"But many do. I've already started to ask around. Subtly."

"You?" He made a sound that on anyone else she would have called a snort. "Subtle?"

Now Miranda gritted her teeth. "It's possible, you know."

"I have not seen evidence of this."

Pastor Jake returned and slid behind his desk, saving her the need to respond. He wiped his hands on a cloth, then stuffed the cloth into his pocket. "It is strange to be talking about Christmas preparations, when next week it will only be Easter."

Miranda suddenly perked up. "I love the Easter services. But I haven't heard anything about your Easter cantata."

Pastor Jake quirked one eyebrow. "Cantata?"

"Your Easter cantata."

He turned to Ted. "We have no special cantata planned for Easter. Do we? It is not our way to do that."

Ted shook his head. "No. We do not."

Miranda's heart sank. "But . . . this is the celebration of the resurrection. This is the reason Christ came, the fulfillment of His purpose for coming to Earth. Easter should be more important to celebrate than Christmas. We have to do something special."

Pastor Jake rubbed his chin with his thumb and forefinger. "This is true. Ted, please add something to the service, to be special for Easter."

"But Easter is less than one week away. That is not enough time to organize anything."

"Then only do one song, but I think we should honor Miranda's request. This also will show Miranda how much we appreciate her." Miranda stared at Ted. She wasn't sure what he felt for her, but she was pretty sure it wasn't exactly appreciation.

Ted turned to her. "Our church has never added a special song for Easter before. Since your church has, how would you like to plan and organize this?"

"In less than a week? That's not enough time. Besides, I'm too busy with the Christmas drama. What about your church choir?"

Ted crossed his arms over his chest. "We do not have a choir."

"Not even for special occasions?"

"No."

"Surely you have a couple of people who could do a duet? Or a quartet?" Miranda's mind spun with possibilities. Since no one except Ted had ever sung from the front, this was a good time to see who would be brave enough to sing in front of a crowd and see how they stood up to the pressure. With two, or even four, people singing together, no one would feel alone, making it a good introduction to being on a stage, even though the church didn't have a stage. Yet. But they would.

Ted leaned back in the chair, his arms still folded across his chest. "Who do you think would do this, and who would have time to practice?"

"Sarah Janzen, first of all. Then Elaine. We need two men, but the only one I can think of who could do this on short notice is Brian."

Ted nodded. "Yes, I think this is possible. But we still need a tenor voice. What about Leonard?"

"He's too busy right now with exams at the school. Besides, I've heard him sing, and he wouldn't be my first choice."

"This is not enough notice to ask anyone else."

"What about you? Whatever song we pick, you'll know it. After all, we'll be selecting something from your music library."

A range of emotions flitted across his face, ending with resignation. "Do I have a choice?"

"Uh . . . no."

He sighed. "Then I suppose that we will select something on Thursday evening, at my house, while Brian is there."

She forced herself to sit still, and not jump up and do a Snoopy Dance in front of the two men. Doing her best to keep a straight face, she glanced quickly at Pastor Jake, then concentrated on Ted. "Whatever works for you, works for me."

He made that strange almost-snort sound and stood. "It is time for me to return to work. I will drive you back to Leonard and Lois's home."

She shook her head. "No. If you wouldn't mind, can you drop me off at your house? I just got a great idea for the play, and I do my best work when I know no one else can hear me."

He hesitated for just a second but then looked up at the clock on the wall and sighed again. "Should I invite Brian over for supper?"

Mentally, Miranda calculated the time. "Yes, you should."

The ride in the car was silent, but she suspected that when Ted arrived at his house, her good fortune would be over.

One look at him as he stopped the car told her she was right. Instead of following his established pattern of getting out first and running around the car to open the door for her, he grasped the brim of his hat and straightened it, remaining seated behind the wheel. If his car had automatic door locks, she was positive this was a time he would have used them. Here, parked on the street, they could talk in private, yet be in full view of all his neighbors.

The day they talked long enough for the windows to fog up, he might have some explaining to do.

She hoped today would not be that day. She had ideas. Lots of ideas. And not a lot of time.

"Since you are obviously going to start writing today, is there a way I can get you to change your mind? I am not convinced this idea has the most wisdom."

"You've already changed my mind. I wanted to set this in a big city so it will be applicable to more people."

Ted leaned back in his seat, crossing his arms over his chest, although he looked rather cramped behind the steering wheel. "But we are not doing what I wanted, either. My plan would be to show our culture and our heritage, to set this in the days when our church was founded."

Miranda turned sideways so her back pressed against the corner, half on the door and half on the seat, and crossed her arms, imitating his position. Although her knitted cap in no way conveyed the same intimidation factor as Ted's wide-brimmed hat.

"The thing we did agree on was that the purpose is to attract new people from the demographic area. We have to show the positives about who you are, and what you're doing now. This can't be a history lesson."

Ted raised his hat, ran his fingers through

his hair, then plopped his hat back on his head. "But we are changing now. Only a few weeks ago for the first time we have had husbands and wives and their children sitting together, on both sides of the church." His eyes narrowed. "And not everyone has noticed this, but I have seen your friends have been wearing . . . denim jeans, when they are together. I do not want to think of what will be said when word of this gets back to Pastor Jake. Or to their fathers."

"That wasn't my fault. I took them to buy blouses and pretty shoes that weren't black. I tried to get them out of the jeans department, but they wouldn't listen. But I don't know why it matters. They aren't little girls. All of them are grown women, the same age as me. They can wear whatever they want, as long as it's not indecent or disrespectful."

His body sagged, and he closed his eyes. "I try to tell myself that very thing, but it is difficult. It is not our way." He turned his head to look out the window, swiping his hand on the glass to wipe off the condensation that was beginning to accumulate. "I am not sure what *is* our way anymore. The young ladies are getting jobs, often outside of our town, and many of our young men are not coming back when they get their education. Even some of the older ladies are beginning to wear pants during the week. The young ladies have stopped wearing their prayer *kapps* except for Sunday and to Bible study. We have added musical instruments to our worship service."

He turned back to her. "These are not all bad things. But they are changes. Where will they stop? I do not want to become lost as they have in the ways of the cities." ◆

There it was. As if a switch had flipped in her head, Miranda suddenly understood what his issues were. She wasn't sure what she could do about them, but she needed to reassure him that not everything was evil outside the boundaries of the ways of his father and forefathers. True, at her own church, even though it was fully and completely Mennonite to the core, most of the old-world traditions he so valued had been lost, just as he feared. This community was in a vulnerable position. Protected as they kept themselves from the outside world, whatever she put in the play, whether acted or sung, would expose something, or someone, that up until now had been kept private, whether individually or by the community. Whatever was exposed was vulnerable to injury.

"Why are you looking at me like this? I

spend much time in the cities, and I see what happens there. How people act. They have cast God aside. I cannot allow that to begin here."

"I know that. You've got to trust me." Miranda yanked her hat off her head and wiped the entire passenger side window with it. "I'm going to go inside now, and you get back to work. Don't get out; I'll be fine. All I want you to think about is that I'm going to be making your supper."

He reached for his keys and began to wiggle his door key off the ring. "I am not sure how I am supposed to respond," he muttered as he pulled off the right key and handed it to her. "And I would like to know, what exactly is a trans fat, anyway?"

Miranda sighed as she watched the taillights of his car disappear around the corner, then closed the door without locking it. Here, she didn't need to.

Of all the people she had known in her lifetime, Ted was the most stuffy and the most reserved, and definitely the most predictable. Yet the combination also made him the most reliable and the most trust-worthy. Even though he drove her crazy most of the time, she understood why so many of the single women, including those who were the closer friends she had made since her arrival, had their eye on him with marriage in mind.

She had no idea why he didn't seem interested, especially since he was a couple of years older than she was. But then in this community, the second he decided it was time for him to get married, there would be a lineup around the block, each woman loaded down with armfuls of food. And for those who knew him best, a package of good guitar strings.

Thinking of the need to feed him, Miranda headed to the fridge before she made her way to the piano. This time she only had the distraction of her own thoughts, without needing to teach piano lessons, so today she could prepare something for the men that needed more attention than the usual fare. Besides, she had been stockpiling many of the same staples that she had at home, so she was now more comfortable in Ted's kitchen. Yet she doubted that he looked past the first row of the top shelf of his fridge when she wasn't there.

If not, then this was going to be a surprise.

By the time Ted and Brian arrived, Miranda was ready. She hadn't actually composed any music, but she did have some basc mclody lincs and thcmcs, and in her head, she could hear Sarah's voice singing the female lead and Ted's voice singing the male lead.

"Have you accomplished what you set out to do?" Ted asked before he'd even removed his hat.

Miranda nodded so fast her hair bounced. "Yes!"

Ted reached to hang his hat on the peg beside the door. "Can I hear it?"

She shook her head so fast a lock smacked her in the eyes. "No!"

Brian smirked as he began to unbutton his coat. "Now that we have this established, what is for supper? Something smells *zehr gut,* although I am no longer going to ask if it is something my mama makes."

"Brian, when are you getting married?"

Both men froze. She wondered if Ted was even breathing.

"I . . . have not thought about it," Brian stammered. "Probably within two years." He pressed one hand to his chest, over his heart. "But if you are asking me, it could be sooner."

She couldn't be positive, but Miranda was almost sure Ted rolled his eyes.

"Why are you asking me this?"

"Curiosity."

Ted's eyes narrowed. "You are not going

to use this in your play, are you?"

Miranda shook her head. "Of course not. But maybe that's not a bad idea . . ." She turned and dashed off to the piano, where she had been making her notes.

Brian's voice lowered, but she still heard him. "She would not, would she?"

She stopped writing, waiting longer than she thought she should have, for Ted's reply.

"No."

She resumed writing and was interrupted before she had finished her sentence by Ted appearing in the doorway.

She waved her left hand in the air, then kept writing. "Don't look at me like that. A little happily-ever-after would be the perfect finishing touch. Everyone loves a happy ending."

"The happy ending is the joy of the birth of Christ."

"Of course it is. But there is a plot besides the Christmas story, you know. That's what's going to appeal to the guests. For the most part, as long as we appeal mostly to the women, the men will come."

"This must appeal to the men as much as the ladies."

"It will, but we don't have the budget to include high-speed racing and car crashes."

Ted's mouth opened, but no sound came out.

"That was a joke. Not really. Seriously, I've got to present something that can be done with a very simple stage set, and that means a quiet and low level of action. You've got to trust me."

"You say this often."

"I guess I do," she muttered, then stuck her tongue between her teeth as she finished writing her thoughts. "That's it," she said as she stood. "Now it's time to get supper on the table and talk about Easter Sunday."

13

As Ted adjusted the music stand in front of him, the church fell silent. Somehow, in just a few days, word had spread.

When trying to decide on which hymn to do as a quartet, Miranda expressed her opinion that she didn't want to do one that everyone in the congregation knew. He didn't know why Brian agreed with her, but once he said so, both Sarah and Elaine did as well. His protests that he had no music in his library for an Easter service meant nothing. Using his computer, Miranda happily went onto the Internet and found a song she promised would be easy to learn.

She was right, but he refused to admit it.

However, this wasn't the time to feel dissatisfied. This was the time to worship his Lord and Savior.

He looked up at the congregation. For the first time since he could remember, there were no empty seats near the front on either the right or the left side. The only empty seat in the front half of the church was the third row aisle seat, formerly on the ladies' side, next to Miranda.

Without an introduction, Ted strummed one chord on his guitar, the four of them hummed their opening note, then began to sing.

At the end of the song, a collective hush filled the room, finally broken by some "amens," and a few sniffles. He tried not to show his surprise that Miranda wasn't the only woman with tears in her eyes. Instead, he turned back to his music stand, uncovering his hymnal.

"Please turn with me to page 107, and we will sing 'Christ the Lord Is Risen Today.' "

Brian, Sarah, and Elaine returned to the congregation after the singing had begun, the sound of melody occasionally broken by some people blowing their noses. This also was something none of them had ever experienced until the arrival of Miss Randi with an "i."

Pastor Jake took his place at the front at the end of the worship time. "Thank you for sharing in that special way. Everyone, please turn in your Bibles to Luke 24:50."

As he took his seat, Miranda leaned toward him. "You all sounded wonderful up there. You did great. Thank you."

"We did not do it for you. We did it for our Savior."

She winced. "Of course. Thanks for the reminder."

He waited while Miranda opened her purse, but this time, in addition to pulling out her cell phone, she took out a strange-looking pen.

"What are you doing with that? I thought you took your sermon notes in your cell phone. Do you think you will again lose your data?"

Miranda shook her head, pressed a button on the pen, then rested it on a bare spot on the pew between them. "No. Shh. I'm recording, so don't talk."

He looked down at the pen. "Recording?"

"Shh. Pastor said he was going to do a really different Easter Sunday sermon. He's going to talk a little about redemption and then relate it to the book of Revelation. I'm recording this for Daddy."

"I have seen this pen before." His mind whirled as he struggled to remember. "You had this same one at your first church board meeting."

"That's right. Now please be quiet. I want to pick up Pastor Jake, not you."

Ted ground his teeth so hard his jaw

196

ached. At the meeting she had asked if she could take notes, so he had been aware of being recorded. Just not in this way. Apparently, she did not have a photographic memory after all.

Just knowing about the recording device between them distracted him from Pastor's words. Like the previous week, every time Pastor Jake mentioned a Bible verse, Miranda's cell phone appeared between them, but this time he was careful to remain silent even when she flipped the page too soon. The longer he sat, the more uncomfortable he became, until his left leg fell asleep. All he had to do was move, but he could not, lest the sound of the rustle of his clothing would be picked up by the microphone beside him.

Even as a child sitting through an hour-long sermon, he'd never been so relieved when the sermon was over. He hobbled up to the front to close the service with the final hymn.

Behind the podium, he tapped his foot while the prickly sensation subsided. "Let us end with page 109, 'I Serve a Risen Savior.' "

The last resonant chord had barely faded when people from the congregation began moving forward instead of exiting the sanctuary.

Sarah was the first to arrive.

"Ted, many people in the congregation think we should sing like this again. I agree with them."

Brian appeared behind her. "Yes. Others have asked if they may join our choir."

Ted shook his head. "But we do not have a choir."

Brian grinned. "It appears that we do now. Which night is practice night, and what song are we going to sing next Sunday?"

He forced himself not to grind his teeth. "I think you should go ask Miranda."

Sarah grinned from ear to ear. "I will do that. I know she will listen to me."

Before Ted could say that he had his doubts about that, Sarah dashed off and Brian moved closer. "Well, my friend, it appears that we must expand the music selection in your library. Which I happen to know consists only of our own Mennonite hymnal and hymnals from other denominations that you purchased while you were away at college."

Instead of looking at Brian, Ted was watching Sarah talking to Miranda so excitedly that she was waving her arms as she spoke. "I do not have time to go to the cities to look for music." He turned his attention back to his friend. "This means I must use the Internet, as Miranda has done to find the song we sang this morning."

Brian nodded. "*Ja.* I have been using the Internet more since Miranda has come to us. She has shown me much I did not know about shopping with my computer. Instead of paying money for long distance phone calls when I need parts for my shop, I am now shopping using the Internet. Most of the time I have been able to save money by comparing prices. She has also given me other ideas."

Ted squeezed his eyes shut. Their community and lifestyle had been changing for years, but since Miranda had arrived, the changes were coming faster.

Before he could respond, a few of the men from the congregation arrived to stand beside Brian. Ted nodded in greeting, then turned to Frank, who stood closest.

"Good morning, Ted. I wanted to tell you that the song with the four of you singing made this Easter service very special."

"Thank you."

"Susan has heard that we will now have a choir at our church. She wants to join, and so do I."

Ted looked up. Women now surrounded

Miranda, many talking at once, and one of them was Frank's wife.

"It appears that is so. You are welcome to join."

"When will the first practice be?"

Ted kept watching Miranda as some of the women's husbands joined the circle of people around her. "I cannot say. But from the look of things, Miranda is deciding that right now."

Frank stiffened. "Miranda? Then who is leading the men's choir?"

"There will be only one choir for both the men and the women."

"A woman is leading the choir?"

Once again, Ted caught himself grinding his teeth. If he'd had time to think of this, he would have realized that many men would have difficulty with a woman leading a group of mixed gender. He was one of very few men in their community who had frequent dealings with the rest of the country outside their own community, and that meant he was accustomed to women in management positions. But for people the age of his parents, like Frank, most dealings were in their small town, where it had only been within the past five years that women had dealings with business outside their homes. They had never experienced a woman in leadership, much less in their church.

From his own experience, he suspected that many of the businesses who supplied Frank and Susan's store deliberately chose a man to deal with Frank when he called. He didn't know if that had made things better or worse.

He lifted his guitar to slip the strap off his shoulder, then held the guitar in front of him. "We are both leading the choir, but Miranda will be the one to direct the singers, because only one person can do that at a time. Miranda and I will decide together which evening is the best for the group to assemble."

As Frank walked away, the other men, all of whom had heard the conversation, nodded and left as well, leaving Ted standing alone beside the podium. He sighed and turned to tuck the guitar back into its case. To be honest, he liked the idea of having a choir, and even if he were not the worship leader, he probably would have joined the choir himself.

The zipper on the guitar bag was only halfway done when Miranda's voice sounded behind him. "Ted? I think we need to talk."

He turned. "*Ja.* We do. But today is Easter

Sunday, and I will be joining Onkel Bart and Tante Odelle after the service."

"Uh, yeah . . . about that . . ." Her voice trailed off as Tante Odelle came forward from the crowd.

"Did you tell him, my dear?" Ted froze. Turning to Ted, she said, "Your Onkel and I, we have not been able to talk to Miranda, and you spend so much time together. We have already asked Leonard and Lois, and we have their permission. Miranda will be joining us for our Easter dinner today. We will be having a big ham and your favorite Easter treat!" She turned to Miranda. "He loves chocolate eggs rolled in coconut," she said with a wink, her voice lowered. She smiled and rested her arm around Miranda's shoulders, then turned back to Ted. "Brian tells us of the good healthy suppers she cooks for you, so I have been eager to learn her good recipes."

Miranda's cheeks turned pink. "She wants my secret recipe for Shake 'N Bake chicken with oven-baked fries."

Ted tried not to choke. "*Ja.* There is no trans fat." He sighed. "I will be a few minutes. I have some things to put away."

"Take your time," Tante Odelle said, still smiling. "Miranda will be coming home with us. We will talk."

Miranda leaned over the table, glanced quickly at Ted over her shoulder, then finished drawing the notes on the poster board. "These are the technical vocal ranges for the soprano, alto, tenor, and bass voices, and I'm going to do each one in a different color." In her best legible handwriting, she wrote the names of everyone who had come out for choir in the colors of their vocal ranges. "Remind me, we have to get Pastor to call someone to get the piano tuned. This is really good timing that so many people want to be in the choir. Everyone can get used to singing on stage nice and early, way before we have to start the Christmas play. Are you going to audition?"

"No. What exactly did Tante Odelle say about me on Sunday when I was not there?"

"Not much. She just told me all the embarrassing things you did as a child. I didn't realize Hank could sing so well. Did you? Do you think he'll want to be in the drama?"

"*Ja.* Just like at the school, he likes to be a good example to his students. As a teacher, he also will not be shy in front of people." Ted leaned forward, resting his palms on

the tabletop. "I did not do anything embarrassing. I was a good student and a hard
worker. I think it was you who did the
embarrassing things during your time in
public school."

"I was a straight-A student until twelfth
grade." She bit back a smile and tapped her
pencil on Brian's name. "Brian is the only
true bass, but you have quite a low voice
when you speak. Are you really a tenor, or
do you just sing tenor because it's the same
range as most of the other men?"

Ted stood straight, crossing his arms over
his chest. "This is not important. I do not
wish to sing for the Christmas play. I sing at
the front every Sunday. What is important is
what Tante Odelle said to you about me."

Miranda sighed. "It was just girl talk.
Okay?" Still bent at the waist to write, she
moved her head to look up at him, hovering
above her. "She hasn't seen as much of you
as before, and she wanted to make sure you
were eating okay."

His eyebrows arched. "That does not
make sense. Lois is a very good cook, and
you are very sure not to feed me trans fats,
so I am eating well." He rested his hands on
his stomach. "Maybe I am eating a little too
well."

Miranda stood and watched Ted as he

struggled to figure out what was so impor- tant about his aunt's concern about how he was being fed. It was more than just a ques- tion about Ted eating well. Odelle had wanted to know that Ted was happy, and to her, a big part of being happy was being married. Miranda had no answer as to why Ted was still single. She had been here long enough to see that most, if not all, of the single women his age wanted to marry him. She paused. "She also thought that lately you've been looking a little stressed."

"Stressed?"

"She didn't exactly say it that way. She said that whenever you go there for supper you're either in a hurry or you seem tired. She is worried that your uncle has given you too much responsibility at the furniture factory, and it's been putting too much strain on you lately."

"It is not too much strain. I have been busier lately, but it is not from the factory. I am fine."

Despite his aunt's concern, he really did seem fine, and he certainly didn't ever seem unhappy. The only fault she could really see with him was that once he got something in his head, he became focused to the point of excluding anything else.

"I'm sorry to get you involved in the choir.

I really didn't plan this."

"But it worked very much in your favor."

"Yes, it did. If you don't mind, I think that we should also start the auditioning process. The earlier we start, the more time it gives me to write a production that will suit everyone involved to their own individual strengths."

"I am not so sure of this. I do not think it is the right thing to do."

Miranda sighed. "We have to start somewhere. I just wish I could give Sarah the lead part, but I can't."

Ted nodded. "*Ja*. It is too bad, because she sings so beautifully. She was fine during the Easter song, but today when we asked her to sing even one line by herself, she could not do it."

"Yes, I would have liked her in a lead part, but it looks as if I was right about her being too shy."

"Yet she was not shy to sing with Brian. Maybe we can ask Brian to help her."

Miranda tried not to giggle. "I'm sure that would help her a lot, but not so much with her singing."

"What do you mean?"

"Don't tell me you haven't noticed the way they look at each other?"

He didn't answer, but his blank expression told her that he didn't have a clue.

"Never mind. I think this is going to be interesting."

"Interesting?"

"If I'm not mistaken, you're going to be seeing a lot more of Sarah." She looked up at the clock on the wall. "It's getting late and you've got to get up early for work. I think it's time you took me home."

14

Miranda sat behind the newly tuned church piano. Alone.

She didn't know which hurt worse, the shock that no one had come to audition, or the sinking in her gut that her entire project, the reason she had left her home for a year, and the way she had tried so hard to integrate into their community, had been rejected.

In the past week everyone who had expressed any interest — those who had joined the choir and a few who hadn't — had been invited to come to audition tonight.

At home, aside from the first performance, audition night was always the most exciting time of any project. Enthusiasm was contagious because everyone's hopes were so high. This was the night that the top roles were wide open, and each person arrived pumped with the hope that they could reach for their own personal star.

Blindly staring at a blank spot on the wall, Miranda pressed the sustain pedal and played one perfectly harmonious chord. The piano was ready for a lineup of enthusiastic singers. The strings echoed their rich tones around her like a melodious waterfall, then faded . . . to complete silence. The only sound in the room was her breathing.

She had set the entire evening aside rather than making specific appointments. In this Mennonite community, the clock did not have much meaning. People opened their businesses to the public on time each day, and they were on time for church and Bible study, but otherwise, time concerns were more like the women's cooking. Everything simmered for hours, and the longer it sat, the better it would be.

In the complete silence, the squeak of the main door opening jolted her like the whistle of an oncoming train. Footsteps approached. Her heart pounded. Male or female? She couldn't tell. All the women wore practical flat-soled shoes with heels that didn't click. It didn't matter. One individual didn't make for an extravaganza, but it was a start.

Miranda suppressed the urge to jump up and embrace the visitor. A shadow approached the door.

Miranda held her breath.

"Miranda?" A male voice echoed from around the corner. A boot appeared in the doorway. "Where are you?"

Her heart sank.

"Ted." She dropped herself on the piano bench with a thud. "It's you."

He removed his hat and pressed it to his chest. "I came to see how you were doing and to take you home if you were done."

Home.

She might as well go home. To her real home, not the bedroom she had borrowed from Len and Lois.

"Yeah, I'm done." More than done. She was truly finished. Miranda sighed, unable to keep the defeat out of her voice. She couldn't believe how wrong she had been. Despite her good intentions and best efforts, she had failed. "I'm definitely done." Her throat tightened. The backs of her eyes began that burning sensation. "I just have a few things to pack up. Let's go."

She turned her back so he wouldn't see her swipe her nose with the back of her hand, then picked up the notes she'd made and the beginnings of the melody lines she had prepared. For nothing. A sniffle escaped.

"Miranda? Are you crying?"

She swiped her nose again, then turned to him. "You're as diplomatic as always."

"What is wrong?"

She swished one arm through the air, her palm open. "Look around you. No one came."

He turned and scanned the pages laid out on the nearby table and the few sheets of music arranged on the piano. "Not even Frank?"

She plopped back down on the piano bench, facing outward, not toward the piano. "No."

"You knew that we have never done such a thing here before, did you not?"

"Of course I knew that." She turned to that familiar blank spot on the wall. "That's why I made sure I told everyone that tonight was auditions. I thought there was a thread of excitement in the crowd, especially those who joined the choir. But nothing. No one was interested enough to want to partici-pate, only to watch from a distance."

Ted slowly lowered himself onto the bench beside her. "That is not true. There is much interest. But this is not our way."

"I don't understand."

"We have been raised since childhood to do God's will, and to trust in God for our

211

many blessings. For those who would be blessed to use their talents for God's glory, we wait for God's timing. We would never compete with our friends for this. This is not God's way."

Miranda's thoughts stalled in her brain. "But I do believe this is God's way to open up the doors to your church to the surrounding communities. That's why I came. I don't know how we all could have been so wrong."

"This is not wrong. Do you have your cell phone with you?" Miranda pulled her purse out from under the piano bench beneath her. She didn't know why he asked. She always had her phone with her, and he teased her about it mercilessly. Except she hardly used it as a phone anymore. Instead of paying expensive roaming and long distance charges, she e-mailed her friends and her father or used the webcam. Since she arrived here, she'd used it as a phone exactly once — to call Ted from the parking lot. Her main use now for her cell phone was as her Bible with all her notes and a full concordance available at a tap of her fingertip.

She handed the cell phone to him. "Here. Did you forget your Bible somewhere again?"

He pulled a small notebook out of his pocket and dialed a number.

"Hello, Theresa, this is Ted. I am calling from the church. Miranda and I have decided that we would like you to have the part of Mary in the play we will be doing at Christmas. Can you do that?"

Miranda's breath caught. He hadn't asked if she would *like* to do it. Only if she *could.*

He nodded as he listened to Theresa's response. "Yes, of course we are sure." He nodded again. "Certainly we will pray for you." He smiled. "You are welcome."

He flipped the phone shut. "There. You said you wanted Theresa to take the part of Mary. It is done. I remember that you wanted William to play Joseph. I will inform him at the office tomorrow. If you give me your list, as I recall you had conceived the same number of parts as the number of people you thought would want to participate. Assign the parts as you deem best. No one will turn this down; they will be honored and humbled to be chosen. I will phone the men and you can phone the rest of the ladies."

"That's it? That's all there is to it?"

"*Ja.* That is all."

"Really? I don't know what to say."

Ted smiled ear to ear. Little crinkles

formed at the corners of his eyes. "There is nothing to say. It is done."

Miranda couldn't remember the last time he'd smiled at her like that. Or if he ever had. She also couldn't remember ever being so close to him. She'd always sat beside him when teaching him piano lessons, but the other times they'd been side by side on the bench, they both faced the piano, and she never looked at his face, only his hands. Now, with the piano keyboard at her back, all she could do was stare up into his eyes.

They were brown. Like her favorite chocolate bar. Dark and rich. Except his eyes had little flecks of gold and a dark olive green. His eyes were beautiful. And kind.

She tried to smile back, but it came out wobbly. Along with a quivering smile, a telltale tear leaked out of the corner of her eye.

Ted's smile wavered and dropped. "I do not understand this. When I talked to Theresa, she began to cry. Now you are crying. I thought this would make you happy. It did not make Theresa happy either."

Another tear escaped. "You really don't get it, do you?"

His clueless expression was all the reply she needed.

She turned sideways on the bench to

reach and take his hands in hers. "I'm not sad. You've made me very happy. It's just like one of those television shows with a sappy ending that makes all the women in the room weepy."

"Women do not come to my house, and I do not have a television."

Another tear leaked out. "Of course you don't." The only rooms of his house that she had been in were his living room, his kitchen, and the room where he'd put her electric piano, but she knew he didn't own a television. No one here did. The only person who might have had one would have been Ted, only because he was the most contemporary person here, but he would have considered it an act of rebellion, and that wasn't in his nature. He had a significant pile of books in his living room, so she knew what he did with his spare time. She had even borrowed a few, with his permission.

She gave his hands a gentle squeeze. "Thank you."

He smiled again. At the sight of those adorable little crinkles, despite her efforts, her tears welled up again. She didn't want to cry in front of Ted, of all people, but the harder she tried to fight it, the more her eyes watered.

The right thing to do would have been to let go of Ted's hands, stand up, wipe her eyes, and leave. Except she didn't want to lose the contact. Again, his smile faltered. She could only guess at how awkward he felt. She felt awkward too.

"It's okay," she sniffled. "These are happy tears."

"I do not understand how tears could be happy. I must admit that I do not know what to do. Would you like to borrow my handkerchief?"

Her lower lip quivered. "I would like a hug." She sniffled again, released his hands, and leaned her face into his shoulder.

Ted was trapped. In slow motion, one of his hands settled at her waist, the other at the small of her back. The warmth of being enclosed made her feel both better and worse. She probably shouldn't have, but she leaned closer to him and raised her hands to his shoulder blades and held on. When his hands pressed her closer, she lost it.

To her credit, she didn't sob outright, but she created a sizeable wet spot on the front of his shirt.

The wetter his shirt became, the tighter he held her.

Telling him that she was PMSing probably wouldn't help. But this felt so good.

This was Ted.

Miranda pushed herself away and stood. "I feel much better now," she mumbled without looking at him. "Let me pack up my papers. I'll finish this up later. I think it's time for me to go home."

15

Ted left the busy group to find a quiet spot in the middle of the sanctuary, where he spread the photocopies on the pew beside him to look for the right piece of music.

Halfway through the pile, he still hadn't found the right song when Len's voice came from behind him.

"Ted, can we speak now, while we are away from the rest of the group?"

Ted raised his head. Len's mouth was set in a thin line, his brows drawn close together.

Ted remembered this expression well from his high school days, and it never meant good. At times like this it was difficult not to address Len as "Principal Toews" or even "Sir." But Ted reminded himself that since high school, not just the principal but the entire community looked at him differently. In the cities, he would have been called "geeky." Here, they had simply considered him odd for preferring to read a book rather than go swimming or fishing with the other boys.

Now, a decade later, as the biggest employer in town, he was one of the most prestigious members of the community. Not that he deserved this honor; the business had already been a success when Onkel Bart had given him the position as general manager. He had simply used what he learned at college to help the company grow. Yet people looked up to him, and he could not insult them by reminding them that he was no different in God's sight than the sick and the widowed.

Ted sat straight, keeping his fingers in the stack of paper so as not to lose his place, and met the eyes of his former principal. "Do not worry, Len. The song I need is probably at the bottom of the pile, so this is a good time. What is your question?"

Len jerked his head in the direction of Miranda and the group of people at the piano. "Miranda has been so busy like this every day, only taking the Sabbath to rest. In the month since you have decided who will sing, every day she is either at the piano or with different people from the time she wakes, until late in the evening, teaching and coaching them both here and at our home. In the middle of the night I have seen her sneaking through the house in her nightclothes to go to the piano. She looks at it but does not play, then writes music. Lois tells me that in the morning as soon as Miranda knows we are awake, she runs to the piano to play what she has written at night."

Ted let out a sigh. This was not a surprise.

He turned to watch Miranda, listening as she played a few phrases of one her songs for Bess. The short melody rang out, clear and unique in its beauty. This was probably one of the songs she had heard in her head and wrote down before she actually played out the notes the next day.

"She does this because her electric piano is at my house so she can teach her lessons back in Seattle by using the Internet. I think it is time for me to go to the cities to buy my own piano so she can use her own for what she had intended, which was to do her composing at night with headphones."

Len nodded. "I would not mind if she played piano in the middle of the night, except at night she should be sleeping. Look at her. She has circles under her eyes. She is so tired that many times in the evening she falls asleep on the couch with the dog on her lap."

Ted nodded. "Miranda is very fond of Fidette. She tells me she has always wanted a dog but could not have one at her father's home. Many times she has brought Fidette to my house on lesson day." In fact, Len's dog was at his house so often he had purchased a dog bowl and a blanket for Fidette. "So I think that having the dog in her lap is something she enjoys. It is probably not bad that she falls asleep."

"But she has also stopped knitting in the evenings. Lois tells me that she knits to relax, but Miranda has stopped."

Ted smiled. "The last time I took Miranda to the store for knitting supplies, I heard her telling Bess that it was the last thing she was going to make. It seems she must stop because she has too much to take home."

"But Lois is worried about her, and so am I. When we talked about this, the committee members did not mean for her to do nothing else for the time she is here. We can understand this taking all her time in the fall, but it is not yet even summer."

Ted shook his head as he continued to pick through the pile of music. "Do not forget that she is also doing work for the accounting firm in Seattle while she is here. I suspect that some of the time you think she is doing our play, she is doing her job."

"Then she is doing too much."

"Miranda has told me that she likes to keep busy. If there is one thing she hates, it is being bored."

Len crossed his arms over his chest. "She has been so busy that often Lois takes Miranda's dinner to her so she may eat in her room as she is working. Even so, Lois tells me that Miranda is losing weight."

Ted's hand stilled. *"Daut's schlajcht,"* he muttered. That was bad. In the cities, so many women were as thin as Miranda because they were always on a diet, eating so little he didn't know how they stayed alive. He knew she ate well on Thursdays when she cooked supper for him and Brian. With Lois feeding her the other days, and Lois never skimping on portions, that wasn't the problem.

"She is probably not eating lunch then."

Ted turned his head at the sound of her laughter and watched the group. They had all moved so Miranda sat at the piano with everyone else standing around her in a circle. He pulled his finger out of the pile of music and stood, watching her from the distance.

She was thin, for sure. The day he held her as she cried, at the small of her back his outstretched hand had spanned her entire width.

Ted's thoughts stalled in his brain. Thinking of that moment made his heart beat faster. As she'd cried, he'd never felt so helpless in his life. The only thing he could think of was to hold her until it was over, which was what he did. Yet, at the same time, in her moment of weakness, the way she had pressed herself into him had made him feel stronger, empowered. He'd never been big or muscular like the men who did physical labor on the farms for their daily jobs, but as he cradled her in his arms, he'd felt he could have protected her against a grizzly bear attack.

"You are right. She is too skinny. I will speak to her."

"Thank you. Then you will bring her home tonight?"

Ted nodded, and Len returned to the front to take his place in the circle he had left. As soon as Miranda noticed Len, she turned to Ted and motioned at him with both hands in the air.

"Don't worry about that song," she called out across the large room. "We'll pick something else."

As Ted rejoined the group, she handed him a photocopy of a new piece of music.

"We'll be doing this one. I wrote all the guitar chords out for you on this copy, so don't lose it. This is what we're going to do when the townspeople meet up with the nativity people. We're going to try to keep the contrast between the old ways and . . . uh . . ." her voice faltered and she looked up at everyone in the circle around her. "More old ways, I guess." Most of the people around her smiled, but Ted did not.

This was their main point of disagreement in the presentation. What she considered the old ways of the townspeople, he considered new. Between the two of them, they agreed on very little of the interaction in the play between the townspeople and the people from the nativity scene. The only thing they agreed on was that both groups were to be on stage at the same time.

Even though he hadn't practiced this particular song, Ted managed to play through it at a satisfactory level. From what he'd seen so far, the group songs were fairly simple because she'd written them to be easy enough for everyone to memorize.

At the end, she stood and drew everyone into a circle as she pointed to one particular phrase.

Being the only person in the group who wasn't singing, Ted remained seated. From his lower vantage point, he watched Miranda. As she spoke to Elaine, Miranda turned her back to him to point to the music. He noticed that she was wearing the same jeans she had worn at the airport on the day he had picked her up. Not that he ever paid attention to such things, but that day he had noticed how her jeans had fit her because he had compared her to some of the other ladies from the same plane whose jeans were far tighter.

His breath caught as he studied her from behind. She leaned over more to play a few notes on the piano without sitting on the bench. Her jeans surely did not fit the same as they had that day; they were, indeed, looser.

He couldn't stop thinking about this. Even though he had been raised in the town, he knew that farm families kept track of the weights of their animals because it was an important tool to monitor good health. He'd heard his mama talking about the weights of babies and young children. A healthy weight must therefore be important for adults as well, although he suspected it was more difficult to monitor.

He had never had a scale in his house. His pants fit him the same every year. The day he no longer needed suspenders to keep his pants up would be the day he would begin to monitor his own weight.

He had a scale in the shipping department at the factory. He could not imagine how he would be able to get her to come there and stand on it for him. Yet even without the scale, it was obvious that she had lost weight. She was already the thinnest of all the ladies.

Ted stood and rested his guitar on the chair. "Frank, can you please come with me? I have something I must do and I need your help."

No one said anything, but Ted's abrupt departure caused an agitated stir in the group.

"Please, everyone, we've got to concentrate," Miranda said. "This is our third time going through this song." She plunked the soprano and alto lines out with two fingers. "Like this. Let's try again."

As she began the introduction, a few of the ladies were still glancing toward the doorway. Miranda gritted her teeth. She had no idea what could have been so important that Ted needed to leave so suddenly, especially to drag Frank off with him. In this town, she doubted there could have been an emergency at the furniture factory or Frank's grocery store.

She had been depending on Ted's guitar-playing. Even though she had composed the songs, she needed to focus her concentration on teaching the singers, not accompanying them on the piano.

If only Ted had taught himself to play piano as fast as he had taught himself guitar. He was learning the piano quickly, but not quickly enough to accompany the choir, even for practice time, which was another reason that she had to find another accompanist. She couldn't direct the play while playing piano, especially for the performances.

Miranda pulled out her cell phone and made herself a task reminder to find a piano player.

She slipped her cell phone into her back pocket, then slipped down onto the piano bench. "Okay everyone. Let's try again from the chorus. Elaine, watch that high note, and Frank . . ." Her voice trailed off. Frank, her best bass, was gone. With Ted, her guitarist.

"Men . . ." she grumbled.

"Ach, ja," Elaine nodded, half grinning. "What can we do with them?"

All the ladies giggled. A few of the men blushed.

Miranda checked the time. "I guess with those two gone we'll end our practice a little early. Let's just do this song one more time, and then everyone can go home."

Brian cleared his throat. "I will be driving Sarah home, but if Ted does not return, I will take you home as well."

She opened her mouth to say that she could go home with Len and Lois, but Lois was watching Sarah and smiling like the Cheshire Cat.

Miranda captured her lower lip between her teeth to hold back her own grin. This was probably less an offer of a ride than it was asking if she would accompany them so they could spend more time together. "That would be great," she said, but she was really thinking that she wanted to go home and go to bed. However, without an escort, Sarah wouldn't be allowed to spend any more time with Brian than the time it took to drive five blocks, which barely allowed time to start a conversation, much less to actually finish one.

Lois's grin never stopped. "I will call your papa and let him know this."

"All right, let's start at the first verse and this time . . ."

The main door banged, disrupting their focus again. Everyone turned toward the entrance to the foyer. Part of her felt relieved that Ted had returned, but part of her wanted to reprimand him for his timing.

The timbre of male voices in the hall told her that Frank had returned with him.

"They're back, so we're going to do . . ." Ted and Frank stepped into the sanctuary, carrying large grocery bags. Miranda pressed her hand onto the sheet of music. "What is that?"

Ted and Frank both grinned as they set the bags down on the pew closest to the piano.

Ted reached into the first bag and pulled out a large plastic bottle filled with brown liquid.

Miranda stared. "Root beer? What are you doing with that?"

Frank reached into one of the other bags and pulled out a tub of vanilla ice cream.

Ted jerked his head toward the doorway. "If some of you ladies could bring some bowls and spoons from the kitchen, I have a surprise for everyone."

Practice was over. All the ladies left to go into the kitchen, leaving Miranda with the men.

She tightened her hands into fists. She'd seen nothing that was cause for this sudden celebration. "Would you mind explaining what in the world you're doing?"

"I am going to make root beer floats."

"Why?"

He smiled that heart-stopping little smile with the little crinkles in the corners of his eyes. "It is a special treat for everyone for working so hard."

She stared into his eyes, mesmerized. Her mind whirled with things she could have said, but the women returned, clattering dessert bowls and spoons. Lois hurried in front of them to drape a tablecloth over the pew beside Ted to protect the wood from spills.

Frank ladled a large scoop of ice cream into the first bowl. Very precisely, Ted poured root beer over the ice cream, waiting for the fizz to die down before pouring just a little more. He reached into the bag and pulled out a spray can of whipping cream and squirted a generous amount on top. Frank was ready beside him with a jar of maraschino cherries. Ted spooned one out and gently set it in the middle of the whipped cream.

"Done," he muttered as he extended his arm and held it toward her. "The first one is for you."

Miranda had never put great emphasis on desserts before, and she had certainly never before been presented with one like this. It reminded her of her friends' descriptions of their boyfriends' proposals, although no engagement ring had ever been presented with such flair. And from Ted, of all people. She hadn't known he had a sweet tooth, nor had she ever seen such an artistic root beer float. It was a masterpiece, so pretty she almost hated to ruin it by eating it. Almost.

"I . . . I don't know what to say," she stammered, her throat tightening up.

Ted's smile faded. His opened his free hand and pressed his palm onto his shirt, just below his left shoulder. "You are not going to cry, are you?"

"No, no . . . of course not." Before she actually did, she reached out with both hands to cup the bowl.

But instead of releasing it to her, Ted moved his hand from his shirt and rested it over her hands as she held the bowl, preventing her from moving. "First we must pray."

"Of course," she mumbled, unable to believe that she had almost forgotten.

Ted bowed his head and closed his eyes, but instead of the expected volume used when praying in a crowd, his voice became low and quiet, almost beseeching, only loud enough for herself and Frank to hear.

"Dear Lord, I thank you for this day, and for this opportunity to share. I ask that you watch over all of us, for health, and for endurance, and that all will work together for Your glory, amen."

"Amen," she replied, and Ted removed his hands, releasing the bowl to her.

Beside her, Sarah handed her a spoon. "Wow . . . I have not ever seen something like that."

Ted smiled. "My mama used to make these for me as a treat."

Instead of making the next float, Ted stayed still, watching. As if he wouldn't continue until she tasted it and gave her approval.

Miranda felt the eyes of all in the room on her.

Slowly, she dipped in the spoon and took a generous helping.

It was as good as it looked. Maybe better.

She closed her eyes and let the sweet blend of flavors and thick texture of the ice cream roll around in her mouth. "This is so good. I haven't had one of these for years." She opened her eyes and smiled at him. "Thank you. But I want to know, if you can make these, how come you can't cook yourself a decent supper?"

"This was not exactly difficult, although my mama would not be pleased that I bought whipped cream in a can and did not make it myself."

With all eyes on them, Ted and Frank produced the rest of the floats in assembly-line style, scooping a portion of ice cream into each bowl as the ladies lined them up along the covered pew, then pouring the root beer in the same fashion, followed by the whipping cream. Unfortunately, the last few ran out of cherries, but no one, including Frank or Ted, seemed to mind.

Miranda couldn't help but notice that hers had the most whipping cream, and was the prettiest. She was almost sure that hers had the most ice cream, too, because after Frank did the first scoop, Ted had been very careful to measure properly in order not to run out before every bowl had one scoop. She was half done by the time Ted started eating his.

Everyone broke into small groups to talk while they enjoyed their desserts. Ted stayed with Frank and Len, so she didn't have a chance to thank him, but she didn't feel pressured because she would have plenty of time in the car when he drove her home.

Miranda joined Sarah, and the two of them sat side by side on the piano bench.

Miranda turned her head toward Sarah so she didn't have to stop eating to talk. "You know, it was really strange, but when Ted gave this to me, his grace felt more like he was praying over me. Kind of like being anointed with oil, except it was ice cream."

Sarah giggled. "You are silly," she said so softly it was almost a whisper. "But now there will be more talk, for sure."

"Talk about what?" Miranda asked around the spoon in her mouth.

"Ted is sweet on you. Many thought so when he asked you to be with him at his onkel and tante's home for Easter dinner, but now this. He did this for you. I also saw how he looked at you."

Arguing would only create more talk, so Miranda didn't dare deny what everyone thought. Besides, it would be more than a little embarrassing if she had to admit that it wasn't Ted who invited her for Easter dinner, but his aunt and uncle. Worse, the "look" he gave her wasn't that of dreamy expectation. It was fear that she was going to start crying again — not one of her finer moments.

"We'll see. Just remember that I'm not going to be here for very long. After Christmas, after this is all over, I'm going back home."

"This is only May. December is a long time. Much can happen."

"That's true, but I think you can safely keep Ted in the bachelor pool."

Sarah sighed. "Ted is not in the bachelor pool. Ted has made it very clear that he does not wish to seek a wife."

Miranda glanced at Ted, who was laughing at something Frank said. "No. But from what I've seen, that hasn't stopped the ladies from trying. He gets invited out to the home of a single woman almost once a week. Before you tell me that he hasn't accepted any of those invitations because of me, that's only half true. The reason isn't because he's got a thing for me. It's because I made a deal with him to cook him supper once a week in exchange for using a room at his house for my piano lessons. So it's kind of like paying for room and board."

"Say what you want. I know he is sweet on you. I have seen this."

Miranda turned to Sarah. "You're only saying that because Brian is sweet on you. I've seen how he's been so quick to pick you up and drive you home. Next thing, he'll be sitting in church with you."

Sarah actually blushed. "Maybe. But Ted is already sitting in church with you."

Miranda sighed. "He's the worship leader.

He's been assigned to sit with me. It's not his choice." She felt a quick pang of realization that if he hadn't been told to, he wouldn't sit with her. "Hey, it looks like everyone is finished eating. Are you?"

"Yes. I will help do the dishes. Since Ted is now here, Brian will take me straight home. Unless you and Ted would like to join us and go somewhere."

It was all Miranda could do not to yawn. "Not tonight. I'm really tired. I was going to go to bed early but it's not early anymore."

As soon as she stood, it was as if Ted had been watching her. He approached and stopped her before she could join the rest of the ladies on their trek to the kitchen with the dirty dishes.

"I need to ask a favor of you."

"Sure. Name it."

"Len tells me that you have been making trips to the piano at night, so it is time for you to have your electric piano with headphones at Len's house. I have it in my car to take to Len's when I take you home tonight."

"That's thoughtful of you, but that's not going to work. I need it more at your house on Thursday afternoons so I can do my piano lessons before you get home from work. You also need it for your own lessons."

"*Ja,* I need a piano, but I should not have yours. I am enjoying learning to play the piano, so it is time for me to buy my own. I would like you to come to Bemidji with me on Saturday to help me pick the right one."

Knowing how much he hated going all the way to Minneapolis, Miranda didn't want to suggest that he would probably get a better deal there. However, it was just as likely that the additional cost of gas and the expense of having to buy supper instead of eating at home would eat up his potential savings.

"That's a good idea, but I have a practice arranged with the nativity group tomorrow so I can't go with you."

"I know nothing of electric pianos. I would really like for you to come with me. What if we go early, and I have you back in time for your practice?"

A little clock flashed in Miranda's mind. So much for her plan of sleeping in. "I guess I could do that, but that means we have to leave here at eight-thirty to be back for noon." Which meant she had to get up at seven. Miranda nearly groaned out loud.

"That is good. Also, I was thinking that we should be talking more about the practices and what needs to be done. For at least a few weeks, I would like to meet with you at lunch time. I usually pick up my lunch at Elena and Mary's on my way to work, and I will have enough food for both of us."

"Every day? Do you really think that's necessary?"

Instead of answering her right away, Ted glanced at her face, then at her arms, then skimmed up and down her jeans.

"*Ja,* Miss Randi." As the words left his mouth, he reached down and grasped one wrist with both hands. "It is necessary."

Miranda struggled to keep her mouth from dropping open. Not only was he touching her, but he'd called her by the nickname she liked — something he said he couldn't do. Of course he had to qualify it by putting "Miss" in front. But he'd done it. With Ted, nothing was random. If he had just called her by the name she liked, it could only mean one thing.

Something was wrong. And he didn't know how to tell her, so he was going to do his best to tell her nicely.

His voice dropped in pitch as he brushed his thumbs over her wrists. "I think everyone is finished cleaning up and has gone home. Let us make sure everyone has left, and I will lock up the building. Then I will take you home, and I will see you in the morning."

16

Miranda waved at Anna, who was on the phone, and continued on to Ted's office. As she stood in the doorway waiting for him to also finish a phone call, the wonderful smells of good food wafted toward her.

She leaned into the doorframe and closed her eyes, lost in the delightful aroma. Whatever it was, it was not charbroiled McDonald's. She was pretty sure this was beef. The rich bouquet of simmering meat caused her stomach to rumble.

Afraid the dream would end, she refused to open her eyes. It was almost like being in Lois's kitchen when she'd been cooking all day, except this was Ted's office — a place of business. The fact that it was so out of place emphasized the goodness of it.

With one hand pressed over her noisy tummy, she inhaled deeply to try to identify what he'd brought. Besides simmering meat, the teasing scent of onions promised a rich and tasty meal. Some kind of spices enhanced the earthiness of the onions, but she couldn't identify them. She only knew that whatever this was, lunch promised to be great, and she was going to eat too much.

"Miranda? Why are you like that with your eyes closed? Are you sick?"

Her eyes popped open as Ted pushed his chair out from behind his desk and stood.

Her cheeks burned. She raised her palms in the air toward him. "Don't get up. I'm fine. I was just trying to figure out what it is that smells so very good. Or should I say, *zehr gut?*" She grinned. "For sure, it ain't sandwiches."

Ted's eyes opened wide. "Your accent, it is very bad."

"You may or may not find it surprising that it's not the first time someone's said that to me."

He sank back down into his chair, smiling. "I have brought *Yum Zetti.* It is Elena and Mary's lunch special today. They gave me a slow cooker and told me to plug it in as soon as I arrived in my office. They said it would continue to cook and be ready for lunch time." He checked his wristwatch. "Which is in ten minutes. How did you get here? I was going to get you as soon as I finished my phone call."

"It's a beautiful sunny day outside, so I walked." As she spoke, she approached the slow cooker. Beside it were two plates, cutlery, and a scoop. The condensation on the glass lid prevented her from seeing exactly what was inside, but the closer she got, the better it smelled. "There seems to be a lot in here. Way more than the two of us are going to eat for one meal. I think we should divide this in half and save half for tomorrow." She gently lifted the lid, allowing the steam to escape, then peeked inside, confirming her suspicions. She turned to make eye contact with him. "You do have a microwave here, don't you? I know most people don't have one in their homes, but I would think it's different in a place of business."

"*Ja*, there is a microwave oven. But many do not use it."

"Do you?"

"*Ja*. Sometimes. Because often I burn things in the pot, and it is so much work to try to clean it. When things are burned on, it cannot be put in the dishwasher."

"Dishwasher?" In just a few months she had spent more time with Lois washing and drying dishes by hand than she'd done in her entire life. "You mean there actually is a dishwasher somewhere in this town?"

"This is a place of business, and we must meet our promises to our customers and be done on time. Onkel Bart did not agree, but I purchased a microwave and dishwasher so that the ladies would spend more time at their jobs and less time cleaning the kitchen."

"You're lucky everyone cleans up their own mess here. Where I work in downtown Seattle, sometimes the kitchen is so messy I hate going in there. I feel sorry for the cleaning staff. Your cleaning staff probably has it pretty easy."

"We do not have cleaning staff. Everyone keeps their work stations clean. In the same way, the people who use the kitchen must clean up their own mess."

What he probably meant was that the men used the microwave because they weren't capable of heating anything in a pot without burning it, and the women cleaned everything else. She glanced around his office, which was spotless. "I can't imagine you dusting and washing your own floor in here. After all, you're the general manager. I can see factory people sweeping up sawdust every day, but you don't make Anna or William clean the office, do you?"

"No, I do not. Tante Odelle comes in on Saturdays to mop the floors and do the dusting so everyone else can be with their families on the weekend."

Miranda froze. "The owner's wife cleans the office?" She couldn't imagine Zane's wife in Seattle cleaning the office. The woman didn't even clean her own house. Not only did she have a housekeeper, she also had a nanny.

"She says she will not pay money for someone else to do what she can do herself. Enough of this talk. It has been difficult to concentrate on my work with the *Yum Zetti* cooking all morning. Let us eat."

Miranda inhaled deeply once more. "You're not going to get any argument from me on that." Before she reached for the lid of the slow cooker, she looked around, hoping to find something to put the hot lid down on so she wouldn't damage the fine wood surface of the credenza. Unlike her office in Seattle, where the office furniture was sterile metal, everything here was hand-crafted wood, probably made personally by Ted's uncle when he expanded the business into the factory building.

Ted left his desk and set a thick pile of folders beside the slow cooker. When Miranda lifted the lid, Ted picked up the ladle and one of the plates.

She hadn't expected him to serve himself,

but being one of the few single men who lived alone in their community, he was obviously accustomed to not being waited on when not at someone else's dinner table. While she settled the lid on the pile of folders, Ted scooped a generous portion of a meat and macaroni mixture onto one of the plates, then dipped back in to scoop out some of the cheese that had melted on top.

He smiled and held it toward her. "This is for you. Eat and enjoy."

Miranda stared at the plate, almost double what she would normally eat for supper, never mind lunch. She looked up at Ted, still smiling and holding it for her.

She could hardly believe that a tradition-honoring man was serving her food. Maybe he felt territorial about his office. Ted obviously ruled his office, and that apparently included lunch. "Thank you," she said quietly as she accepted the plate from him.

In the back of her mind, she noted that he hadn't taken her to the lunchroom, but they seemed to be staying in his office to eat. She didn't know if it was because he didn't have enough in the slow cooker to share with the entire staff, or if he didn't want anyone to overhear their conversation.

Her stomach turned over. That meant this was it. This was the time that he was going to tell her whatever it was that she wasn't going to like when she heard it.

But even that wasn't going to stop her from eating. She had been so busy lately, between her regular accounting job, composing music, writing the play, and coordinating everything, that most of the time she'd worked past lunch time, then didn't want to impose on Lois to make her a lunch in the middle of the afternoon, so she'd gone without eating. Then by the time supper came, often she felt too sick from being too hungry to eat a decent supper. Sneaking a little yogurt in the middle of the night tided her over until morning, but then the cycle repeated most days.

Ted spooned himself a portion only slightly larger than what he'd given her, and returned to his desk. He set his plate on top of a pile of papers he'd been working on, so Miranda picked up a file folder and did the same. "I do this at home too. Use customer's files under my plate. It must be an office workers' thing."

"Perhaps. I eat in my office most days. Now let us pray." He folded his hands on the desk in front of him and bowed his head, so Miranda did the same. "Thank you, dear Heavenly Father, for this day of good health and this day to share. Thank you for this good food and the ease with which you have provided such a feast to us in the middle of a busy day. Amen."

Miranda ate her first forkful without speaking. And the second. And the third. After the fourth, she finally slowed her pace. "I didn't realize I was so hungry. This is so good, part of me wants to eat it too fast, and the other part of me is saying to slow down and make it last longer."

"*Ja.* I agree."

Miranda took another mouthful, slowly savoring every chew. "Lois has never made this, which I find strange. She loves to cook, and I know she's spoiling me by giving me a huge variety of all the traditional dishes. But she's never made this."

"This is not a dish from our area. This is from the Pennsylvania Dutch Mennonite area, which has differences from our own Low German heritage. But this is very popular in Mary and Elena's restaurant, and they make it often."

"I know there are many differences among different groups of Mennonites. Those of us on the West Coast are less traditional, because civilization is newer there. You and your people are in the middle, and the most traditional and old-world communities are on the East Coast. I've only thought of all of us as Mennonite Brethren without digging into much history. When I get home, I think I'll sit down with our older members and ask some questions."

"That would probably be very interesting."

Miranda sighed. "I've never been away from home this long before. Actually, I've never really been away from home. I've been to camps, but they were always a few hours away, and I knew I could go home whenever I wanted."

Ted stopped eating and watched her. "You must miss your friends and family."

"Not as much as I thought. In fact, I'm in contact with some of them more now that I'm farther away. E-mail is a wonderful medium."

She noted that he didn't comment. Everyone here, including Ted, frowned on technology, except that Ted was forced to use it.

"I know you travel for your uncle's business. Have you ever been to Seattle?"

"*Ja,* I have been there once. It is a very busy city with many hills. I was warned not to drive there, that the traffic was very bad. I have never experienced traffic like that, both in the city and on the highways, or in any other city I have been in."

"Yeah, it's pretty bad. And there's always

something under construction."

While they ate, Miranda told him some of the tidbits and interesting things about living in Seattle. When they were done, she pressed her hands over her stomach. "I can't believe I ate all that. I don't think I'll eat for a week."

Ted sucked in a breath. "But you must. I brought dessert."

Miranda held back a burp with great effort. "I really couldn't eat another bite." Yet as overstuffed as she felt, visions of all the desserts Lois served danced through her head like a PowerPoint slideshow. Lois served a dessert with supper every day. Miranda didn't want it to become a habit to have dessert so often, but it was already too late.

"Uh . . . what is it?"

"Elena's famous breakfast cake." He reached beside him for a paper bag that had been sitting at the corner of his desk and pulled out two pieces of rich-looking coffee cake. "When I was a boy, Mama made this for breakfast on the weekends, and we ate it dunked in milk. But at this time of day, it is simply a good cake."

"One of the ladies at my church makes coffee cake to die for. It's loaded with calories."

Ted put one piece on a napkin and pushed it across the desk toward her. "It is loaded with goodness. This is my favorite cake, so I would like to share it with you."

With a line like that, Miranda couldn't refuse.

She ate about half before she couldn't take another bite. "I think I'm going to explode," she groaned, "and it's not going to be pretty."

"You will not explode. Even horses do not explode from eating too much grain."

Miranda didn't want to think that Ted had just compared her to a farm animal. "Didn't you want to talk about what's happening with the play?"

Ted checked his watch. "I did, but it is too late now. The lunch break is over, and I must get back to work. I will pick you up tomorrow, unless you again decide to walk, and we will do this again."

This time, Miranda couldn't hold back a burp.

Ted's eyebrows raised. Her cheeks turned red as if she'd spent a day in the hot summer sun.

She stood straight, trying to recover a little dignity. "Sure. That would be good. I'd like that." Even though the words came out automatically to be polite, she found she meant them.

Ted walked her to the front door, pulling his keys out of his pocket when he reached the door. Miranda pressed her fingers into his arm, causing him to freeze.

"I know you mean well, but I don't need a ride. After all that food, I don't know if I can sit down. I need to walk this off. Still, this was great, and the best lunch I've had in a long time. I'll be back tomorrow. But tomorrow, if you don't mind, I would like to serve myself."

"*Goondach,* my friend," Brian said as he closed the car door behind him. "Is there something you would be wishing to tell me?"

Ted put the car in gear and turned toward home. "*Goondach* to you too. No, there is not."

The silence didn't last more than a few seconds. Brian turned and leaned back in the seat, tipped his hat forward, then clasped his hands and rested them in the center of his chest.

"But I have heard some very interesting things. Mary tells me that you are bringing food to Miranda — that you are feeding her every day. Elena tells me that you are also bringing her all your favorite desserts and sweet things." Brian waggled his eyebrows. "I have been wondering when our charming visitor would turn your head."

"Mary and Elena talk too much," Ted grumbled.

The silence hung again, but not long enough.

"She is at your office every day."

"Anna talks too much as well."

"When Miranda returns from lunch, there is sunshine in her cheeks from thinking of you."

"Lois also talks too much." Ted gripped the steering wheel tighter. "I have been worried that our charming visitor is not maintaining her health, so I have been feeding her a nutritious lunch. My office door is kept open so anyone may see that we are talking. Then she has chosen to walk home instead of allowing me to give her a ride. I am making sure that she is eating enough to regain her strength."

Brian grinned. "Are you sure you are not feeding her trans fat?"

"Mary assures me that she is only providing healthy food that will put some meat on her bones." Automatically, one hand went to his stomach. "I know my efforts are successful because in less than two weeks I can feel that my own pants are not fitting as they did."

"So you are only doing this because you are concerned for her health?"

"Of course." Ted turned onto his street. "She is only here to help us in our outreach mission. What other reason would there be?"

Sarah slipped her hand out from between the curtains and backed up a step. "They are almost here. I see Ted's car down the road."

Miranda gave the vegetables another stir. "Finally. When he said he was going to be late, I had no idea it was going to be this late. This is on the verge of being overcooked. We'll have to do his piano lesson after supper."

Sarah giggled. "I certainly do not mind staying later. Brian will just phone my papa and let him know."

Miranda smiled. "You've been seeing a lot of Brian, haven't you?"

"*Ja*. But you have been seeing Ted more than I have seen Brian. You have seen Ted every day." Sarah turned to her, beaming.

"Don't get any funny ideas. We're only meeting at his office so we can talk about the play without anyone interrupting us."

Sarah peeked through the curtains quickly,

one more time. "Has this happened?"

"Not exactly. By the time we finish eating, his lunch break is over. The only thing we've agreed on is that I want the men in the town group to wear their hats onstage, and that he is going to ask William, since he's playing Joseph, to grow a beard."

Sarah took the milk out of the fridge and set the bottle on the table. "Mary tells me that Ted is bringing you so much good food. This can only mean one thing."

"It means that he's using our meetings as a good excuse to eat all his favorite things, including the most fattening desserts I've ever had in my life. I don't know if he thinks I haven't noticed, but his pants are a little tighter around the middle than they were a month ago. If he keeps this up, he's not going to be needing those suspenders for much longer."

"*Ach,* it is you he is trying to fatten up. He is sweet on you."

"That's ridiculous. If he liked me, he'd want me looking my best, not like the neighbor's pregnant goat."

Sarah scanned her from head to toe. "You will never look like that. You will be thin even when you are pregnant."

Miranda didn't want to think of that one. She pressed one hand onto her stomach.

"I'm not so thin anymore. There's no scale at Lois's house, so I don't know how much I lost when I was scrambling to get the harmonies figured out in the first scene where the nativity group and the town group meet up. But whatever I lost, I gained it all back, and then some." She stopped stirring and turned to Sarah. "Speaking of scales, you wouldn't believe what Ted did to me. The second day we had a meeting at his office, he needed something in the shipping department. When we got there, he tried to get me to stand on the freight scale."

"The freight scale?"

She tried to keep the hurt out of her voice. Despite his overall graciousness and his overwhelming generosity, every time they talked about the play and her plans she felt his disapproval in almost everything she suggested. Their first day at lunch he'd asked if she missed her friends and family. She hadn't thought anything of it at the time, but in hindsight, she should have realized what he was thinking.

"He said he wanted to see how much I weighed so he could find out how much it would cost to ship me back to Seattle."

"*Ach,* Ted was just telling a joke. We all know that he is sweet on you. We have been wondering when this would happen."

255

Miranda added more soy sauce to the mixture, probably a little too much from shaking the bottle too hard. "He has a strange way of showing it." Her hand froze in midair above the pot. More soy sauce dripped out. "Wait. We? What do you mean, we? Is everyone in this town talking about us?"

Sarah's hands rose to her cheeks. "*Oba nijch!* No! That would be gossip! We have been praying for you!"

"Great," she muttered, making no attempt to keep the sarcasm out of her voice.

"We have been praying for Ted too."

The sound of the door opening saved her from having to give a response.

"I am sorry we are late," Ted's voice echoed from the doorway a split second before he came through. "The truck . . ." His voice trailed off as both Ted's and Brian's noses wrinkled. "What is that smell?"

"Ta dah!" Miranda sang out as she lifted the lid to the frying pan. "It's a special surprise. Susan managed to get some bok choy as a sample without ordering a whole case. I made vegetarian chop suey!"

Ted and Brian leaned over the stovetop. "I have never seen anything like this before."

"It's a Chinese vegetable stir fry. It's a

little overcooked, but it's still okay. This green stuff over here is the leaves from the bok choy. And this is tofu. These long white things are mung bean sprouts. I ordered the seeds on eBay and sprouted them myself." She beamed, proud of all her hard work.

"This is strange. I was expecting you to cook the ham I had in the refrigerator." Ted sniffed, then made a face. "This does not smell good."

"Don't worry, that's just the oyster sauce. Or maybe it's the broccoli. It tastes better than it smells. It's very nutritious." And low in calories, to counteract all the high-calorie lunches he'd been feeding her.

Instead of making his way to the table, Ted picked up a fork and poked at some of the vegetables, speared a limp bean sprout, then put the fork down. "I do not care about the nutrition. I will not eat this."

Miranda rested one fist on her hip. "What do you mean you won't eat it? I worked hard to get all this stuff and cook it for you."

"It is slimy and it looks and smells like my grootmutta's compost bin."

Before Miranda could think of a response, Ted spun and strode out of the kitchen.

Behind Miranda, Sarah gasped. "*Mein seit!* Oh, dear," she whispered to Brian. "I think they are going to have their first fight."

Miranda banged the lid back down on the frying pan. "You're going to have to eat without us," she ground out between her teeth.

Taking a deep breath, she stomped out in Ted's wake.

17

Ted dropped down on the couch and sucked in a deep breath. Doing so did nothing to relax him. He needed to pray, but praying in anger was wrong, especially when he didn't know why he was so angry.

Instead of being allowed to calm down in the privacy of his living room, he heard footsteps approaching from down the hall.

She'd followed him.

Ted hunched his shoulders.

He stood, raising his palms toward Miranda as she rounded the corner. "Do not say anything," he snapped. "I admit I was not gracious. I apologize, but I still will not eat what you have cooked."

"Not gracious?" Her voice dripped with sarcasm. "Now there's an understatement."

Ted's stomach tightened in a way that had nothing to do with hunger. In fact, he had completely lost his appetite. He waited for her to say more, but for once she had nothing to say.

He flexed his fingers, then rammed one hand into his pocket. "I think it is best that we miss the piano lesson. I will just take you home."

"I would rather walk than get in the car with you," she hissed back.

Rather than say something he would surely regret, Ted glared at her while she glared back at him.

But while she glared, something changed. She tipped her head to one side. Her face softened, and she held one elbow and cupped her chin in her hand. "This is so not like you. You were fine at lunch. What happened today?"

Ted straightened his back and crossed his arms over his chest. "Nothing."

She waited for him to say more, but he didn't. "Then did anyone who works for you complain about their part in the play?"

"No."

She raised her eyebrows. "But . . . ?"

"But nothing. Everyone is very pleased with the way it is going."

"But you're not."

"You are aware of how I feel."

Again a silence hung between them, but it wasn't long enough and she started talking again. "We agreed to meet in the middle. I still think it would be a more interesting plotline if we had the contrast between the nativity people and regular city type people."

"I do not want contrast or a plot. We need relevance with our community, which means to have my people portrayed as they really are."

"You got your way. Besides, that's not the issue here. I think you should at least give the Chinese food a try and if you don't like it, then I'll make you something else."

"I do not want something else. I want to be left alone so I may pray."

Her mouth opened, but for once no words came out. She glanced around his empty living room, stepped beside him, then slowly sat next to him on the couch. "You look like you could use a friend right now."

Automatically, Ted turned his head to look down the hallway toward the kitchen.

"Not Brian," she said, as if she were reading his mind. "Me. I'd like to pray with you."

He gave up and turned back. He'd learned the hard way it was pointless to oppose her, regardless of how he felt.

She raised her hand as if she was going to pat his knee but then retracted it and folded her hands primly in her lap. "What were you going to pray about?"

He stared out the window. Despite the late time, the sky was still bright. "I had not decided."

"Then let's start with why you're so cranky."

"I am not 'cranky.' "

She chuckled. "Oh, but you are. Let's go back and find out why. Did you and Brian have an argument in the car?"

He turned and looked at her face as he recalled his conversation with Brian. "No. We did not argue." Every week, more people in town seemed to think that he was courting Miranda, when nothing could be further from the facts. He didn't know when the talk started, but he suspected it was when Tante Odelle invited Miranda for Easter dinner and people assumed he had been the one who had sought her.

It was Brian that everyone should now be talking about — Brian was courting Sarah, who obviously cared for Brian the same way he cared for her. Ted suspected that soon they would be married.

Which meant that besides the elderly widowers, that would leave him as the oldest man in their church who was not married.

Miranda waited for him to elaborate, but

those were thoughts he did not care to share.

"Okay. . . . What about before that? Did something happen at work that set you off?"

He'd been busy at work, but no worse than any other day. "The truck was late, but I was assured that the order would be delivered on time."

She stared into his eyes, no doubt waiting for him to say more. He was annoyed, but not angry that the truck had been late. It had only meant that that he'd been late for supper, which, as it turned out, he wasn't going to eat anyway.

"Then if it wasn't business, did something personal set you off this afternoon?"

"No."

"Aha!" Miranda raised one finger in the air. "You were too quick to answer. What happened?"

The words of Rachel's mother's phone call repeated in his head. "Nothing happened. I received an invitation for supper today, and I turned it down."

"Why?"

He turned away. He could have said that he told Mrs. Reinhart he'd declined because Thursday was the day for his piano lesson, and Miranda wouldn't have known any better. But that would not be the truth.

He turned back to her, looking directly at her as he spoke, not breaking eye contact. "I am tired of being invited for dinner when they are only looking at me as a good husband for Rachel."

Miranda blinked. "Don't you like Rachel?"

He maintained eye contact. "She does not particularly like me."

Miranda's eyes widened. "Oh . . . I'm so sorry . . ."

"Do not be sorry." Ted looked at her, looking expectantly at him. He bowed his head. "I do not know why I am telling you this."

She reached over and patted his knee, which made him flinch. He raised his head to look up at her.

"I'm a PK. You wouldn't believe what people tell me."

"PK?"

"Pastor's Kid. It gives me an 'understanding' gene. It's true. Also, being a girl, people tell me more than if I had been a boy."

Ted stared blankly at her. He couldn't imagine men opening their hearts to her, but in the time she had been here, he'd seen all the young ladies do exactly that, with the exception of Rachel.

"Tell me about Rachel, and how you feel

about her."

He pictured Rachel as she was the last time he saw her, which was at church on Sunday, sitting with her parents. "Rachel is a wonderful young lady. She is smart and a hard worker and an excellent cook. She loves the Lord and she is good with children."

"But?"

"I do not wish to marry Rachel. Yet she wishes to marry me, which is clear every time her mama invites me for dinner."

"Do you feel guilty about that? It's okay if you don't feel the same way, as long as you haven't been letting her think that you like her when you don't."

"The only place I see her is during church with the rest of the congregation." Or when he accepted a dinner invitation, which had stopped when he figured out Rachel and her mama's primary motives. Only now, it had started up again. But Rachel still didn't feel any different about him, nor did he feel different about her.

Miranda shook her head. "Have you been encouraging her to think that you like her in a special way?"

"No. But she does not think of me in that special way either. Yet she has made it very clear that she wishes to be married to me."

He sighed and swept his hand in the air, in the direction of the book he'd been reading, still open and face down on the coffee table, where he'd left it last night. "In my spare time, you can see that I read mystery novels."

"Yes. You've got some good ones in your library. I've read a number of them. I see you've already got *Dead Reckoning* by Ronie Kendig. A friend told me it's really good."

"I have not read it yet. But it is next in my pile. Like many others, the back cover summary hints that the principal characters will fall in love when the crisis is solved. God's word also speaks specifically of the love between a husband and his wife. I witnessed this special love between my mama and papa." He paused, waiting for a sudden tightness in his throat to clear. His mama and papa loved each other so much that neither would leave the burning house without finding the other, and they died together. "This is what I want for my own life. I desire a wife who will love me in the same special way I will love her. If that does not happen, as God's word directs, I will remain unmarried."

Miranda's voice lowered in volume, her words coming soft and gentle. "That's what most people want. It's the way marriage is supposed to be."

"But I have been unable to find this. Rachel wants to marry me because she looks upon me as a good provider, and because I am reasonably intelligent and in good health, I will be able to produce healthy and intelligent children. I believe in God as the ultimate authority in marriage, and I will be faithful until death. Likewise, Rachel possesses all the qualities of an ideal wife, so marrying her would not be a hardship. She talks to me with respect and does her best to win my favor, including offering me an endless supply of good food. Today Rachel and her mama had prepared stuffed meat loaf and yams for supper, with shoo-fly pie."

"Then you came home instead."

"Yes. To be offered something that looked and smelled like what I used to shovel out to my grootmutta and grootfoda pigs."

Miranda cringed. "Ouch."

"I am sorry, but I have never seen anything like that in a kitchen."

From the kitchen, the sound of Sarah and Brian's laughter echoed down the hall.

Ted's jaw tightened.

Miranda sighed. "Sarah has asked me if I will help sew her wedding dress. She thinks it won't be long, and Brian will ask her to marry him."

"I do not think it will be long, either." He turned to Miranda and looked into her face. Rachel's mama had not been subtle in reminding him that he should accept Rachel's invitations before she stopped inviting him. She very bluntly pointed out that regardless of how everyone assumed he felt about Miranda, at the end of the year she would leave and take all her city ways with her. Then it would be too late. Rachel would have another man courting her, she probably would accept, and it would be too late for him.

The reminder did nothing to change his feelings toward Rachel, or any of the other ladies who had wanted to attract his attention with the ultimate goal of marriage for the same reasons. "Is something wrong with me, that the only reason a young lady wishes to be married to me is that I will be a good provider?"

"I don't know if I'm such a good person to ask that. Things are different here than what I'm used to. Still, being motivated to hold down a good job and being dependable are important things, no matter where you live. Money and financial issues are a major cause of divorce. But since you asked . . ." She tipped her head to study him. "It's not like your uncle's business is a Fortune 500 company, but you're doing pretty well, considering the cost of living out here compared to paying a lease on a high-rise condominium near downtown Seattle. You're stable and your faith is rock solid, and that's always good too. How tall are you? I'm five foot seven, so I'm guessing you're about five foot ten? So as far as being tall, dark, and handsome, you're not tall, but you're reasonably good looking, I guess. Considering you work in an office, I doubt you have washboard abs. You also look a little washed out after a long winter. Maybe you need to spend some time in the sun. I've noticed you've put on a few pounds around the middle lately. So you're not exactly a stud muffin, but you have a kind spirit, and you're a nice guy."

That was it? *Nice guy?* Who had a few recent pounds around his middle? Ted sucked in his stomach. "I did ask for your honest opinion. I suppose I should thank you for keeping me humble."

Her cheeks turned pink. "Don't take it wrong. If you were filthy rich and drop-dead gorgeous, then you'd be out of reach for the average nice Christian girl who's honestly looking for an average, nice Christian guy. If you had an accounting job downtown and drove a nice little gas-economy hybrid, you'd be just the kind of man I'd look for. If I was looking."

"When you do start looking, I hope you plan on improving your cooking skills."

Her eyes flashed. "If I have to change things about myself in order to impress someone, then they won't be getting the real me." She made a sound halfway between a sniff and a snort. "Maybe that's why I'm still single too."

"I thought Lois told me you have a young man waiting for you when you get home." Not that he'd asked, but she'd told him anyway.

She shrugged her shoulders. "At first he was, but we've been e-mailing and we do the occasional live chat. We agreed it wouldn't work, and we're going to be just friends."

"You split up with your fiancé over the computer?"

Her eyebrows knotted. "We weren't really engaged. When I left Seattle, Bradley asked if I'd think about marrying him when I got back. It wasn't the most romantic proposal in the universe, and that should have been my first hint that it wasn't right. We've been almost like best friends ever since we started kindergarten, and while we're probably the most compatible people you could ever imagine, there's much more to a satisfying marriage than companionship. There's got to be sparks." She stood. "You know, I've been feeling guilty about telling Bradley that, but talking to you today has helped. I think this is probably the same thing as you and Rachel. I'm sure you're compatible, but that doesn't mean you're necessarily the right marriage partners. You're doing the right thing. And now I know that I am too."

Ted stood as well. He didn't feel any better, but at least he was sure he had done the right thing by declining Rachel's offer — even if he did remain single for the rest of his life. "Thank you. It appears that your PK gene is effective." As he spoke, his stomach rumbled. He made a nervous laugh. "I think I am starting to feel hungry after all. Perhaps I can try what you have made, since you say it is so healthy."

He started to follow her back to the kitchen, but suddenly she stopped and spun around. He skidded to a halt, just short of bumping into her. Not backing up to allow more space between them, standing nearly toe to toe, she tilted her head and looked up at him. "You know what? I think I'll do as you say and throw it in the compost bin after all. I know it won't be the most balanced supper in the world, but how about if I make us some French toast?"

"French toast? I did not know that toast could be prepared in different languages."

She giggled. "Trust me." She reached between them and patted his tummy as she spoke. "You're going to love this. It's fried in butter, and coated in sweet syrup."

All Ted could do was stare at her hand, which had now stilled. Her red nail polish contrasted like a stoplight against the light brown of his shirt as it rested on his stomach. He felt the shape of each of her fingers, almost burning him through his shirt.

He should have backed away. He shouldn't have allowed her to touch him. But he didn't want to lose the contact. He didn't care if it was foolish or foolhardy. Instead of stepping back, he reached forward and slowly put his arms around her almost like a hug, but without drawing her in. He didn't know if his ego would shatter if she pulled away at this moment, but something in him needed a confirmation.

In slow motion, her hand slid from his stomach, around his side, and to his back. She shifted slightly forward and turned her head so her cheek rested against his throat. Both her hands pressed into his shoulder blades. He sucked in his breath at the sensation when she leaned into him and held him tight.

His arms tightened around her, holding her solidly and warmly against his chest. He wasn't that much taller, so he turned his head slightly to rest his cheek at her temple.

He'd held Miranda once before, but he wasn't prepared for the rush of feelings holding her like this evoked. Standing instead of sitting, the warmth of her pressed against him from his knees to his nose. His heart beat faster than it should have, and he couldn't remember ever feeling so cherished as he felt now.

If he wanted to, and he did want to, all he had to do was turn his head slightly and lower his chin just a little, and he could kiss Miranda right now, making the moment perfect.

Miranda squirmed slightly, pressing herself more firmly into him. "Rachel's an idiot," she mumbled into his shoulder.

Ted's heart stopped, then picked up in double time. He had no feelings for Rachel, and if how he felt now was the way a man was to feel when he properly embraced his lady, then he never would have feelings for Rachel.

But neither could he ever have feelings for Miranda, despite how she felt in his arms.

Not only did she come from the cities, in just a little over six months, she would be gone.

A scraping sound from the kitchen indicated the movement of chairs being pushed away from the table.

He released Miranda and stepped back just as Brian and Sarah turned the corner in the hallway, a smile on Brian's face. "You would not believe this, my friend, but what Miranda has cooked was very tasty, even without meat. We did leave some for you, but I am afraid that it is not very much."

Miranda's cheeks flushed, and when she spoke, she focused on the light from the kitchen instead of Ted or Brian. "That's okay. I'm going to teach Ted how to make French toast."

"Teach me?" He almost protested, but keeping busy was probably a wise idea. He had a lot to think about.

"Yes. Then I'd like to do your piano lesson. Except today I'm going to teach you a basic version of one of the songs for the Christmas play. I can't find another piano player, but I need to help the vocalists with their difficult parts, if you wouldn't mind."

"Not at all."

He nodded as Brian and Sarah passed by them into the living room, and continued into the kitchen with Miranda.

He should not have touched her.

He should not have embraced her, regardless of having a weak moment. This was how the devil used good things to tempt God's people. The reason he wanted to kiss her could only be wrong. They shared nothing similar except a liking for the same kind of books.

Even if he did something stupid and began to care for her as more than a partner in ministry, that would be foolish. He could never marry Miss Miranda. As Rachel's mama had so rightly reminded him, Miranda would go home to her city life and her city friends after Christmas.

Besides, already everyone was watching him and talking about everything he did with Miranda. He could make no mistakes, nor show any signs of impropriety. What had just happened could never happen again.

18

Miranda made a fist and feebly punched the center of the ball of dough with the last of her strength. Extending her lower lip, she blew out a weak breath to clear her hair out of her eyes. A puff of flour erupted in a cloud around her head, and she spoke over her shoulder to Lois. "Are you sure he's going to like this? I never realized cinnamon buns were so much work."

"Everything that is good is worth the work."

"Maybe. But I didn't realize the dough would fight back." She gave it one last bang to show it who was boss, then gave up. "When I make cinnamon buns at home, it's not like this."

"How is it, then? Please do not tell me that you use baking powder instead of yeast for rising."

"I don't know what makes them rise. I buy the kind that comes in a tube, and then you break them off where they're presliced and put them in the oven. They even come with a plastic bag of that white icing glaze stuff."

"*Mein hoat!* My heart cannot take this. After you make these buns, which is my grootmutta's own recipe, you will never buy those despicable things again."

Miranda waved her hands over the mess of open containers, their contents spread over every square inch of the countertop. "This isn't a recipe. You just had me put in a little of this and a little of that. I have no idea what we did. I can't do this. I'm destined to be forever enslaved to the Pillsbury Dough Girl."

"Who?"

"No one special," Miranda mumbled as she pushed the dough into a round lump, set it into the bowl, and draped a tea towel over it. "How long do we wait?"

"We do not wait. We will soak the raisins and mix the filling."

The doorbell rang, echoed by Fidette's shrill yapping.

Lois peeked through the curtains. "This is strange. It is Ted. Why is he not at his office?"

"Ted? Here? Now?" Miranda thumped down the jar of cinnamon, making even more of a mess when it erupted in a cloud, and ran for the door. Ted would never take time off work unless something was very important, or . . . some disaster had happened.

She flung the door open so fast he stepped back, reached up to touch the brim of his hat, and blinked.

"What's wrong?!" she blurted out.

"Nothing is wrong. I have come to ask a favor." He removed his hat and pressed it to his chest. "May I come in?" His eyes swept her from head to toe, pausing on her arm, her shirt, then stopping at her face. "What is that on your nose?"

Miranda brushed her nose with the back of her hand, hoping she made it better instead of worse. "Flour. And probably yeast. Lois and I are baking."

She led him inside, but instead of leading him to the living room, she led him to the kitchen while she still could remember how much cinnamon she'd sprinkled over the raisins.

"This is a mess. Where is Lois?"

Miranda looked around the room and sure enough, Lois was nowhere to be seen. The corner of the counter where Lois had been mixing her cookies was also strangely clean and bare. "I have no idea. She was here a minute ago."

He studied the covered bowl in the middle of the table. "I see you have dough rising. My mama made bread often, almost every day. But my mama's kitchen never looked like this. Did you do something wrong?"

"No, I'm just not very good in the kitchen, so not everything went as smoothly as it does for Lois. I'm supposed to do the next step now, but Lois isn't here, so I guess I can't." She pulled out one of the kitchen chairs. "So we might as well sit down and talk. What kind of favor do you need?"

Ted sank down into one of the other chairs. "There are two things. I must leave on a business trip tomorrow, and I would like you to pray for this with me. It is a very important new customer who insists on talking to me immediately, in person."

He waited, absently tapping one finger on the tabletop.

Miranda leaned back in the chair. Aside from Sunday at church when they sat together, or church business with the rest of the board, they'd never really prayed together for anything that wasn't related to food and eating together.

"I would be honored to pray with you. What else?"

"If you can spare the time, I do not like to

leave my car parked at the airport. I wish to ask if you can come with me, then drive my car back home and then pick me up when I return."

Visions of the Mall of America danced through her head. She hadn't done any real shopping since she finished her Christmas shopping last November at Bellis Fair Mall, north of Seattle. She'd never been to the Mall of America. But knowing she was going to be living within a few hours of it, she'd googled it and downloaded a list of all the stores onto her phone. Until now, she'd never been able to go.

Now she could. An unlimited shopping excursion. Two, actually, if both his departure and arrival times coincided with mall hours. She would have plenty of time to browse for a new perfect purse, which also meant a gorgeous pair of matching strappy shoes. Then she could buy the perfect summer outfit to go with them. Maybe two perfect summer outfits. Maybe more, to mix and match. And then another pair of shoes. And some sandals. Which meant a new shade of nail polish. And nail decals. It was too early for the fall clothes to be out, but the stores would all be packed with great summer fashions. She could also buy a kit and touch up the streaks in her hair. And maybe a few new sets of earrings to finish it all off.

But she would be doing it alone. Suddenly, the shopping trip didn't feel so fun anymore.

She turned to Ted, who was watching her strangely, probably because she was taking so long to reply. Ever-patient Ted. In his boring blue button-down shirt and semi-casual black slacks, black suspenders, and his practical black loafers. He'd left his utilitarian black hat on the rack at the door. Plain and functional Ted, who matched perfectly with his plain and functional community. A mental slideshow of all the people she knew in Piney Meadows, male and female, passed through her mind's eye in vivid color. Or maybe not so vivid. None of the colors of these people were bright, none were showy, and Ted was the closest to anyone who dressed in any form of the latest fashion. Sometimes, anyway.

Of the women, no one cared that they all wore only slightly different versions of the same thing. Their only concern with what they wore was that it was clean and pressed, and that their shoes were comfortable and fit well.

She had been shopping outside of Piney Meadows with a few of her new friends exactly once. They hadn't made it to the Mall of America. They'd gone to the factory outlet, bought what they came for, and happily returned home. They didn't care about going to the mall, where the variety of shopping and entertainment opportunities was endless. They had only cared that they were together to accomplish their goal.

They'd had more fun yakking and giggling in the car than shopping. Naturally they'd prayed together before they left.

Suddenly, Miranda felt very shallow. She didn't need a new purse or a closet full of clothes. Rather than flitting around the mall, jostling alone through crowds of strangers, she would be happier here, with her new friends, sewing, working on music, talking, or even cooking.

She glanced around the kitchen. It would take nearly as long to clean up her mess as it would to drive all the way to Minneapolis. But here, in the kitchen, she would talk and laugh with Lois, which would deepen a wonderful friendship.

Once she left Ted at the airport, she would be alone to shop. But she didn't need time to buy more clothes. She needed time with a friend.

"If this would be too inconvenient for you, then do not worry. I will leave my car at the airport."

Miranda smiled weakly. "It's not that. I would love to do the favor for you. Under one condition."

"Condition?" Ted's eyes narrowed. "Does this have something to do with the mall?"

"Yes. Before your flight, I'd love it if you would go to the mall with me to check out the aquarium. I think it would be fun, and we both need a break. And then I'll gladly take you to the airport."

"Just the aquarium? I do not have to go shopping with you?"

She thought of the skirts and dresses she wore to church on Sunday, and her limited selection of T-shirts and jeans that she wore from day to day. She'd been wearing only four pairs of shoes. Her black clogs for Sundays; her tennies for the rest of the week, which were showing more wear in two months than in the three years since she had bought them; her big, padded winter boots, which hadn't come out of the closet since the snow melted; and the red ones she'd bought on eBay, which now, in the warmer weather, she wore when it rained.

"I don't need to do any shopping. Everything I need is right here."

"A little to the right. Before the orange one

swims away. Come on. Smile. I know you can do it."

Ted moved over, but he didn't smile.

Miranda took one more of what surely had been hundreds of pictures, then turned to watch the bright orange fish swim happily around its habitat, not caring that he, or anyone else, was watching every move it made.

"I do not understand why you need me to be in so many pictures. You know what I look like."

"I don't have that many. Quit being such a spoilsport."

"I am not being a spoilsport. I simply do not like my picture being taken."

She lowered the camera. "Am I going to have this problem during the Christmas presentation? You're not the only one who feels that way, are you?"

"No, I am not." No one in their community except Brian liked being photographed.

She shoved her camera into her pocket, then pulled out her phone and started typing a message into it. "Then I'll have to be sure to make an announcement before each performance that no pictures are allowed until the end. We don't want anyone to be distracted and nervous."

"You made me promise not to talk about the Christmas play today."

"Oops. But this isn't really talking about it." She dropped the phone back into her purse, retrieved her camera, and handed it to him. "Can you take a few of me looking at that fish that looks like a rock over there? I need to be in at least a few to prove I was here."

"Will no one trust you and take you at your word?"

"It's a joke. Come on, let's keep going. You don't want to miss your flight."

He took her picture as requested, then stepped back on the moving walkway, which transported people through the tunneled section of the aquarium at a speed slow enough for people to enjoy the fish, but fast enough to keep the flow of people orderly.

Miranda had barely joined him when she took her camera, then stepped off the walkway again, arched her back, pointed the camera up, and started taking more pictures. Ted couldn't help himself. He also stepped onto the nonmoving section, pulled the camera Brian had loaned him out of his pocket, and took a picture of Miranda taking pictures. He didn't know what was more enjoyable to watch — the fish, or Miranda. Although he had to admit that the unique construction of the aquarium with all the varieties of fish was as fascinating as the website had promised.

"I caught you. You're taking pictures too."

"Not so many." He pressed the button on the display screen to discover that he had taken many more pictures than he thought. Not that he would admit it to her. Out of the corner of his eye, he saw Miranda take a picture of him fiddling with Brian's camera.

"You know what?" she piped up. "We need a couple of pictures of us together."

Before he could agree or disagree, Miranda interrupted an elderly couple and began to show them how to work her camera.

"Is this necessary?" he grumbled while positioning himself in front of a fish that looked interesting; the sign identified it as a stingray. Miranda hustled toward him while the lady aimed the camera, preparing for the best angle.

The woman waved one hand in the air. "Step closer so I can also get the shark behind you."

Without warning, Miranda pressed herself against his side, slipped her arm around his waist, and squeezed. The top of her head brushed the brim of his hat, setting it crooked. Not wanting to look foolish, Ted righted his hat with one hand while he slipped his other around her waist.

"Smile, both of you," the woman sing-songed.

Against his will, Ted smiled for the camera, only because he knew Miranda was grinning cheerfully. The woman took a few pictures, then returned the camera. "Are you two newlyweds?"

Ted opened his mouth, but no words came out. After being confronted by Rachel's mama, he'd briefly projected what it would be like being married to Rachel. But he'd never considered what it would be like being married to *Miranda.*

He couldn't imagine it. One thing, he would probably starve. But it would be interesting, and they would never lack for conversation, even if most of it would be one-sided.

Beside him, Miranda giggled. "No. We're not. It's kind of funny you should ask that."

He looked sideways to Miranda, who hadn't left his side. Suddenly, the concept wasn't so funny.

She flipped through the three pictures the woman had taken. "Do you know that these are the only pictures I have of the two of us together?" She flipped back to the last picture and held the camera up for him to see.

Ted glanced briefly at the display, then he locked his attention onto her face. The color of Miranda's eyes was pretty from a distance, but up close the mixture of shades of green was fascinating. More than interesting, her eyes were warm and kind, eyes that hid nothing — a mirror to her soul. Her nose was a little too long to be called cute, but it suited her because she was too intelligent and efficient to be thought of in any way that could be related to anything childish.

His gaze lowered to her lips, which were not too full, not too narrow, but perfect. He'd seen those lips do many things, from tightening in frustration when they disagreed on yet another facet of the Christmas production, to laughing heartily when Fidette pulled a stunt that Lois allowed her to get away with.

Right now, her lips were slightly parted, almost expectantly, while she waited for him to say something.

Watching her as she watched him, his heart beat a little faster. Miranda was a beautiful woman, inside and out.

If he wanted to, he could kiss her. They were standing so close he would barely have to move, and no one around them would notice. The few people nearby were busy watching the fish, not other people.

"Ted? Is something wrong? Do I have something on my nose?"

Ted raised his hand to straighten his hat and stepped back while she wiped the tip of her nose with the back of her hand.

"No. Your nose is fine." *Your lips are fine. Everything about you is fine. Very fine.*

What wasn't fine was him. This was neither the time nor the place to think about such things.

Actually, there was never a time or place to think such things about Miranda. She had none of the qualities he needed to look for in a potential wife. Even if she did, she was leaving after Christmas.

She took one more swipe at her nose. "Are you feeling okay? Maybe nervous about your flight?"

"I am not nervous about flying. I just do not like to leave home." He checked his watch. "Which is a reminder that we cannot be late. Even though you showed me how to get my boarding pass online, I still must be there at the right time."

"Of course."

He followed her through the rest of the exhibits, and he didn't complain when she asked another stranger to take their picture together, this time with Brian's camera.

While he was gone, he would buy a camera for himself.

After they left the aquarium, most of the drive to the airport was in silence as she flipped through hundreds of pictures on her camera, oohing and aahing at the ones she considered the best. Every time he stopped at a red light, she treated him to a fast replay of her recent favorites.

According to plan, Ted drove to the departure area instead of going to the parking lot as he usually did. When he found a place to stop, he tried to get out of the car and hurry around to the passenger side to open Miranda's door. But as usual, she was out and had the door closed by the time he'd rounded the car. She waited on the curb while he removed his suitcase from the trunk and closed the lid.

"Thank you for doing this. The journey through the aquarium was also fun. I have never done anything like that before except when I am on a trip, and the people I visit take me out. Why do you have one hand behind your back?"

When she brought her hand to the front of her, she held a small bag. "I made these for you. For before your flight."

He accepted the bag and looked inside. "Cinnamon buns. Thank you. Is this what you were baking yesterday?"

Miranda nodded quickly. "Yes. I wanted to have them finished to take to you at lunchtime, but they took longer to make than I thought. You can't take them through security, but you can find a nice quiet corner and eat them after you check your suitcase."

"Did you make these for me?"

"Yes. I hope you like them."

He stared down into the bag and inhaled deeply as the sweet aroma wafted up at him. She'd even iced them with the white glaze he liked so much. He closed the bag so they wouldn't become dry before he had a chance to eat them, and looked at Miranda.

"Why did you do this?"

She shrugged her shoulders. "Because Lois said you liked cinnamon buns. You were so down the other day, I thought you could use a pick-me-up. They're not exactly Cinnabons, but they're pretty good."

Words failed him. No one besides his mama had ever cooked a special treat to please him rather than impress him.

Miranda glanced up at the sign, then back to him. "You should probably go check in. We don't want to cause a traffic jam. Cars

291

are only supposed to stop here for a few minutes."

The thick smell of exhaust drifted around them as traffic crawled past. Another car pulled up behind his and cut the engine. Trunks slammed and people milled about toting suitcases and parcels.

He didn't want to go.

In front of them, near the curb, a couple leaned toward each other to exchange a farewell kiss before one of them began a journey.

Ted lowered his head so the brim of his hat shielded his eyes. He didn't want to intrude on this couple's private moment, but their image as they were about to be separated burned into his mind. Unless he was forced to make another business trip, in six months he would be back here doing this same thing, except it would be Miranda who was leaving.

And she wouldn't be coming back.

In six months, he would never see her again.

He stepped forward so they were toe-to-toe and raised his right hand to rest his fingertips on her cheek. Her skin was soft and warm and delicately smooth.

Ted cupped her cheek with his hand. "*Goonaudee*, Miranda," he muttered, his voice coming out strangely rough and low-pitched.

Then, instead of telling her that he would miss her, he tipped his head down slowly, eyes drifting closed, and kissed her.

At first she went stiff, but in a split second she relaxed and tilted her head just a little to increase their lip contact. Her hands settled in at the sides of his waist, and she kissed him back.

On the street beside him, a car horn honked. Ted didn't care. He slid his fingers into her hair and slipped his other hand around her back, wishing he didn't have to hold the bag of buns, vaguely aware that he shouldn't drop them.

Her lips were warm and soft, and the press of her body against his was exhilarating. Reluctantly, Ted raised his head and stepped back. It took him a few seconds to find his voice. "I will see you again in three days."

Before he could say something stupid, he pulled out the handle of his suitcase, turned, and walked into the building.

It was going to be a very long three days.

19

"Ted, can you give us all the SATB notes for the word 'joy,' nice and loud?"

Obligingly, Ted struck the notes on the piano one at a time, bass, tenor, alto, ending with soprano. In sequence, everyone hummed and held their notes until the harmony was complete.

"Okay, now everyone change to the word 'joy,' and do your best to round it out and take the harshness out of the 'oy."

While they worked to even out the sound, Miranda reminded herself that this group had never been together as a choir. They didn't know the nuances of tone and resolution, nor how to smooth out abrasive syllables and words. For a new group, they were doing quite well, and she was quite proud of them. But they still needed a lot of work.

Good thing it was only July. When September came, she would step up the practice schedule and start to demand more from the soloists. They wouldn't know what had hit them as they climbed the difficult road to excellence.

Miranda smiled. It truly was going to be an excellent performance. The final scene would surely bring tears to the eyes of all the women and probably even some of the men, and that would mean many would return to this church to learn more about the love of their Savior, which was their goal.

"Good! Let's finish the verse, then we'll all take five and get a big drink of water."

As they finished off the song, she could hear every point when Ted struggled with the music. Yet, considering the short amount of time that he'd been taking piano lessons, he was doing extremely well. She would have to find some way to thank him for all his hard work.

Maybe more cinnamon buns.

Miranda started to cough, which distracted the choir. She waved her hand in the air to signal them to keep going, then turned her back to lessen the distraction.

She would never be able to think about cinnamon buns in the same way again, ever since giving him that bag at the airport.

The airport.

The strangest things with men happened

to her at airports. Back home, Bradley had proposed to her at the Sea-Tac departure curb. Then he had given her a little peck that produced more noise than contact.

Then Ted. But that had been more than a peck, and there had been plenty of contact. That kiss had nearly melted her socks off.

Those cinnamon buns were good, but they weren't *that* good.

Later that day, she had e-mailed her father to ask if there was some old Mennonite tradition that involved a parting kiss. He hadn't been aware of anything. She knew she couldn't ask such a question here in Piney Meadows. Everyone knew she had taken Ted to the airport, and it wouldn't take a rocket scientist to put two and two together if she asked such a thing. Already there was enough gossip — or rather, prayer — going around on that topic. She didn't need to add more fuel to the fire.

Her coughing abated on the last note, after which everyone filed away to the kitchen.

Everyone except Ted.

"I am not doing very well with that song. When will it be possible for me to direct and cue the singers, and for you to return to the piano?"

"You're doing great. I really appreciate all

your work in learning the song. But I
understand how you feel. I think by next
week we'll be at a point where I can go back
to the piano and you can direct."

"This is good. Are you going to work with
any of the soloists this evening?"

Miranda checked her watch. "Yes, if
they'll stay."

"Then I will return after I drive the ladies
home."

Miranda shook her head. "You don't have
to do that."

"I want to. I will play my guitar for the
soloists, and then I will drive you home."

She almost told him she could walk the
short three blocks, but she knew he would
insist, so she didn't waste her breath.

"Did those people from Los Angeles call
you this afternoon like they said?"

"Ja." He broke out in a huge grin. "They
placed the largest single order we have ever
had. It appears that my trip was a success."

"That's great. Have you figured out that
camera you bought yet?"

His smile faded. "I have not had much
time. It is simple to operate, but I have not
yet finished reading the manual."

"You read the manual?"

He tilted his head to one side. "How else
will I learn all the camera can do?"

She didn't even know where the manual to her own camera was. Probably still in the box. "What are you doing tomorrow? Will you be working, or can you join us for another afternoon practice?"

"Tomorrow is Saturday. I will not be working. I was thinking that I could arrive at your home early, and we could go for a walk." He rested both hands on his stomach. "I have been eating too much and moving too little."

She didn't know why he had included her in his desire for a little exercise, but even without a scale, she knew she'd put on a couple of pounds too. "Sure. Practice is at one o'clock. What time?"

He cocked one eyebrow. "How about if instead of walking through the town, I can take you to one of my favorite places. I will pick you up at eight."

Miranda opened her mouth to respond, but she snapped it shut before she said something she would regret. If he wanted to start walking at eight a.m., by one p.m. she would probably need a nap. However, she had dragged him through the aquarium, so in order to be fair, she couldn't refuse. Maybe it would be a welcome change, even nice, to go someplace without crowds of people.

"Sure," she said, just as the choir turned the corner, returning from their break. "Now let's get back to work."

Wanting to end on an encouraging note, Miranda worked on the easier songs for the second half of the practice time. Everyone left with a smile and a feeling of accomplishment of a job well done.

As promised, Ted drove everyone home who had not come with a driver, leaving her alone with Theresa and William.

She smiled. In the last month, William's beard had grown nicely. By December, it would be perfect. By then, he might even have to trim it. Overall, he was being a very good sport. Ted had told her in confidence that William had been teased about it at work but had handled it graciously.

"I'd like to go over your first duet, where Mary tells Joseph that she's pregnant with God's child. Not much is said about this in the Bible except that Joseph planned to divorce her after he found out. We can only guess what was said, but until Joseph was told in a dream that the baby was from God, he could only have thought that Mary had been unfaithful to him, and was pregnant with another man's child. So this is the mood we have to portray in this scene. Joseph is angry, hurt, and feeling betrayed.

299

Mary is trying to defend herself because she's being accused falsely, and God has not yet spoken to Joseph to tell him what really happened. Are we ready?"

Both William and Theresa nodded, so Miranda led them to the piano, where she did her best to play and coach at the same time.

Through all the key parts, William tended to overact, while Theresa was unusually half-hearted.

Miranda stopped the second Ted returned. She had already spread out his music, so all he had to do was take his guitar out of the case and sit down. "We're at bar thirty-seven, where Mary is trying to tell Joseph to trust her. Theresa, you look a little tired, so let's just concentrate on getting our pitch and timing, and we'll work on the emphatics another time."

Both of them nodded, so Ted began to play.

While William and Theresa sang their parts, they didn't need Miranda's intervention most of the time, so Miranda watched Ted play.

He played the score of the Christmas production differently from how he played from the front of the church on Sunday mornings, where he only played hymns.

Here, his style of the music was similar to that of contemporary choruses. He managed the difference in style with remarkable finesse.

He was exactly the type of guitarist that she would choose as a partner for a special duet. Or he could be a perfect member for a four-person worship team — guitar, piano, bass, and drums. His playing was strong and distinct, he chose the perfect times to play a few single notes versus solid chords, and his sense of rhythm was flawless.

All this from a man who lived in a community that had added musical instruments to their worship time only two years ago. With some real lessons and a bit of practical theory behind him, he could be phenomenal.

When the song ended, Miranda studied Theresa. "You don't look like you have any more energy in you. Would you like to call it quits for the night and go home?"

Theresa nodded weakly. "That sounds very good. I do not feel well. I think I will go to sleep right away, and hopefully I will feel better in the morning."

William stood. "Then I will drive you home. Let us go." He nodded first at Miranda, then Ted, and the two of them left in silence, William retrieving his hat from the rack by the door.

That made Miranda think of Ted and his identical hat. Ted did look good in his hat. Not quite dashing, but definitely eminent, even a little enigmatic. Maybe he was a bit of a stud muffin after all — in a traditional sort of way, of course.

"Why are you smiling? I did not hear what William said."

She couldn't wipe the smile off her face, even as she looked at his messy hair. "No reason. If you're finished packing up your music and stuff, let's go. After all, we're getting up early tomorrow morning. Don't forget your hat."

Miranda watched the trees whiz past as they sped down the country highway. "Where exactly are you taking me?"

"To a place I go when I want to get away from everything."

"Uh . . . Piney Meadows *is* getting away from everything."

He smiled, as though he thought she was joking. "I'm taking you to Cass Lake. I go fishing there, but sometimes when I need to rid myself of excess energy, I do not bring my fishing pole, but just jog down the trail around the lake."

The few times in her life that she had

actually jogged, Miranda had done it on the nice even oval track at the local park. She couldn't imagine jogging down an uneven trail dodging tree branches and avoiding wild animals. Suddenly the trees ended, and to the right she could see a calm, still lake.

Miranda gasped. "It's beautiful! Is that an island in the middle?"

"*Ja.* It is called Star Island, and the island also has a lake in the middle. It is a very interesting piece of property."

"Where exactly is this trail? And how long is it?"

"The trail is about a quarter of a mile long. When I was a boy, my papa would take me here with my toboggan. There is a steep hill down to the lake. Brian and I would race our toboggans down the hill and see how far we could slide onto the lake."

"You had a real toboggan? Made of wood?"

"*Ja.* What else would a toboggan be made from?"

"Plastic, and the one I had was called a Super Saucer."

Ted's eyebrows raised. "Super Saucer?"

"A Super Saucer is kind of like a heavy-duty molded plastic circle, with small handles on the sides for steering."

"If it was circular, it was not a toboggan."

"I know, but you also have to remember that some winters Seattle doesn't get any snow at all, or it's mostly just snow showers and gone in a few hours. When it did snow, though, the schools closed and I was always ready to go meet my friends at the one of the local parks along the water with my Super Saucer. Otherwise there aren't many places to sled in the city of Seattle. It was a major outing if anyone really wanted to go. The only places that had enough snow every winter, all winter, were in the mountain passes, like Snoqualmie."

"Is it not dangerous to do this in a mountain pass?"

She shrugged her shoulders. "Not any more dangerous than what I did when I was in my first year at college. Everyone used to go sledding on Queen Anne Hill, which is quite steep. I didn't do very well. Most of the time I just fell off and hoped no one rode over me before I could get out of the way. Most of the students didn't have anything proper to sled with, so they used plastic garbage can lids."

Ted cringed and his mouth opened, but Miranda held up her hands to stop him from commenting.

"I know. It wasn't safe, but we all thought we were invincible. When Justin broke his leg, we found out the hard way we weren't. So it wasn't such a bad thing when the next few years it didn't snow enough in the winter. I haven't been on my Super Saucer since then."

"I cannot imagine a winter without snow."

"Now that I've experienced the amount of snow you get every winter, my next winter at home is going to be pretty boring."

Ted stopped the car in a sheltered area. "I will show you how to get to the path."

It wasn't far off the highway, but unlike what he'd led her to believe, it wasn't much of a path.

"You don't really expect me to run through here, do you?" Miranda said as she pushed a branch away from her face while they walked.

"The branches do seem to be a little overgrown, so it appears that we will not be able to jog after all. Would you like to walk to the lake?"

Miranda whipped her camera out of her back pocket. "I'm ready if you are."

Ted grinned, reached into his back pocket, and drew out his camera as well. "I am also prepared. We should not linger. Everyone will be waiting for us at the church at one o'clock, and we should be there early to open up the building."

"No, we can't be late. If we are, I can just imagine how everyone will be praying for us."

"But that would be good if everyone was praying for us."

"Not what I'm talking about. Let's go."

20

As Miranda approached Ted's office, Anna waved her to the side. "I wanted to tell you how much I am enjoying being a part of the Christmas musical for our church."

Miranda smiled. Enthusiasm was often more important than talent — and that was especially true of Anna. As a high soprano, Anna simply wasn't capable of being smooth and melodic on the notes needed for the solo parts — the optimum voice for that was a low alto. If they performed any of the songs in Anna's vocal range, it would sound as if they were doing an opera.

"I'm glad you're enjoying it. It's great when a ministry project can be fun."

"*Ja.* I had a dream last night that many would come to our church and join God's family because of it."

"I hope and pray that's true." It was certainly their goal, and the reason she was here.

Anna glanced through the open door of Ted's office, where he was talking on the phone. "I also want to tell you that you have made the right choice in asking Theresa to play Mary. When she sings she sounds the way I imagine Mary would sound."

"Thank you for telling me that. It was a hard choice to make. They all were."

"They were all good. Having Elaine and Len and young Barbara and Walter play the townspeople family is perfect."

"They're doing very well, yes." The reason Miranda had selected Elaine was not so much her singing ability but that Elaine was the person in her age bracket who had shown the least fear.

"Of course, William is perfect for the part of Joseph." Anna giggled. "Everyone thinks he will not shave the beard after the play is over."

Miranda tried to sneak a glance over her shoulder at him so he wouldn't notice. She wasn't fond of beards, although it was necessary for this part. But it wasn't his willingness to grow a beard that had gotten William the part. He truly had a beautiful voice. Not as beautiful as Ted, but Ted had refused to be part of the cast.

"Ryan and Steven and Edward are good Wise Men."

"Only because Ryan is always quick to stop Edward from fooling around so much." Miranda didn't know there could be such a jokester in a community like this, but she supposed that God had to have a sense of humor, even in such a straight-laced society. "I almost made him a shepherd, but since we're using real animals, I had to pick the people who actually owned the animals to lead them."

Anna nodded. "I hope and pray the animals behave during the performance when people are watching. I think it is a wonderful idea to have real animals, but very strange."

"Not really. It's not like there's a whole herd. It's only one donkey and one sheep and one goat. Back home, Llinkie always loves his part acting as a camel. Of course, there is a certain liability following behind him, but one of the boys in the youth group is always prepared with a bucket and a small shovel in case of an accident."

Anna stopped typing. "Llinkie?"

"Yes. Llinkie Llama. One of our members has a llama ranch. Llamas are pack animals, so one of our congregation made a pack for Llinkie that looks like a camel hump. Every year Llinkie proudly shows it off as he walks up the center aisle with the Wise Men leading him." She smiled, thinking of the latest new member of Nathan's herd — Mama Llama's new offspring, Shamma Llama, a sibling to her older brother, Rhamma Llama, who would probably be the next camel when Llinkie retired. This year, no one attending Piney Meadows Mennonite Church owned llamas, but next year, maybe someone who owned llamas would join, if they even had llamas around here.

Although next year, she wouldn't be here. Next year she would again be sneaking faithful old Llinkie more treats before his grand entrance.

Anna hit save and folded her hands in her lap. "I guess what I am trying to do is thank you for the part you have given me. I was not sure that we could do it, but now that we have been practicing for two months, we know we can. The four of us singing our parts boldly with no instruments truly will be a heavenly chorus, worthy of telling the world of the birth of our Lord and Savior."

Miranda smiled with relief. Fortunately, none of the congregation had admonished her that the Bible did not have any angels of female gender; in the Bible all angels were men. For the play Miranda had written a joyful and triumphant four-part a capella harmony for two men and two women, giving Anna a strong high soprano part. Anna was the only one who could pull it off, and she was doing a spectacular job. Still, it wasn't a solo part, which was what Anna had wanted. Each person suited his or her role so well.

The only weak link was Pastor Jake. Since he was the pastor, she'd set him up to play himself, and he was playing himself badly. She didn't know how it was possible, but it was happening.

"Ted is finished with his phone call. You may go in now. You are really going to enjoy your lunch today, but Ted made me promise not to tell you what it was."

Miranda inhaled deeply. She'd never eaten as she had in the past seven months of her life. The only reason she could think of that the women who lived here didn't all weigh five hundred pounds was that it was so much work to do all this cooking.

She walked into Ted's office and plunked herself down in the chair in front of his desk. "That smells so good. You're going to make me fat."

"That is not true. Today I have brought *Kartoffelkrapfen*." He smiled proudly and extended his open hand toward a loosely covered casserole dish on the counter.

"Meat and potato cakes with gravy. Meat

with added carbs, and then some added fat for good measure. But ya gotta love it." She scooped a few onto each plate and set them on the desk. "You've been feeding me for lunch for two and a half months now. Isn't this getting rather expensive?"

"Elena and Mary give me a good discount. I have told you this before. I buy my lunch from them every day, so to add a little extra is not a hardship for me. Let us pray." He folded his hands on the desk and bowed his head. "Dear Heavenly Father, I pray Your blessings upon this food and this day. I pray that our thoughts and our words and our actions are pleasing in Your sight as we continue about our day, and that You and Your glory are shown in everything we do. I pray this in the name of our Lord and Savior Jesus Christ, Amen."

"Amen." Miranda began to cut the first meat cake. "Tomorrow I'm going to bring lunch. So don't buy anything."

"But —"

Miranda raised both hands to silence him. "I made my own lunch most of the time at home, and I obviously haven't starved to death."

The second he glanced at her stomach, she regretted her words. She had discovered to her embarrassment that the reason he'd originally invited her to share lunch with him wasn't because he needed to discuss the details for the Christmas production, as he'd hinted. It was because he thought she was too skinny and possibly malnourished. Between Ted's efforts and those of Lois to keep her healthy, Miranda was thankful for her high metabolism.

"Are you sure? It is no trouble for me to buy lunch."

"It bothers me that you're spending so much money. Please, let me bring lunch tomorrow. I'm not promising that it will be fancy. It won't be as good as this, for sure. But I can promise that the price will be right."

"In that case, I will accept." He took his first bite of a meat cake, savoring it for an unusually long time, probably wondering if he was making a mistake, then set his fork down on the plate. "We have had our first criticism of the Christmas production today."

Miranda sighed. She hadn't really expected any complaints from a community like this, but people were people, and there was always someone who wasn't happy. Not that complainers usually were willing to do anything to fix the problem. Most just liked to hear their own voices.

"I guess it was bound to happen. What is it?"

"One of the men in the townspeople group objects to wearing his hat inside the church. He says it is disrespectful."

"But the scene he's talking about is set outdoors. I know it's inside the church, but the stage is supposed to look like it's outside."

"I tried to explain that, but he has refused to wear his hat in church."

Miranda bit her lower lip. She wanted to set the play in the city to make it more applicable to more people, but he'd insisted that they set it in their own town with the way their people were a hundred years ago when the church was founded. After many arguments, they'd met in the middle, setting the town in modern times, but keeping the Mennonite dress and traditions as they were in Piney Meadows. So she had added the story of the birth of Christ side by side to the town as it was, and they were both happy.

But she hadn't seen this coming. The men's hats were as much a part of their society as the women and their prayer bonnets. Even though the younger women no longer wore them all the time, they still did on Sunday, Bible study days, or any time they thought they would need to pray.

They were going to have to wear them often to work through this. Part of the appeal of Piney Meadows was the consistent way all the people followed their old-world traditions and customs. Miranda hadn't thought that by telling the men to wear their hats inside, she was asking them to violate their traditions in order to show them.

"I don't know what to do."

Ted looked out the window as he spoke. "I have a thought. You had a good idea to ask everyone to wear part of what could be their costumes whenever we meet to practice to help get everyone in the mood for their part. Yet we have no scenery. I would like to make some clouds and hang them from the ceiling, and that might remind people that they should act as if they are outside. We all know this play is for ministry for God's plan, so if we show a visual reminder that this takes place outside, he may feel more at ease with his hat."

"It's probably also been hard for them to pretend to be out in the snow, when it's really the hottest part of the summer. How exactly are you going to make these clouds?"

Ted broke out into a smile and shrugged his shoulders. "Constructing scenery is Ryan's job. I will trust him."

"Done. Is there anything else that might be a problem?"

"Not that I can think of. By now whatever has been a problem has been fixed, and everything is now running on schedule."

Miranda closed her eyes and sighed. This production was her dream come true, and it was, indeed, coming true.

Everything was written, and the singers, soloists, and chorus members were happy. All the volunteers were learning their parts and were comfortable with them. The templates and plans were well underway for construction of the sets, including blueprints to enlarge the stage at the front of the church. They had already booked and confirmed spots with all their advertisers, and Pastor Jake had even been invited to be a guest on a few radio stations and a local cable channel. All details were in place — something that never happened at home this early. The only thing missing was a camel.

Miranda opened her eyes and looked at Ted. "Don't you love it when it all comes together like this?"

21

"Well?" Ted asked as Miranda flipped her cell phone shut and turned to him. "Where is she?"

"This is so odd," Miranda replied so softly only Ted could hear. "Theresa's mother said she left over an hour ago. I hope nothing's wrong."

Ted checked his watch, although, as he raised his arm, he didn't know why. They knew exactly how late Theresa was. That was why Miranda had phoned.

"I can't wait any longer," Miranda muttered as she trotted over to the middle of the nativity group. He knew she would figure out what the group could practice the most efficiently until Theresa arrived so it would involve the least amount of disruption.

When he scanned the room, he realized that he didn't see Evan, either. Evan was one of the townspeople, so his part was not as critical, but since it was now September, Miranda had increased the number of practices per week, making it clear that all should attend practices, regardless of the importance of their roles. People were not usually missing.

Theresa and Evan's absence was cause for alarm also because Evan had been courting Theresa since spring. The affection between them was strong and obvious to all. Ted knew that could mean that temptation was also strong. Because of Miranda, Ted now knew more about temptation than he ever had. The same things that annoyed him also drew him like a moth to a flame, which he knew usually spelled destruction for the moth.

He had found that she never backed down from any disagreement, even when their conversation was turning into a full argument. Yet no matter how frustrated she became, she never raised her voice or became angry. She didn't appear to know the meaning of defeat, but turned every potential loss into a compromise, even if it meant more work for herself. While her stubbornness exasperated him, he admired her strength.

She used the same unwillingness to give up when a situation required patience. All the ladies he knew were patient with children. It was the Mennonite way. Miranda was no exception, but he'd never seen anyone, male or female, exhibit such a level of patience. Her patience wasn't only with people. She had even taught a goat to jump through a hoop. Why anyone would want to do such a thing was beyond him, even if the goat was fat and needed exercise. It wasn't even her goat.

With her patience came much kindness. To help him become more active, she had forced elderly Mr. Reinhart to use a cane that she had bought for him on eBay. Then she'd assigned him a part in the play and argued with him until he gave in and took the part. Immediately after she had badgered the elderly gentleman, she cried when she found a baby bird with a broken wing that had been abandoned by its mother. She had faithfully nursed it back to health, protecting it from neighborhood cats. She had cried more when the bird flew away for the last time than she had when she'd found it near death on the ground.

He couldn't describe her cooking skills. He had no comparison for most of the things she tried to feed him, but he'd learned a lot about trans fats and cholesterol. He would never look at bacon and eggs the same way again.

The woman had more quirks than he could put in a bucket.

But whenever he didn't see her, he counted the hours until the next time they would meet, even if she brought strange things to feed him. Yet she hadn't brought anything worse than the bok choy stir fry, nor had she attempted to cook that again, even though Brian had requested it.

When they did meet, not all his thoughts concerned their assigned project, and that was why he never had her at his house with him without Brian being present as well. Since their parting at the airport, he had never been able to look at cinnamon buns in the same way.

He watched as she told the two groups where to stand as they prepared to practice the next scene, allowing extra time for Mr. Reinhart to take his place.

Over the course of his lifetime, Pastor Jake and his mama and papa had quoted 1 Corinthians 10:13 to him many times. He hadn't understood why until now.

No temptation has seized you except what is common to man.

She didn't know it, but Miranda had

taught him the meaning of temptation. One kiss was not enough. But at the same time, it was too much, because even a month later, he found himself being distracted from his work, even when he was in the middle of a critical project, wondering what it would be like to kiss her again. He suspected that men throughout the ages felt much the same way as he did. Lately, when he had been talking to Brian, he would catch his friend not paying attention to what he was saying. Instead, Brian would be staring off into space, smiling. When asked, Brian would grin even more and admit he'd been thinking about Sarah. Ted suspected he knew what those thoughts were. Now he understood them. He could also understand why, in their Mennonite community, there was no such thing as a long engagement, such as happened in the cities.

And God is faithful; he will not let you be tempted beyond what you can bear.

So far, Ted had been able to bear his temptations because Miranda was not as distracted by him as he was by her. Yet he knew she felt something, because when they were together in a crowd, unless she had joined a group of women, she always stood beside him instead of wandering in the crowd talking to people, and she did like to talk. He had noted that when she stood with other men while waiting for him, she never stood as close to another man as she did with him, not even Brian, whom she knew well. Which was a good thing. He would hate to have to punch his friend in the nose.

But when you are tempted, he will also provide a way out so that you can stand up under it.

God had indeed provided a way for Ted to stand up to the churning feelings in his heart. After Christmas, the play would be over and Miranda would be gone. Her flight home was already booked for late Christmas Eve, so she could be home with her father for Christmas Day.

The pending finality of her departure was an effective deterrent.

The introduction to the first song when the nativity group met the townspeople on-stage brought his mind back to where it should have been.

He had to find Evan, and where he found Evan, he knew he would find Theresa.

He walked to the piano and leaned down to speak privately to Miranda. "I am going to look for Evan and Theresa. If they are together, I may know where they have gone."

Miranda made a mistake with the notes, but recovered and kept playing. "Evan is missing too? Oh, no."

"I hope to be back soon. They will have much explaining to do." This would be worse for Theresa, since explaining the reason for her absence would not be easy with her papa. Since Theresa's mama knew she was not at practice, by now her papa also knew, and her papa was a strict man. He didn't want to think of what Theresa's punishment would be, but it was now too late. Ted would not lie. Depending on what they were actually doing, though, he could ask for leniency.

Even as Theresa's papa's employer, it was probably unfair of Ted to intrude on family matters, but the punishment had to fit her transgression. Theresa was in her early twenties, not a child. A lapse in judgment for a young adult was not a punishable offense — unless the transgression was severe enough.

Ted almost hoped he would find Theresa in a ditch with an injured leg. Then the only consequence for not being where she was supposed to be would be a long recovery with restricted activities, which would be punishment enough.

The first place Ted looked for them was at Evan's parents' home, which was deserted. Just in case, Ted pressed his ear to the door. Relief filled him when all he heard was silence.

His next stop was the soda shop. It was the custom of many young Mennonite couples to come here for a root beer float, and even though the food was not as hearty as at Elena and Mary's small restaurant, it was a popular place.

Ted only took one step inside. This evening he didn't see any Mennonite couples. Most of them were at the church with Miranda and the rest of the cast. Today there were only people here from the rest of the town, surrounding farms, and outlying burgs.

He returned to the car, but couldn't think of anyplace else to go. He had been sure they would be at the soda shop, and they were not. The last place he could think of that they could have gone would be to the movie theater, but he couldn't go in there looking for them without buying a ticket. Even if he did, he wouldn't be able to see them in the dark. He would have to wait for the show to be over, then catch them as they were leaving. He left the car in the no parking zone long enough to run to the door to check the movie times, then ran back to his car before he got a ticket. The movie had just started fifteen minutes ago. Even if this was where they had gone, by the time it ended it would be too late to drag them back to practice.

Ted checked his watch. He should go back to the practice. Miranda depended on his guitar playing so she could stop playing small sections on the piano to help people who needed it as they practiced the songs.

With regret, Ted returned to the church. As he pulled the door open, he absently looked down to the pin lock at the bottom of the door. Every time he opened the door, he heard the scrape of it dragging on the floor, a never-ending reminder that it needed to be tightened. Today there was no scrape, indicating that someone had finally fixed it. He looked down to see if it had simply been tightened, or if he would see a shiny new mechanism. Instead, an envelope was folded in half and lodged behind it, preventing the pin from slipping down.

Ted stopped and stared at the envelope. It had his name on it. He didn't know how long this envelope could have been there, but it could have been there all day. No one would have seen it as they entered because there was no reason for the average person to look down as they opened the door. He had looked down only because so often he was the last one to leave the building and was aware of the malfunction.

He hunkered down, pulled the envelope from behind the loose pin, and unfolded it. Instead of just his name, in bold blue letters, it said *"To Ted and Miranda."* Printed in red pen and underlined beneath their names, were instructions to read the contents after the practice was over.

A cold chill ran up his spine.

Practice was only half over, but he had not given his word that he would follow this request. The contents were obviously important.

He had three choices. He could wait for another hour and do as the instructions said. He could interrupt the practice and take Miranda somewhere to read it in private, which would cause a stir and alert everyone in their church that there was a problem. Everyone was already fully aware that Theresa was missing, and a few perceptive people would by now have realized that Evan was also missing.

Or he could read the contents himself, then interrupt Miranda if it was warranted, and something in his heart told him it would be.

He turned and sank down to sit on the landing with his feet resting on the top step, instead of going inside. The worn wood of the structure still radiated accumulated heat from the hot Indian summer day, making the step almost uncomfortably hot to sit on. He needed to be by himself, where it was quiet, which wouldn't happen if he went into the hub of activity inside. He needed to pray for wisdom and discernment concerning the contents of this letter. With his free hand, he removed his hat and rested it on his knee. Ted inhaled deeply to clear his mind, closed his eyes, and bowed his head to beseech his Heavenly Father.

The click of the door lock being engaged from the inside broke through his concentration. The creak and whoosh of the door starting to open gave him barely enough time to snatch his hat and jump up. The solid wood door brushed his back as he rose.

"Ted? What are you doing? Did you find them?"

He swayed for a second while he regained his balance halfway down the steps. Miranda stood in the open doorway, alone, her eyes wide, watching him as he barely prevented himself from falling.

He held up the envelope with one hand as he returned his hat to his head with the other. "I did not find Theresa or Evan. I found this instead. I fear we have a problem."

22

Miranda stared at Ted, two steps down, clutching a white envelope in his hand.

"What is that?"

"It is a letter I found tucked behind the locking pin. It appears we were meant to find it when the practice was over and we closed up the building. Why are you here? Shouldn't you be practicing with everyone?"

"I gave everyone a water break. I thought I heard your car, but you didn't come in, so I came to see if you had a problem."

"If you heard the car, then there is a problem — that I need a new muffler."

Miranda didn't know what to say. This didn't seem like the time to make a joke.

As Miranda had spent so much time in Ted's office over the past few months, she had learned something about him. Ted spent a lot of time on the phone. She often heard him use obscure changes of subject when he was dealing with his business clients. He was a powerful negotiator because people commonly underestimated him with his old-world accent and ways, and he used it to his advantage — something she'd also learned the hard way until she figured it out.

He was stalling. That meant he hadn't made up his mind yet on his best course of action with the letter. Therefore, she had to *un*-stall him.

"I only have a few minutes before everyone will start coming back. When they do, they're going to see us talking and know something's up."

"I do not think we have time to read this now. We should wait until everyone is gone. By leaving it this way, I think they wanted us to read it in private."

She looked him straight in the eye. "You're probably right. But this is going to bug me all during the rest of the practice time. Quick, I think we need to pray."

Instinctively, she moved forward as she would have done at home in a similar situation. She walked down one step, reached out, grasped Ted's hands, and looked at him. As she stood one step up from him, they were exactly eye to eye.

"Wha . . . what are you doing?" he stammered.

"Where two or three come together in my name, there am I with them. There's trouble here, so just like God's word says to do, we're gathering. We're also running out of time. Let's pray." ✦

Miranda started to bow her head, but she hadn't figured on being so close to Ted because of the way they were standing on the stairs. When they both bowed their heads at the same time their foreheads touched. The thought flashed through Miranda's mind that even though they were only praying, with their faces hidden beneath the brim of Ted's hat, anyone watching would get the wrong idea of what they were doing on the church steps.

Miranda chided herself. No one was there to observe. Everyone was in the kitchen.

Miranda forced herself to focus. "Heavenly Father, I don't know where Theresa and Evan are, but both Ted and I are worried about them. I pray for their safety for whatever they are doing, and that you'll give us peace as we finish off the practice and read the letter later, according to their wishes. I pray we will both be faithful servants as we work together to get this project done for You, for Your ministry to call more of Your children into Your kingdom. When the practice is done, please guide our hearts so we can help Theresa and Evan and guide them in whatever their problem is and why they aren't here with us today."

The echo of people returning to the practice area sounded behind them. Ted flinched, and instead of adding to her prayer, he sighed and said, "amen."

She squeezed his hands, then released them and backed up, nearly stumbling as she stepped backward to the top step. In the silence before he'd said, "amen," a thought of what she could have done hidden beneath the brim of his hat had run through her mind. It had absolutely nothing to do with prayer. She would have to say an entirely different prayer about that later.

Ted stared at her, his eyes narrowed. "Do not ever do that again," he hissed. He rammed the envelope into his back pocket, then stomped up the stairs around her and strode into the sanctuary where he picked up his guitar and flipped through the pages to the song they had been doing when he arrived.

Miranda sucked in a deep breath and returned to the piano. As soon as she was facing the piano and her back was toward all present, she heard a little giggle behind her. She peeked over her shoulder to see a few of the ladies separating. To her left, a couple of the men nudged each other with their elbows, and grinned at Ted as he concentrated on tuning his guitar.

Miranda squeezed her eyes shut, pressed her lips together, and pounded out the first chord of the song after what was supposed to be Theresa's solo. Next time she would coach them on how much to lower their volume to hum along with Theresa, but for now, they had to move on.

"Okay, everyone, let's get back to work. The pickup to bar forty-eight. Here we go."

As Miranda played through the song, she found herself getting distracted by the envelope sticking out of Ted's pocket. Part of her willed it to fall out so she could jump up and grab it, then excuse herself to run to the ladies' room and read it. But God had other plans because it stayed firmly in Ted's pocket.

She dismissed the practice a few minutes early and tried not to look as if she was giving these good people the bum's rush, as she encouraged them to leave as quickly as she could without pushing them out the door.

When the last person finally left, she turned around to see Ted hunkered down, securing the pin lock on the left door.

"Come, let us go."

"Go? Aren't we going to read Theresa and Evan's letter?"

He rose, picked up his guitar, and held the right side door open. "*Ja,* but not here."

She didn't question him, since he appeared adamant about leaving. She followed him to his car, where he opened the passenger side door and held it for her while she got inside. However, he didn't close the door when she got herself settled. He left it wide open and walked around to the driver's side, opened his own door, tucked the guitar behind the seats, and took his place at the steering wheel, also leaving his door wide open.

"I am doing this so the car will cool down after such a hot day. We can read the letter here."

Ted leaned to one side to pull the letter out of his back pocket. Holding it over the top of the steering wheel, he ripped the envelope open.

He cleared his throat and began reading.

Dear Ted and Miranda,

We're so sorry to give you the news this way, but we had no choice. Theresa and I can no longer be in the play for our church, and I have to quit my job with you, Ted, because we have moved away. Our parents do not yet know and we ask that you tell them because they respect both of you very much.

We have left Piney Meadows because we are not yet married and we are going to have a baby. Instead of embarrassing our families with this situation, we have decided to move to the city, where we will take care of ourselves.

I have already found a job and we have a place to live, so do not worry. We will be fine.

God bless you,
Evan and Theresa

Miranda gasped. "Theresa is pregnant?"

"Offya fallen Mennoneet," Ted mumbled, staring at the handwriting.

Miranda cringed at his harsh tone. "What?"

Ted turned away. "It is an expression."

"I figured that out already, thank you very much. What does it mean?"

He turned to face her. "It literally means this is a Mennonite who has fallen off the wagon."

"Fallen off the wagon?" Miranda's hands rolled into fists. "Let those who have never sinned cast the first stone," she retorted, not caring about the sharpness in her own voice.

"I am not casting a stone. They admit they have sinned, and they have chosen to run and hide." ❧

The memory of girls who had become pregnant during the time she was in high school flashed through her mind. Nothing had changed with unplanned pregnancies, except that it seemed to be happening more often as time went on. Theresa was much older than the teen girls in her high school, but less wise in the ways of the world. While Miranda was in high school, most girls who became pregnant when they were too young and unprepared had abortions. Two had given up their babies for adoption. Only one had kept the baby, but then she ran away from home when she found out how much work it was to raise a child, abandoning the baby with her parents. Instead of being able to build toward their pending retirement, the baby's grandparents had ended up struggling with another mouth to feed.

But this was not the same situation. Theresa and Evan were obviously together and staying together.

"I don't understand why they ran away. Why wouldn't they stay here, where family and friends can help them?" She glared at Ted. "This community wouldn't shun them, would they?"

Ted crossed his arms over his chest with the letter dangling from his fingers. "We do not do shunning. We care for our brothers and sisters in Christ."

Miranda's chest tightened at the memory of some people back home who were supposed to care. She tried to shake the thoughts away, but they bombarded her anyway.

"For some reason, Theresa and Evan don't feel the same way." Her throat tightened. "I can understand why a single girl who is pregnant might want to run away, but the letter sounds like they plan to get married. Certainly that would make a difference."

Ted turned his head and looked out the open car door as he spoke. "I know people would help them, but Theresa's papa is very strict. I do not like to say this, but while I am positive the church would help them, I fear her parents would not. I fear her papa would banish her from their family."

Her head swam. "That's awful," she choked out. "My dad was my biggest supporter."

Ted's head moved so fast his hat nearly flew off his head. He grabbed the brim to steady it. "You have had a baby?"

Her eyes burned with the memory of

everything that had happened. "No. I never had a baby. The issue was about me being pregnant." Her chest constricted, and she started to choke up as she struggled to push back all the memories.

His eyes softened, and he swallowed hard. He pulled off his hat and pressed it to his chest. "You lost a baby . . . I am so sorry."

Miranda shook her head. "No. That wasn't it. I was never pregnant. Without going into a bunch of embarrassing details, it was a girl thing, and it ended up being just a hormone problem. But between the symptoms and all the medical stuff, it caused a lot of . . ." Her voice cracked. She let her voice trail off until she could regain control of herself. ". . . issues."

Ted didn't speak, nor did he move. He simply sat, waiting, being a good listener.

She swallowed hard, fighting the burning in the back of her eyes. "I haven't ever been able to talk about this. Everyone knew everyone else, so I couldn't say anything to anyone except Bradley. I know I said some things that weren't kind, but Bradley was always safe to talk to. I couldn't talk too much to my dad because he's the pastor and knows everyone. Dad was already so angry on my behalf. That's probably why I'm so close to Bradley. He stuck up for me so much that everyone thought he was the father." She fought against the burning in her eyes. Over the years she had already shed too many tears over it. She refused to ever cry about it again.

"What happened?" Ted asked softly, still not moving.

"When I was in my last year of college, my period stopped."

At the word "period" Ted's cheeks and ears turned red, but like a gentleman, he sat still and continued to listen. "My mother had died of cancer at an early age, so I was pretty worried. My father sent me straight to the doctor, and the first test they did was a pregnancy test, even though I told the doctor there was no way I was pregnant. But since those doctors hear that all the time, they did it anyway, plus a bunch of other tests. I told some friends about it, but one of them wasn't as trustworthy as I thought, and word spread that I'd had a pregnancy test. I was feeling really sick and run-down, so then many of the ladies started talking about me in the same conversation as how they felt when they were first pregnant."

Ted squeezed his eyes shut for a second. "And with all the talk, people assumed the wrong thing . . ."

"Yes. It turned out to be a hormone problem aggravated by me being too active and too skinny and not eating properly. My doctor got it under control with a short-term hormone treatment, but he also put me on a strict diet loaded up with lots of vitamins. I immediately gained some weight, and everyone noticed every pound. For four months I could feel every eye on me, waiting for me to completely balloon out, even though I repeatedly told everyone that I wasn't pregnant."

"That must have been terrible."

"That's not even the worst of it. I gained a pants size, and then when I didn't expand any more, one woman started telling everyone that I'd had an abortion. With me being the pastor's daughter, you can imagine the impact that had. From the pulpit without naming names, my father made a big issue of everything people did. The backlash was unbelievable. Many people repented, but many left. It was awful."

Ted put his hat back on his head, reached toward her to hold one hand, and motioned with his head toward the wide-open car door. "I always do my best to avoid reason for gossip."

She smiled weakly, thinking of how often Brian found himself tagging along with them, and then more recently, Brian and Sarah. Today, Ted had been very obvious about not being alone in an empty building with her. Again, she found herself in the car for the purpose of having an important conversation. She had become very familiar with Ted's car.

This time, with both front doors wide open, a nice breeze wafted through. She didn't mind sitting in Ted's car, except he didn't have a CD player.

"I've learned the hard way that while most of our people are good, all it takes is one to start the poison flowing, and nothing you do will stop it," Miranda said. "If they're going to talk, they'll talk. I do my best to follow the narrow path that God has set out for me, and that's all I care about. As long as I'm right with God, that's all that matters. So you're wasting your time and energy making sure we're never alone in an otherwise unpopulated building. Unless you think I'm going to jump up and attack you."

His eyes widened, and his grip on her hand tightened slightly. He licked his lips, and his voice lowered to a tone that for anyone else besides Ted, she would have called seductive. "Would you?"

All thought processes stopped. Ted never watched vampire flicks — he didn't even

have a television. So he could only be referring to what she had almost done earlier
that evening when they had finished praying
together on the church steps. Which she
thought about doing constantly after the
way he'd said good-bye at the airport.
Which was why she hadn't baked cinnamon
buns since then. If she did . . .

Miranda cleared her throat and tried to
smile, but she knew it probably looked as
lame as it felt. "Don't be ridiculous," she
mumbled, then yanked her hand out of his.
"Theresa and Evan need to have God's
people with them to hold them up. I know
what it's like to be tried, judged, found
guilty, and convicted, so I'm not going to
let them go through this alone. I don't care
if anyone starts talking about me and saying
I'm encouraging them to sin. I can't leave
them like this — they need a friend. Besides,
I'll be gone soon, so it doesn't matter what
anyone says. I don't know how, but I've got
to find them."

Ted started to lean forward, but he suddenly stopped, blinked, and his face tightened. He sat back, straightening himself in
his seat until he was positioned firmly
behind the steering wheel. He grasped it
tightly with his right hand, then leaned to
the left to grab the door handle of the wide-

open door, pulling it closed. "I am not sure if this will work, but I have an idea. Close your door. We are going to my office."

23

Ted sighed as he inserted the key in the lock of the church door.

He knew Miranda was inside. Lois had told him so. He ignored the statement she was making with the locked door and entered anyway.

She wasn't hard to find. If the sobbing hadn't given away her location, the echo when she blew her nose pinpointed exactly where she sat. He found her in the sanctuary, sitting in the aisle seat of the front row.

"*Goondach,* Miranda," he said as he approached her.

She wiped her eyes and then her nose with the back of her arm. "What's good about it?"

"I have found Evan and Theresa. He has given me his address. As you said, one must love e-mail."

She responded with a sound almost like a snort. "That's, 'you gotta love e-mail.' You're amazing. I don't know how you did it."

"Many companies in the cities have policies against using the company computer for personal Internet use. I trust my employees to obey the rules that they may do their personal e-mail on their lunch break. I feel some guilt at looking at his personal e-mail, but the computer is company property, and as his boss, I have every right to do so."

"I still don't know why he gave you his address so easily."

"I told him that we would mail his final paycheck and vacation pay on Monday. I suspect he needs the money. I also sent the e-mail using William's address because he prepares the payroll."

"Smart move. You must be very shrewd in business dealings."

He shrugged his shoulders, walked around the pew to where Miranda was sitting, and sat beside her. "I am not here to discuss my job. Why are you crying? What is wrong?"

The second he asked his question, the tears started flowing again, only this time they were silent. Ted didn't know which was worse.

"You remember how the Penners reacted last night," she said.

Ted nodded. "*Ja*. Zeke did not say much,

but he was very, very angry with his daughter."

Miranda sighed and lowered her head to stare at the floor. "He said everything there was to say today, and then some."

He clenched his jaw. "Did you go back to Zeke and Agatha's home without me?"

"No. Zeke phoned me and said everything he didn't say yesterday." She sniffled again. "I don't belong here."

Ted thought of all the good things Miranda had done since her arrival, both the things everyone could see and the more subtle things that had changed.

"That is not true. You may be a little different from the rest of the ladies who live here, but you have a good heart."

She sniffed again. "A good heart. That's like telling a fat woman she's got a pretty face. She's still fat. And I still don't belong here."

Last night he'd felt sorry for Zeke. Zeke had been overwhelmed by his own anger, so Ted had understood. Today Zeke had crossed the line because this was more than shock at his daughter's situation; he had struck out at Miranda to deliberately cause hurt. If Zeke had said something to cause Miranda to feel unwanted, Zeke would have to answer for his words.

"That is not true. You have done much good here, and you continue to do much good. While it is true that many of the ladies have changed their choices of clothing, this was something that was already happening. You have helped them make wise choices. If you had not been here, they would have had no guidance."

She turned toward him, her eyes big and sad like a beaten puppy. "He said the young ladies all look up to me, impressed with my city ways. He says I have no restraint or respect, and I corrupted Theresa not just by my words, but by my actions as well." A big tear overflowed and rolled down one cheek. "He said it's by the example of my loose ways that Theresa let herself have sex with Evan. But I didn't mean to present myself that way. I'm saving myself for my husband, when I get married. I really am." Another tear rolled down her cheek. "But if that's how everyone sees me, it's true. Then I really don't belong here. I've always felt so different from everyone else. I truly don't belong here, and this really is my fault. I've caused my sister to sin."

Anger welled up in him, but he tamped it down. He would deal with Zeke privately, another time. For now, he needed to be here with Miranda.

Slowly, he reached to wipe a tear off her cheek with the pad of his thumb. "You have caused no one to sin. You have not been a bad example to the ladies here but rather a good one. You are showing them patience and lovingkindness. You are also showing them organizational skills and strength of character, and with that, restraint. For those who had already decided to leave us, they will still leave, but they have seen by your example that they do not need to compromise themselves to follow the Lord's ways. It is more difficult to follow God's path in the cities, but it is not impossible. For those who choose to stay and continue on in the ways of their forefathers, you have also shown them that it is acceptable to be happy and content, enjoying a simple life."

One corner of her mouth twitched. "I still haven't figured out how you fit in around here," she said. "You're happy and content with the tradition and the ways of the people here, but at the same time you jet-set all over North America. You quietly and humbly take your place in all the church activities you're involved in, yet I'd hate to be on the opposite end of the corporate boardroom table from you."

"It is my goal to do what is fair and best for all."

"But is that what's best for you, and what God wants you to do?"

He considered Miranda's assessment as she tilted her head to one side, waiting for his reply. "Happy" and "content" were not words he would have used to describe himself. While he enjoyed managing his onkel's furniture factory, he wasn't really challenged by it. Miranda hadn't asked him anything he hadn't already asked himself. There were days when he doubted that God's plan for him was merely to direct the processes of building new furniture that looked old and to convince people that the simple designs constructed the old-fashioned way were better than what the mass-market factories threw together with glue and particleboard.

Besides, outside of work, he wasn't sure if he was happy or content, either. If he were, he would be married and would probably have children by now. Yet he was the oldest of all the single men at church, with no interest in a serious relationship with any of the women he knew, much less marriage. Many of the women had expressed interest in being his wife, but he didn't want the kind of marriage they offered. He needed more out of marriage than just to come home and be comfortable and well fed after a hard day at the office. He had that now. The only difference he could think of was that he would no longer have to sleep alone, and that wasn't a reason to get married, either.

Miranda had been accurate. He didn't know how he fit in here, but he did know that he didn't fit into the fast pace of the cities. He had traveled enough that he'd seen the lifestyles of most single men. He had no desire to live that kind of bachelor life.

She stood. "I guess I'd better wash my face. Everyone is going to be here soon to practice. I'll have to plan around all of Theresa's parts for today, but now that we've got her address, I'm hoping to convince her to move back home. When do you think we can go see them?"

Ted stood as well. "It will take a few hours to drive all that way. I think if we leave right after church we can see them for a short time, then be back before dark."

"What about the paycheck you, or rather, William, promised Evan?"

Ted grinned. "It will be ready. Remember, I am the boss. Now let us get ready for the practice. But first I have one phone call to make."

24

Miranda plunked down a couple of submarine sandwiches on Ted's desk just as he hung up the phone. He made an entry to his spreadsheet and hit save. His usually tidy desk was covered with catalogues, sketches, fabric samples, and a rough layout sketch of what looked like a floor plan. Stacked on the floor beside his desk were a few wood samples and a pile of stain color samples.

"What are you doing?"

"Working," Ted mumbled as he made a few more entries on his spreadsheet, then began running a tape on his calculator.

"I've never seen your desk like this." She waited for him to elaborate, but he didn't. "I'm still in shock that they're really not coming back. I also can't believe that they got married like that, without friends or family with them."

He hit the total, and entered the number

onto his spreadsheet. "I am shocked that they got married at a government institution, not in a house of God. I also cannot believe they are going to live like that. Their whole apartment is the same size as my living room and kitchen."

"But the rent is cheap, and that's what they need right now," Miranda said. "You can't compare a downtown apartment to a home out here in the country." It was also unfair to compare, since Ted's house was larger and newer than any of the other homes in the area because he had rebuilt the house after the original century-old house had burned down. All of his parents' old treasures had been destroyed, but by needing to rebuild the house from the ground up, he wasn't living in the same house where his parents had died. "All you're missing is a plasma television."

If she wasn't mistaken, Ted gave her a dirty look, then returned to his spreadsheet.

Since he wasn't talking, she stepped closer and checked out the mess. "Hey, I recognize this. It's a floor plan of Theresa and Evan's apartment." She studied his pencil sketches, complete with measurements. The wood and fabric samples. The catalogues. "Are you making furniture for them?"

He laid his pencil down. "We had to sit

on the floor yesterday. The only pieces of furniture they had were Theresa's sewing machine, a small cabinet for her sewing supplies, and Evan's toolbox. They also will need something for the baby. We have not made cribs before, so I am checking into the government regulations and safety requirements. This is something we can begin to market, and I will give them the first one off the line."

Miranda studied the sketches on his floor plan. "It looks like you're giving them more than just a crib. You're furnishing the whole place."

"It is not only just me who is doing this. It is the work of everyone who is employed here. I will provide the materials, and everyone has volunteered their time to build the pieces that will go to Evan and Theresa. It is the Mennonite way."

"That's very generous." She picked up the blueprint to study it more carefully. "How did you get this? It's got the measurements of every room."

"I brought my tape measure yesterday."

She waited for him to say more, but he didn't. But thinking back, she had noticed periods of time when Ted wasn't with them. He'd been very discreet in his quest. Suddenly she realized that Ted had planned this in advance, even if he had not known the magnitude of the project until he saw the near-empty apartment.

Like the reformed Christmas Grinch, Miranda felt her heart grow three sizes while she watched Ted planning to construct everything he would give Theresa and Evan.

Why hadn't she seen it sooner? Ted was the biggest stud muffin she'd ever met.

"You have a strange look on your face," Ted muttered as he tore the tape off his calculator. "Do you have a question you wish to ask me?"

Miranda cleared her throat. "I just came from the ladies' quilt circle group. They all know that Theresa is a good seamstress, but she can't sew anything without fabric, which costs more money than they have right now. So they are going to sew draperies and make her a bedspread and a matching sheet set. I was going to ask if you could guess the sizes of the windows, but you have the measurements right here."

"Unfortunately, I measured only the width of the windows; I did not need the height."

"This is good. We can guess. It's okay for the curtains to be long. The important thing is the width. Can I copy this?"

"The photocopy machine is beside Anna's desk." •

"I am so stunned at how everyone has jumped right in to help." Miranda carefully began to roll up the paper so she wouldn't crease it. "Everyone is doing something. Lois and a bunch of the older ladies are doing up preserves and jams and a food basket, and she's asked if we can deliver everything next Sunday."

"I believe we can do that. As well, Pastor Jake told me that he has made up a special collection box for anyone who wishes to donate money if they have not been a part of the furniture or sewing or baking groups."

"I have never seen a group of people like this. Everyone is so amazing. Everyone, except her parents, is giving them something. Oh, speaking of them, Zeke Penner phoned me again this morning."

Ted froze. "What did he say?"

"Not much. He apologized for the other day, then asked when I was leaving and hung up on me. It was really strange."

Ted sighed and resumed his calculations. "I think we need to pray for Zeke. We need to pray for Agatha as well."

"I don't think she's stopped crying since we first told her. I talked to Pastor Jake too. I asked if Kathleen could go pay Agatha a visit. He thought it was a good idea."

"*Ja.* Good idea." She hovered over him

until his hand froze over the keypad. "I am going to work through my lunch, but if you are hungry, do not let me stop you from eating."

"It's not that. I have one more favor to ask of you. And it's a big one." She'd almost made cinnamon buns, but with all the phone calls she'd made, she hadn't had enough time.

Ted lowered his hands to the desk. "What do you need?"

"When I planned out the parts for the Christmas play, I wrote the whole thing based on the talents and abilities of everyone who would be involved."

"I know that. Why are you telling me this now?"

"Theresa had the main part of Mary. I gave it to her because she was the best singer and had the best stage presence, and now she's gone. I can't pull anyone off another part because every song was written specifically for the range and ability of the person who has that part. I can't use someone out of the chorus because those are the people who have the least ability. No one else we've got can handle a part like that."

She could see the moment when Ted realized the point she was trying to make. He laid his pencil down and folded his hands on the desk in front of him. "This is very bad. The key performer is gone, and there is no one who can replace her. What are we going to do?"

"First of all, you're going to have to play the piano for Mary's big solo numbers."

"I cannot play those songs. They are far too difficult for my level of competence on the piano."

"You have to. Everyone else who plays piano will already be up onstage. I'm sorry, but if it helps, I'll rewrite the piano part for you. We don't have any other choice. The only woman left who doesn't already have a part and sings in that vocal range to blend with William is . . ." Miranda gulped. She didn't mention the part about potential death by stage fright. ". . . me."

Ted struggled through the opening bars of the introduction of Mary's first solo, barely able to keep his hands on the keys because his hands were sweating so much. If this was what it was like during practice when the only people listening were people he knew, he didn't know how he would do it with the church packed with strangers.

If he could play his guitar, he would be fine, but Miranda was right. The solos needed the fullness of the piano for the best effect.

He struck the final chord of the introduction, then pulled his hands from the keys and released the sustain pedal so a silence echoed through the building, setting up a dramatic entrance for Mary.

He held his breath, waiting for her first notes.

He had never heard Miranda sing. Every Sunday, he was at the front with his guitar while she sat in the front row, so while he knew she was singing, her voice blended with the congregation. Up until now, she had only sung the occasional note to help the other singers, never alone, singing single notes extra loudly to help the real singer get the pitch.

Out of curiosity, he'd asked around, and no one else had heard her sing, either. Not even Lois. Lois had only heard Miranda walking around the house with her earbuds on, humming. She didn't even sing in the shower, unlike Leonard, whom Lois wished did not sing in the shower, which was more information than Ted had wanted to know.

Today would be the first time anyone here would hear her sing. Were they that desperate? Apparently they were.

A clear, melodic voice so hauntingly sweet

it nearly stopped his heart sang the opening lines of Theresa's song.

He raised his hands to continue the piano's accompanying harmony, but his hands wouldn't move.

He stared at the woman standing in the middle of the stage.

She wore the same denim jeans as Miranda, the same red T-shirt as Miranda, and even wore the same red tennis shoes as Miranda. But he couldn't see her face because it was completely hidden by the page of music she held up high, directly in front of her face — the page of music that shook like a leaf in a March wind gust. One knee trembled at almost the same frequency.

He returned his attention to his own page of music and continued to play so she would continue to sing. The beauty of her voice made it hard to focus. He wanted only to listen. But as he played, the piano background enhanced her voice so much that the more he concentrated on her voice and the less on his mistakes, the better he played.

By the time the song finished, it was the best he'd ever done, and he realized that just as Miranda had told him, he really would be able to do this.

As he turned to look at Miranda, still standing alone in the middle of the stage, he realized the rest of the room had fallen silent. Everyone focused on Miranda, waiting for further instruction. None was forthcoming.

He jumped up from the piano and walked to her quickly, before anyone else could talk to her first.

Instead of being her usual talkative self, she was silent. Her teeth chattered, her eyes were as wide as saucers, and her face was as pale as if she'd been left outside in the snow for too long. She looked like a cow in the path of a freight train, about to be hit but unable to move out of the way.

Ted struggled for the right words that wouldn't overwhelm her. "That was . . . uh . . ." *Magnificent? Breathtaking? Spectacular?* He crossed his arms over his chest. ". . . very good."

She smiled weakly, her lower lip still trembling, and pressed the paper into her stomach.

"Thanks," she said, her voice quivering. "I did much better than the last time I tried something like this. I didn't throw up all over my shoes."

He looked down at her. Metaphors failed him. She was trembling like a rabbit in the field with a hawk circling overhead. This was not the Miranda he thought he knew.

He needed to keep talking to give her the time to recover.

"I do not understand why you are so afraid. You are a good leader and a great director. You are organized and thorough, and you never back down when people confront you."

"That's the thing with our greatest fears. They never make any sense."

"But you could have a huge ministry singing about the Lord's glory." He lowered his voice and hitched one thumb over his shoulder. "You are frequently asking me to buy a CD player for my car. To hear your voice on a CD would cause me to go to the cities and buy one."

Her face paled. "This is exactly what always happens when people hear me sing. They tell me that I'm not reaching my potential and they tell me everything I should be doing. Then they always ask me to sing more, doing something just a little harder than I did the last time, just because I didn't fall to pieces and self-destruct on the stage. A few years ago I let people convince me to sing for a college fundraiser. In the middle of the song I fainted and hit my head and they called an ambulance." She held up her bangs to show a nasty scar just below her hairline. "Seven stitches, and

I can tell you that head wounds bleed faster than any other place on the human body. That's why I don't sing. I write. I compose. I direct. But I do not sing."

All Ted could think about was the waste of the voice of an angel. "But you told me before that you've sung duets at your church."

"Yes. The key word there is 'duet.' That means having someone else right beside me. I also have my guitar in my hands, I'm sitting down, and all my attention is focused on the sheet of music." She hunched her shoulders and covered her face with her hands. "I don't know how I can do this, but I can't let everyone down."

"You did fine." Better than fine. He'd never heard anyone sing like Miranda, live or on a CD.

"I didn't do fine. I forgot the chorus, and I mixed up the words to the third verse, which shows how *not* fine it is because I wrote the song."

He almost asked if there was anyone else who could play the part of Mary, but after hearing Miranda sing, there wasn't. She was perfect in every way and probably a lot like the person of Mary in Bible times.

"During piano lessons you are teaching me how to incorporate use of theory to cover when I make a mistake or forget my notes. Can you not do the same?"

"Right. Like I can just make up new words or change the notes and expect everyone to follow along."

"Perhaps not. But do not worry. We will figure something out."

"When goats fly."

He opened his mouth to tell her that while it was true goats didn't fly, she had taught one to jump through a hoop, which had to count for something. But before he could speak, Miranda turned and walked away toward Mr. Reinhart, who was on the wrong side of the gathering of people in his group, and guided him back to where he was supposed to be.

Ted smiled. *That is the Miss Randi with an "i" that I know and love.*

Love?

Ted felt as if he'd been poleaxed.

It was true. Miranda was unlike any other Mennonite woman he'd ever met or ever would meet again. Bold. Vibrant. Stubborn. And the only thing she could cook properly was cinnamon buns.

Maybe the cow standing in the middle of the railway tracks waiting for the approaching freight train was him.

25

"Breathe. Deeply. From your diaphragm. That means from your gut. Do not suck in your waist like a girl. Like this." Ted rested his palm on his belly and inhaled, his belly moving out instead of in, as he filled himself with air.

"But I am a girl. I can't do that."

"I have done research on stage fright, and the first part of helping yourself is to make sure you have enough oxygen. That means to breathe properly. Let us try this again."

He watched as she tried four times before her stomach actually expanded with her intake of air.

"That is right. You need to breathe this way while you are singing. The next thing the book said is that it is normal to be nervous. If you try too hard to calm yourself, you will only feel worse."

"That's true. By the time you started playing your introduction, before anyone had started watching me, I already felt like I was going to throw up."

"It is okay to be nervous. Use the nervous energy to give yourself strength, and that will help you do a good job. The next point the book made was that most of stage fright is being afraid that you will make a mistake. The more you know your part, the less chance there is of that, so practice often and memorize everything. It should also help you to know that if you forget the words, I will have the words in front of me. You can look at me, and I will help you. The church will be dark except for the stage, but there will be lights over my music. I will move the piano so you will be able to see my face, and I will move my mouth with the words if you need help."

"Technically, that sounds like it would work. But I won't know until we try it."

"Another thing the book suggested was not to become too engrossed in the audience. Since you are not public speaking, you do not have to look at anyone. Focus on something that is not looking back at you. Looking at a spot on the wall is not good, because that reminds you that you are afraid. I have spoken to Elaine and Ryan, and they will make sure they have something for you to always hold in your hands, and you can focus on that if you start to become nervous."

"If?"

He smiled. "If. You can do this, and I am going to help you. Now let us start." He hit the button on his computer, and familiar piano music came from the speakers. Just as Miranda's cue to sing sounded, Anna walked into his office and dropped a note with a phone number on his desk.

"I took a message since you are on your lunch break and Miranda is here. Mr. Parker from that place in Seattle called. He says it is urgent that you call him back as soon as your lunch break is over."

"Thank you, Anna. I will do that." Because of the interruption, he hit stop. As soon as Anna returned to her desk, he poised his finger to start again, but Miranda grabbed his hand.

"Wait! You can't do this here. Anna can hear everything we do!"

"That is good. She is not in the room, but she can still be your audience. I have recorded your first song at home because there is no piano in my office. If you are worried about making mistakes, all I can say is that I know I have made more."

He turned the monitor toward her, where he'd opened the document with the words to the song. "Are you ready?" He reset the sound file and hit play.

As he knew would happen, Miranda didn't make any mistakes, compared to the dozens he'd made while recording himself playing.

She smiled ear to ear. "You know it's different onstage."

"*Ja.* That is why we are working on this now. So you will be familiar with it everywhere and the stage will be no different from anywhere else. Now let us eat. I am hungry."

Miranda sighed and sank down into the chair. "I don't know how to thank you for this. When I arrived in town, Christmas seemed so far away, but now it feels like it's right around the corner."

Ted glanced at the note on his daily desktop calendar. "Twenty-five more practices." Over the span of fifteen weeks.

Week sixteen they would do five performances, and then on Christmas Eve, she would be going home.

Miranda gasped. "You're keeping track?"

"*Ja.* That does not count the small practices you do with the small groups or soloists. That is only the full group practices."

"That's actually a lot. I don't feel quite so nervous anymore. We've got lots of time."

It was not enough time. Every day as he

turned another page on his calendar, he felt the loss spiraling out of control. With her joining him for lunch every day at work, he often saw her twice a day, but it was no longer enough.

"I have an idea. I would like to take you to the soda shop this evening. As it is becoming fall, there are not as many warm days and today seems to be one of the few days left to enjoy a good old-fashioned root beer float."

"Isn't that where the young people go?"

He forced himself to smile. That was where the young people would go on a date as one of the few allowable places that it was not necessary to take a chaperone. "Are we too old to go there?"

She blushed as she stood, ready to leave since the lunch break was officially over. "Of course not. It'll be fun. But I was just thinking, why does so much you do have to involve food?"

Ted grinned. "It is the Mennonite way." He rose to escort her out. "I will pick you up at six-thirty. Since it will be a warm evening, and I know you are mentally calculating the fat content, I think it would be a good idea if we walked."

Besides, walking meant the evening would take longer.

"Sure. Exercise is good. Now I had better leave."

As he did every day, he escorted her through the building and into the parking lot, where he stood beside the door and watched until she jogged out of sight.

Now if only he could figure out how to make the lunch hour longer than an hour.

"It's snowing!" Miranda raised her arms above her head and danced in a little circle. "I see visions of sugar plums and marionettes!"

Ted only saw visions of his snow shovel that he'd stored in the garage all summer. The snow had come a little early this year, and he didn't need his desk calendar to remind him that the days were flying by. Soon Miranda would be gone. "I know you are referring to a ballet that is done at Christmastime, but what exactly is a sugar plum?"

She dropped her hands to her side. "I didn't know either, until a few years ago when I googled it. They're those little purple sugar-coated candies that people put out at Christmastime."

"I have not seen these candies."

"Maybe next year I'll send you some."

Next year. He didn't want to jump ahead

to next year. He wanted this year to last as long as possible. However, with the Christmas play in full practice mode, including construction of the sets and props, and all the ladies busily sewing costumes, time was passing much too fast.

The echo of footsteps around the corner told him that people had begun to arrive for the practice.

"Next week it will be November and time for the full cast to start practicing twice a week."

Miranda nodded. "I know." She pressed one hand over her stomach. "I'm starting to get nervous."

Ted's stomach tightened too. She probably hadn't been aware of the full ramifications of what she'd just admitted, but Ted saw the potential for trouble. In the past month they had joyfully entertained much of the office staff, but they had not made much progress with Miranda's fear of singing onstage. If she was already nervous before everyone had arrived, he could only see trouble.

Since he wasn't very good on the piano, he'd practiced more time than he had to spare so he could do as he'd promised, which was to be able to mouth the words while playing and not make a mistake. For the most part, he could, but he wasn't as good as he wanted to be.

Soon everyone had arrived. Miranda had insisted that by this time, all singers were required to have their parts and their cues memorized so no one had a paper in their hands. So far, most were able to handle the songs, but many needed help with their cues to do the movements and actions onstage.

The first part of the play had only the townspeople group on the stage, so Ted stayed at the side and played his guitar while Miranda played the piano. Since he was able to walk around with the guitar, he spent most of the first act onstage, directing everyone's movements. Since the next song would be Miranda's in the nativity scene, they had to trade places. Miranda waited in the wings while Ted took his place at the piano for her first set of songs.

She did fine with her first duet with the angel as he told her that she would become pregnant with God's Son. During the song she held a blanket in her hands because this announcement was supposed to have taken place in Mary's bedchamber. Ted did notice that when she became nervous, she stroked the soft blanket like a cat. The next scene was a fast forward to a duet of her conversation with Mary's cousin Elizabeth. For this

scene she held a duffle bag, because Mary
would have been traveling, and she would
have brought some of her personal belongings with her. Ted gritted his teeth as he
watched her play with the zipper. The more
nervous she got about the high notes that
were coming, the more she zipped and
unzipped it. He didn't know much about
traveling in Bible times, but he could safely
assume that the travel satchels of the day
were tied with drawstrings, and did not have
zippered pockets. But he wasn't going to
switch bags on her and start over.

Then came the moment he had been
dreading. Mary's first solo, when she sang
glory to her Lord, who had blessed her. For
this, since Mary was a maidservant of
humble parentage, she held a bucket and
scrubbing cloth because she was there to
help her cousin through the last trimester of
her pregnancy.

He played the simplified version of the
introduction, let the pause hang until she
sang her opening sentence, then joined in.
She did fine, although he could hear a slight
tremble in her voice since this was the first
time she'd done the big solo without the
printed words.

She made good progress until she got to
the middle of the chorus — a part she only

got the words right on about half the time. Sure enough, she started to stammer, meaning all was about to become lost.

If she made a mistake now that caused everything to grind to a halt, he knew she would never recover. Sure enough, she looked straight at him, as her cue that she needed his help with the words.

Instead of mouthing the words, Ted continued playing with his right hand and pointed to the bucket with his left. Fortunately she got the message and looked down. She actually smiled when she saw the bottom of the bucket, where he'd taped the words to the chorus. Unfortunately, instead of being discreet, she grasped the bucket with both hands and looked down, making it obvious that she was using a cheat sheet.

A number of people laughed, but she kept singing and made it to the end without further trouble.

When the action continued on the other side of the stage with the townspeople, Miranda and all those in the nativity left the stage. Miranda returned to the piano to accompany the next song.

By the time they took their half-time water break, everyone was more than ready. While everyone else went into the kitchen, Miranda retrieved her water bottle from the top of the piano and sat beside Ted on the pew.

"Thanks for putting the words in the bucket. That really worked."

"You are welcome, but next time you might wish to be a little more subtle when you read."

"I will be. I think just knowing they're there will help, and I won't need them so much."

Before he realized what she was going to do, she leaned toward him, and pressed a kiss to his cheek. "Thank you," she whispered as her lips brushed his skin, and then it was over.

His heart pounded so hard he wondered if she could hear it. "If you found that so helpful, wait until you see what I am going to do for that part in the song at the stable where you always get mixed up."

Her eyebrows arched, making it impossible for him to wait. He walked to the piano bench and sat down, then reached behind the music cradle where he'd hidden his hat. Tucked inside the black ribbon band, circling the crown, he'd stuck a sheet of paper on which he'd written in black felt pen the two sentences she always got wrong. He quickly plopped the hat on his head and turned to her. It was probably disrespectful to the hat, but it would get the job done.

But instead of the reaction he expected, one lone tear wandered down her cheek. Slowly, she joined him on the bench and reached up to brush her fingers where the paper was nestled into the ribbon, then looked him straight in the eyes.

"That looks ridiculous, but I know it's going to work." She sniffled. "How will I ever thank you?"

Ted pressed his lower lip between his teeth as he wiped the tear away. "I do not know. Cinnamon buns?"

For a brief second, her gaze settled on his lips, then back to his eyes. "Yes. Cinnamon buns are a very good idea."

26

"What are you doing? Where are we going?"

"It is a good day, and we need a break. We are going skating."

"Skating? What about work?"

Ted grabbed Miranda by the hand and led her out of his office. "Anna, I do not know if I will be back. If any important phone calls come in, please call Miranda's cell phone."

Anna nodded, then resumed her work.

Miranda shook her hand free of his but kept following him as he made his way to the main door. "I suppose I should give up and stop arguing with you every time you do something like this."

Ted nearly laughed. "If you stop arguing with me, then I will know something is wrong."

"And another thing. Whenever we go somewhere during office hours, you always tell Anna to call me if something comes up.

Why don't you get your own cell phone?"

"The only time I ever need one, I am with you, and you already have a cell phone. Why pay for another new phone? Anna will only call one, so she might as well call yours."

"You are so cheap."

"I am a good steward. It is the Mennonite way."

She remained silent while they trudged through the parking lot. Ted unplugged the block heater and wound up the cord quickly, while Miranda waited behind him.

"I didn't know you had a skating rink in Piney Meadows."

"*Ja.* The caretaker at the school has just put another layer of water on it this morning, so it will be very smooth right now."

"School? You have a skating rink at a public school?"

"*Ja.* In the summer, it is the oval race track. In the winter, it is our skating rink."

"Wait. You mean it's outdoors?"

"Of course it is outdoors. That is how the ice stays frozen. Where did you think it was?"

"Never mind," she muttered as he opened the car door and held it open for her. "If this is just an outdoor rink at the school, where are we going to rent skates?"

"I have my own skates, and I have borrowed Anna's skates for you. They are already in my car."

He waited for Miranda to comment, but she didn't say anything in the entire five minutes it took to drive to the school. Since classes were out for winter break, the parking lot was nearly empty, and only a few people were on the rink as they pulled up.

"I haven't been on skates since I was in sixth grade. I hope you're not expecting too much."

"Then I will leave the hockey sticks in the car."

"Hockey!?"

"I am kidding. I did not expect you to skate well. But I had expected that you would have skated more recently than when you were a child. You told me about how you went sledding when you were in college. I thought you would also have been skating."

"There's no outdoor skating in Seattle. It never gets cold enough for that. Snow usually only lasts a day or two, and it's gone. Most of the time all it does is rain. It's probably raining now."

Ted's breath came out in a puff of white. "I cannot imagine that."

"It's true."

Ted pressed his lips together. He immediately regretted bringing up the subject of Seattle. In a week, she would be gone, and he didn't want to think about that. "Let me help you with the skates."

He tugged off her boots, then squatted behind the shelter of the open door while Miranda remained seated in the car. She had such tiny feet, he felt as if he were doing up skates for his small cousin who attended this very school. As soon as Miranda's skates were securely fastened, he put on his own, and walked around the car to help her out.

She wobbled for a few seconds, then straightened herself. When she was steady enough, he led her through the parking lot and to the newly iced rink.

"There are no sideboards. How am I going to do this?"

He extended his arm. "You can hold onto me."

She grabbed onto his arm and held it in a death grip, but she still didn't move her feet. "I don't know if this is such a good idea. Tonight is opening night, and it won't be so good if I show up in a wheelchair."

"If you are nervous, how about if I pull you?" She released his arm, so he skated a few circles around her, stopped directly in front facing her, and extended both arms.

"Give me your hands. It will be fun."

"You can skate backwards?"

"Of course."

She shrugged her shoulders and offered him her arms.

"You will fall that way. You must balance yourself. Hunch down . . . like this." He bent his knees into a partial squat to show her what to do. When she followed his example, he grasped her hands and slowly started backward. When she adjusted her position to balance out the movement, he increased his speed.

At first the terror on her face made him wonder if he'd done the right thing, but after only a quarter of the way across the rink, her eyes brightened, and by the time they were halfway across, she was asking him to go faster.

He pulled her three times around the rink, then had to stop to catch his breath. "I am sadly out of shape. I have not been getting enough exercise, and I have definitely been eating too much."

"It's okay. I think I'm ready to try skating on my own. But I'll still need your help to catch me when I fall."

He noticed that she didn't say "if."

Miranda didn't do very well, but he was pleased that she tried, at least. In the twenty minutes she took to go once around the rink, she spent more time on her bottom than her feet, but he had to give her credit for trying.

She pressed both hands over the back pockets of her jeans. "This is fun, but if I do any more, I won't be able to sit for a week."

"I understand. Besides, it is past lunchtime, and you are probably hungry."

He led her back to the place where they had entered the ice, but for some reason, he thought Miranda skated slower and slower. By the time they were ready to step off the ice, she was standing still.

"Is something wrong?"

"This is really strange. I've had enough skating, but I don't want to leave here. Can we stay a bit longer?"

"We can do anything you want."

He led her to the car, but instead of sitting when he opened the door, she turned toward him and rested her hands on his shoulders. "You know what I really need right now? A hug."

He didn't ask why. In fact, it sounded like a great idea.

He slipped his arms around her back and held her tight, knowing that with the busy schedule they had in the next few days, this might be the last time they could be alone together.

Holding her wasn't enough.

He lowered his head to press their cheeks together. The cold of her skin against his came as another reminder that if he didn't do this now, he might never have another chance.

"Ich leewe die," he whispered in her ear, then turned just enough for his lips to find hers and kissed her with all the love in his heart.

She turned her head just enough to break the contact but didn't move away. "If you just said what I think you said, then I love you too," she whispered against his lips, then kissed him again.

Ted no longer felt the cold. The whole world faded while he embraced the woman he loved. The heat of her kisses could have melted the snow around them, and he wouldn't have noticed. The only thing that would have made the moment any better would have been if he could unfasten the buttons of their coats and hold her closer.

The crunching of snow and the giggling of children forced him to break the kiss, but he refused to release her from his arms.

"What are we going to do?" he asked, his voice coming out strangely rough.

"I don't know. You know I can't stay here. Don't you? As much as I want to right now, I know for the long term, it wouldn't work."

"I know that." He'd always known that. He knew it from the moment he first saw her when she got off the plane, and he knew it even when she put the finishing touches on the quilt that she'd made with Elaine and the group of women with the Wednesday morning quilting circle. He especially knew it now, after she had lived here for a year. The simple life their community led was perfect for some, but wrong for others.

For Miranda, it was wrong. No matter how hard she had tried, and she had tried, she wouldn't be happy here for the long term. And her happiness was all that mattered.

From the inside of the car, Miranda's cell phone beeped for a missed call. Miranda wiggled away from him, and he let her. She reached under the seat to retrieve her purse and checked her phone.

"It's a text message from Anna. She says that man you were waiting to hear from called you back."

Ted checked his watch. "This is very important. I must get back to work. We do not have time to stop for lunch as I had planned."

"That's okay." She plopped herself down on the seat and began to loosen the laces of the skates. "We can just go through the drive-thru . . . oops, never mind. You don't have a drive-thru here. You don't even have a McDonald's."

"No, but if you phone Elena, she will have a good lunch ready for us to pick up by the time we get there, and we can take it back to the office."

She patted his arm. "No, I have so much to do, you should just drop me off at Lois's house, and you go back to the office and make that phone call. I'll see you tonight anyway."

He sighed and walked around to the driver's side, where he opened the door and sat sideways on the seat to remove his skates. He didn't want to take her home, but they had no choice. Tonight was the start of the five-day run of performances for the play. Regardless of what he wanted for his own purposes, this was why she had come.

They drove to Leonard and Lois's house in silence. When he walked her to the door, instead of kissing her as he burned to do, he gave her a quick brush on the lips to avoid giving the neighbors a show, and stepped back. "I will see you later tonight."

It wasn't enough, so he leaned forward and kissed her again quickly, one more time. "Do not forget, I love you."

"I love you too. Now you go take care of business, and I'll see you at the church. If we don't have a chance to talk, it'll be great, and God's message will shine through, as it should. And that's the reason all this has happened."

Miranda held hands with William on one side and Anna on the other and bowed to the roaring applause. In her own church, for a normal presentation, an audience of believers never clapped for any performance, no matter how good they were. Certainly, none of Ted's church members would ever clap.

This thunder of applause meant that the people who had enjoyed the show were exactly the ones they wanted to host, people from beyond the community of Ted's church and the towns beyond, people who didn't know that Mennonites don't clap in church.

The same thing had happened after every evening's performance.

Today was Christmas Eve, and not only had the sanctuary been packed to capacity, the standing-room-only section had also been filled. All tickets had been distributed, so the number of guests had been divided evenly among the five nights. With the audience numbers preassigned, they had allowed enough extra room so that people who came without a ticket could stay, even though many of them would have to stand. Experience had taught her that many of the people who attended church on Christmas Eve came to church only this one day of the year. With this arrangement, no one would be turned away.

God was good.

In all five performances, no one had wrecked their lines except Pastor Jake, but he bluffed his way through and everyone managed to go with the flow. On the second night, Mr. Reinhart had again placed himself on the wrong side of the townspeople group. When everyone around him figured out that it would take too much time to help him work his way over the cords and wires to move to his proper place, they all rearranged themselves into a mirror image of their positions, so all the motions and movement flowed, just the opposite way from what they'd practiced.

Miranda had only looked into the bucket three times over the five performances, and not once had she felt like throwing up.

God was very good. ⚫

The applause continued, so they all bowed again, smiling for the crowd of strangers, many of whom would hopefully become brothers and sisters in Christ. There would be many prayer meetings tonight. Then everyone would go home, ready to be with their families on Christmas morning.

Miranda squinted through the spotlight, looking toward the piano for Ted.

She had a two a.m. flight out of Minneapolis, and they had to leave soon so she could catch it. Even if she didn't get any sleep, she was going to be with her dad on Christmas morning.

Finally, the applause ended and the crowd began to disperse, allowing the cast to leave. But Miranda had yet to spot the face she really wanted to see.

Miranda gathered up her skirts and trudged off the stage. While the flowing dress she'd worn as Mary was comfortable enough, every time she moved she seemed to step on an edge of the loose skirt. She could hardly wait to change back into her old jeans. She gathered the skirts up in her arms and slowly made her way down the stairs, one step at a time so she wouldn't trip. Just as she reached the floor and released the armfuls of fabric, her cell phone rang.

Miranda smiled. It would be her dad, asking how everything went and confirming that she wasn't going to miss her flight.

The area code showed the call as originating from the Seattle area, but the number on her call display was not one she recognized. The name shown wasn't a person, but the name of a business. Which meant this call was for Ted.

She couldn't believe someone would call for business so late on Christmas Eve. She almost answered to tell whoever it was what she thought of such rudeness, but to do so would have been even ruder.

Instead of rushing off to the ladies' room to change, she headed for the piano to find Ted. She found him talking to a man in the crowd. Of course, the phone had stopped ringing by the time she found him.

"Miranda, it is a good thing you are here. I must talk to you. It is very important. But first, I would like to introduce you to Chad Jones. I think you will find that Chad has an interesting story to share."

She turned to Chad and smiled graciously. "Good evening, Chad. Sorry to interrupt." She handed her cell phone to Ted. "I don't know who this person is, but someone called for you a few minutes ago. It must be terribly important for them to call on

388

Christmas Eve like this. You might want to call them back."

Ted pushed the button to read the number. His eyebrows arched when the number appeared on the screen. "Excuse me. I must find a quiet place and call him back. This is very important. I will not be long."

Ted disappeared around the corner, leaving her alone with Chad. All she wanted to do was change out of her costume, but she couldn't be impolite to a stranger. She turned to him. "I hope you enjoyed our play."

He smiled. "Yes. I did. It wasn't at all what I expected to see in a place like this." He paused. "Please don't take that the wrong way. It was really good, which is why I was so surprised. You have a talented group of people here."

"Yes, we do." The ability and willingness to do their best at something they'd never done before was like nothing she had ever seen. Being here was an experience she would never forget, on so many levels.

She tried to be discreet as she looked at the corner where Ted had gone. She had only hours left here, and she wanted to spend every minute she could with Ted, not a stranger. She again smiled at Chad. "Where are you from? I'm curious to know how you found out about our play."

"It's funny you should ask. I actually didn't intend to be here. I was driving around and got lost, then I ran out of gas down the block. The gas station was closed, and the church looked like something was going on with all the people and lights, so I walked in and got a very pleasant surprise."

So much for the megabucks Ted's church had spent on advertising. Not only that, this man didn't even have a preassigned seat ticket.

"I'm glad you enjoyed it. We —"

Her sentence was cut off by Ted's abrupt return. Instead of looking annoyed at being disturbed by a business phone call, he was smiling like the cat that had just swallowed the canary. He hadn't even left his hat on the rack at the door; he was still holding it in his hand.

Miranda was curious about what had him acting so strangely, but more than anything else, she needed to change out of the cumbersome costume, and then they had to leave for the airport. Her suitcase was already packed in Ted's car, so all she had to do was make a quick trip to the ladies' room, and they could leave. Knowing her time would be short, she had already said her good byes and expressed her thanks to

Pastor Jake, Len and Lois, and everyone else she was leaving behind.

"It was nice meeting you, Chad. I'm going to go change, and then Ted and I have to leave quickly. I have a plane to catch."

Ted shook his head. "I will be dropping Chad off at my house before we go. He is going to stay the night."

Not caring that she looked rude, Miranda grabbed Ted by the elbow and dragged him away from Chad. "Are you crazy? You don't know him or anything about him. It would be one thing to have him at your house while you're there, but you aren't really going to leave him at your house unattended all night while you take me to the airport, are you?"

"It is okay. We had a good talk, and I trust him. Besides . . ." Ted pulled a wallet and a set of keys out of his pocket. ". . . he has given me his wallet, which contains his driver's license, credit cards, and a couple of hundred dollars as a security bond. His car is out of gas, yet he has also given me his car keys. Brian will not open the gas station on the Lord's birthday, but he did remove a few necessary parts so Chad's car will not start, even if the gas tank happened to be full and he had a spare key hidden."

"Oh!"

"If you wish to change, you should do that now. It will take a few extra minutes to drop Chad at my house and show him where to find the things he needs. He is also hungry and will make himself something to eat."

"If you've eaten all the leftovers I put in your fridge, tell him that there's a can of —" The ringing of the phone cut her sentence short. "That's got to be Dad! But the tone means he's texting."

Ted's face paled. "Your papa? Wait!"

Miranda flipped the phone open. "This is weird. It says, *'U shd no tht ur young man asked 4 my'* —"

Before she could press the button to flip the screen to read the whole message, Ted grabbed the phone out of her hand.

"Hey!" she shouted as he held it high above his head. She reached out to grab it back, but he didn't relent. Knowing he wouldn't expect it, she tensed, hunched down just enough, then jumped up high and grabbed his wrist. Ted's eyes widened, but instead of releasing the phone, he dropped to one knee. While Miranda held tightly to his wrist, he pressed his other hand to his chest, covering his heart with his hat.

"Ted? What are you doing?"

"I planned to ask you this in the car, where we could have some privacy, but . . ."

He inhaled deeply. "I love you, Miranda. You have made my life complete, and I cannot live without you. *Wells du miene fru siena?* Will you be my wife?"

"I . . . but . . ." Miranda's head swam. She had prayed every day for the past month for guidance if she should stay in Piney Meadows. Nothing had happened to give her a strong feeling about staying. In fact, the opposite had happened. So much had told her — emphatically — that she did *not* belong here.

"I have asked for your papa's permission, and he has given me his blessing to ask you. I have also been offered a job in Seattle, which I will accept if you will have me as your husband."

"A job? In Seattle? Are you saying that you'll give up everything here just for me?"

"What I have here is not important. I can buy another house, and Onkel Bart has given me his blessing to leave and be with you. The furniture factory will not fail just because I am no longer there. The only thing that will fail will be my heart if I cannot be with you."

"But I know how much you hate it when you have to travel to any of the big cities for your business trips."

He smiled. "That was true, but I have

thought about this. It was not so much that I hated being in the cities. It was that I have hated being forced to leave my home and be compelled to go with other men who, when business is done, took me to places where I did not want to go, to do things I did not want to do, and I could not leave." His voice lowered in pitch. "I will love you forever. Wherever we have our home, it does not matter where that will be. As long as we are together, that is all I want."

Miranda's throat clogged up, preventing her from speaking. Still clenching his wrist in a death grip, she quickly looked around her. Many people were openly watching them, and with Ted down on one knee and not wearing his hat, it didn't take a lot of guesswork to know what he was doing.

He hated being a spectacle. He especially valued his privacy, yet he was exposing his heart for all to see.

She cleared her throat. "I love you so much, but I can't let you give up everything for me. You need to marry a nice Mennonite woman."

"That is what I am doing. I am asking a wonderful Mennonite woman with a kind and gentle heart if she will be my wife."

"You're completely sure this is what you want to do?"

"I have never been more sure of anything in my life. *Ich leewe die.*"

She smiled and released his wrist, then wrapped both her hands around his. "You've got to teach me to say that. Yes, I want to be your wife. Do you want to be my husband?"

Ted jumped to his feet. *"Ja!"* he exclaimed as he threw his arms around her waist and twirled her in the air, making the skirt of her costume billow out as he spun her in a circle. He then set her on her feet and kissed her as she had never been kissed before.

The stranger who would be staying at Ted's house clapped and whistled. Everyone else quietly hustled away, and one woman whispered, "Do not look," as all the footsteps faded into the distance.

"When?" she asked when he allowed her to get some air.

"I must wrap up things here and find a suitable replacement for myself, which I thought was going to take months, but I think God has already provided a way."

"Meaning?"

"As soon as you get home, start planning for our wedding. I do not wish a long engagement."

Miranda thought her heart would burst. She tightened her hold around Ted's waist and looked up at his face. *"Ich leewe die,"* she stammered.

Ted smiled and cringed at the same time. "Your accent, it is very bad. We must work on this. We can start on the way to the airport. The sooner you get back home, the sooner we can get married."

"Yes, but please remember one thing." She reached and removed his hat from his hand, set it on his head, straightened it by wiggling the brim, then raised herself on her tiptoes and gave the top a pat. "Even in the city, never change who you are. And please, always keep the hat."

DISCUSSION QUESTIONS

1. It didn't take Miranda long to realize that the situation in Piney Meadows wasn't what she had expected. Has this ever happened to you? What did you do?

2. Lois immediately accepted Miranda into her heart and home, despite their differences. Have you ever met anyone who didn't quite fit in? What did you do to make them feel welcome?

3. Because Ted frequently traveled to large cities for business reasons and had been exposed to temptations, he is protective of his community. Have you ever been tempted to do something that crossed the line? How did you deal with it?

4. Miranda tried to participate in the women's functions, and even though they accepted her and she made friends with

many, she felt as though she never really fit in. Have you ever been a newcomer and lacked the skills or personality to be "one" with the rest of the crowd? What did you do in this situation? How did you feel about the way people treated you?

5. In chapter 9 Pastor Jake found himself in the middle of an ongoing argument between Ted and Miranda. Have you ever been caught in the middle of two people who both had valid points? What did you do to resolve the issue?

6. One of the hymns had new meaning to Ted when he stopped to read the words and actually thought about them. What is your favorite hymn or chorus and why? When was the last time you really thought about the words you were singing in church?

7. Ted inadvertently hurt Miranda's feelings when he wanted her to stand on the freight scale at the furniture factory (conversation from chapter 16). Likewise, Miranda hurt Ted's feelings when she said he wasn't exactly a "stud muffin" (chapter 17). Has anyone ever hurt your feelings when you knew they didn't mean it?

Describe a time when you might have hurt someone's feelings in the same way.

8. Ted found himself unusually moved by Miranda's simple gift of cinnamon buns because they were given with no strings attached. She just wanted to do something nice for him. How does it make you feel when someone treats you with unexpected kindness?

9. When Miranda's medical problem caused gossip and dissension in her church at home, much harm was done, both to Miranda personally and to the congregation as a whole. When you hear gossip, how do you handle it? Do you listen and agree with the person talking, or do you investigate the facts before passing judgment?

10. Miranda struggled to overcome her debilitating stage fright. What is your greatest fear? What do you do when faced with it?

11. Miranda and Ted come from totally different backgrounds. How do you think they can overcome their differences and

forge a new life together? Is it even possible?

12. Did *The Narrow Path* cause you to change your mind about people who may have different traditions but the same faith? How?

AN INTERVIEW WITH AUTHOR GAIL SATTLER

The theme of this book revolves around the differences between contemporary and Old Order Mennonite church communities. Have you experienced life in both? Which setting is most familiar to you?

I attend a contemporary Mennonite Brethren church that is home to me. It's completely contemporary. In fact, I'm on one of the worship teams and play bass guitar. I haven't personally experienced life in an Old Order Mennonite community, but friends within and outside of my own church have experienced life in various stages of the church's life, growth, and development. Regardless of the differences between modern and traditional churches or locations, the Mennonite church has always had the same solid base of doctrine and values intermixed with history and community.

*What is the main component from the Menno-
nite lifestyle that shaped your story?*

The sense of community within the church
plays a big part in the story. Mennonite
churches range from the most contemporary
to quite traditional, and each has its own
individual personality, depending on per-
sonalities, preferences, and needs. When any
Mennonite group assembles it's always
done with love and fellowship, and I hope
this book reflects that.

*Food and hospitality play a big role in the
story. Why is that?*

Food and hospitality are a huge part of the
Mennonite church. Even in the contemporary church where I am a member and
despite the fact that people are busy and
many of the ladies don't have much time to
cook, there is always lots of food involved.
Recently, one of our deacons went to a
Mennonite men's retreat seminar, and part
of his report back to our congregation
outlined the great food.

*Are there specific people in your life who
contributed to the characters in the story? Is
there a Ted?*

Actually, there have been a lot of "Mirandas," and of course, my pastor and his wife have been huge supporters from the day I sold my first book, and even before that. So no, there is no one person in particular, and no, there is no "Ted." But I wish there was. ☺

There is a rumor that the models on the front of the cover work at your publishing company. Could this be true?

It might be. Okay, yes, it is true.

When Abingdon Press consulted me about the cover I had wanted to have Ted and Miranda center front on the cover, except that because of the nature of the book, we didn't want them to look like posed models but real people. To make them real I had some very specific requests. Ted had to wear suspenders and the hat that he was so fond of throughout the story, and Miranda needed the right accessories: her red cell phone, the red t-shirt, red lipstick and nail polish, and even red earrings.

I think it started out as a joke, but in reality Michael and Christa from the marketing department were the perfect people to pose for the photo shoot. It was amazing how everyone in the office got involved and organized everything. Someone there actually owned a red cell phone, and when Christa posed she even wore red earrings but we can't see them behind the cell phone. So that turned out to be a bit of a funny story. But the result was perfect. I'm thrilled with the cover.

Now that we know the "real" Miranda and Ted, have you continued to work with them?

Christa and Michael were also very accommodating to pose for some photos used on my book trailer as well. (You're invited to see it at www.mennoniteromancenovel.com/page/book.) They even worked together to assemble the paraphernalia for the photo of Miranda's junk on the seat of the car. My request was for them to show the program disc for the Bible program next to the red cell phone, because the idea was that Miranda "read" in the car when she was stuck in traffic. Of course since we needed to use the same phone from the cover, which belongs to one of the office staff at Abingdon, that meant they had to take the photo. When it was done they sent me a series of photos, and it was very amusing. They had arranged the items on the seat of someone's car like I'd requested, then in the next photo they added a few more items, took a few more shots, and then kept adding more and more items. So every couple of shots, there was another item added until you see the end result. I must say it is perfect, and I absolutely love the purse!

The whole experience between the cover and the book trailer has been very special, and I can't thank everyone enough to have made it so personal and extraordinary.

So now that you've read the book, watch the book trailer and you'll see that everything in the video is actually from the book or mentioned in the book.

Speaking of the book trailer, except for the photos from Abingdon we talked about, did you take all of the photos used in the shoot?

Almost. With the exception of Ted and Miranda and the junk in the car, I took all the photos but one. The picture of the "special guest" from next door was taken by the daughter of my friend Naomi from my writing group, and the sound clip that goes with it was recorded by Kim, another friend from the same group. The closing shot really is the Minneapolis airport, taken from the observation deck while I waited for a connecting flight. You didn't ask but I also put together the sound track. (Great bass line, isn't it?)

The main event in The Narrow Path *is the Christmas pageant. I understand that Christmas and nativity scenes are special to you and your family.*

It has always been important to me to emphasize the true meaning of Christmas in our home. While I love the tree and decorations, that's not the true meaning of Christmas. Children need to touch things to understand that they are real, so I crocheted all the characters for a nativity scene when my children were younger. This way they could interact wth them on the floor instead of admiring (and never touching) them on the mantel. They were always set up on the floor where the children could move them and play with them and reenact what really happened without fear of breaking anything. Then every night at bedtime, I would pick up all the characters and put them back in their places for the next day.

The wise men and the camel were kept on the dining room floor, the eastern most spot in our house. The shepherds and sheep were on the hearth, the innkeeper and the stable were under the Christmas tree, and Mary and Joseph and the donkey were set up in the middle of the living room carpet, moving a little closer to the stable every day as Christmas drew nearer.

Then on Christmas morning they made it to the stable, the angel came out, Jesus was born, we said a prayer, and then we opened our gifts.

Do you still do this now that your children are older?

Yes, even though they laugh about it and are too old to play with the set. I still put it out all over the house each Christmas, except now before bed I have to recover the characters from the dogs instead of the children.

Do you have a favorite novel from your early life? Did it shape the way you built your story?

Charlotte's Web is my favorite novel from early in my life. It didn't shape this story, but I love the unique solution they found to a common problem and how it saved the day, or rather, how it saved Wilbur.

So is red your favorite color too?

Yes and no. I had a look in my closet, and

there are a lot of red items, but really my favorite color is purple.

Gail, you've shared with us about your life and how The Narrow Path *came to be. You've told us that now you'd like to hear from your readers.*

Yes, definitely! I've added a message board to my website, www.mennoniteromance novel.com. Come visit and tell me what you thought about the story and the characters. I'd love to talk with you, answer questions, and let you know what happens next!